Redemption of Fate

S. Simone Chavous

eISBN: 978-0-9895701-2-1
ISBN: 978-0-9895701-3-8

Visit my website: http://www.ssimonechavous.com

Like me on Facebook: http://www.facebook.com/ssimonechavous

Follow me on Twitter: http://www.twitter.com/ssimonechavous

To Brian, for giving me the opportunity to pursue a dream.

Contents

Prologue

October 25, 1911

"I am to meet the High Commander tomorrow. Perhaps it is unwise for me to proceed. I am told he can read the thoughts of even the most powerful among us. How can I be expected to face him without exposing everything?" the anxious vampire asked; turning away from the one he'd sworn his loyalty to so many years before. "Even if I manage to control the direction of my thoughts in his presence this time, what of the future?"

"My dear Christopher, you do worry so. Have you no faith in me, in my plans?" Lucias asked; approaching the other vampire slowly.

Christopher swallowed hard and shifted nervously on his feet.

"Of course I have faith in you, my lord."

"Christopher, how many times must I tell you? To you, only to you, I am simply Lucias," he responded; gently placing his hands on the man's shoulders as he stepped closer to his back.

"What would you have me do?" Christopher asked; turning towards Lucias.

"You will proceed as planned. Go to him tomorrow. He will be as impressed with you as I was when we first met," Lucias replied with a mischievous smile; as he leaned closer and inhaled deeply. He closed his eyes, carefully savoring the rich scent; knowing their time together was limited.

"And what of his telepathy?"

"Ah, yes; that little inconvenience. I believe I can assist you with that," Lucias said; running his fingertip slowly up the side of Christopher's neck as his fangs elongated. Without another word, Lucias struck hard and fast, pulling roughly on the surprised vampire's vein as he clutched Lucias's body desperately, partly out of shock but mostly due to the overwhelming pleasure the harsh bite evoked.

Lucias slid his fangs from the fresh wounds and gazed into Christopher's desire-filled eyes. He brought his wrist up to his mouth and sliced into the tender flesh, offering his blood.

"Lucias, no, we must not; we cannot, it is forbidden. No mate bond is allowed without approval from The Agency, and never like this, between two men." While his words protested, his eyes and body told another story. His arousal was a tangible force filling the space around them and his eyes hungrily followed the flow of blood down the other vampire's arm while his fangs punched eagerly through his gums.

Lucias tossed his head back with laughter before reaching up and taking Christopher's head in his hands, his ancient blood trickling down the inside of his forearm. "You mistake me for someone else, dear Christopher. The Agency has no authority here; not in my house. Their rules mean nothing; they mean nothing. By their doing, our people hide in the shadows, bowing to an inferior species. It is utterly ridiculous; a shepherd does not fear his sheep, nor should we fear the humans."

He stroked a stray piece of Christopher's straw-colored hair from his forehead. "But it is of no consequence. No one can know of our union, not yet. One day, I will raise our people to their rightful place with you by my side. To accomplish that, you must do this," he said shifting his eyes to the blood still flowing down over his skin. "It is the only way I can help you face him. You must take my blood; forge the bond."

Christopher lifted his hand and ran his thumb over Lucias's bottom lip, smearing his own blood as he did.

"Is this not what you desire most in your heart, Christopher? Why should you not have it?" Lucias asked; once again offering his wrist. With a sigh of acquiescence, Christopher gave in and licked at the trail of blood that flowed down Lucias's arm before latching on to his wrist. The strength of the blood hit him immediately, sending an overwhelming flare of lust through his body. Lucias groaned his approval and resumed his position at Christopher's neck as he moved them back towards the bed.

CHAPTER 1 - *Losing Friends*

Present day

Elijah and Barb sat silently in his BMW across the street from his former clinic, talking of the future and watching carefully as the day wore on.

"I will certainly miss this place," Elijah said wistfully; as he looked to the building which had housed his pediatric medical practice for more than a decade.. "Especially the children. At the rate she's going, Chloe will be a grown woman in a matter of weeks, and I do not see any more grandchildren in the foreseeable future. Perhaps when all of this is over, Ethan and Alexa will consider expanding the family. God knows, the chances of Cami ever settling down are dismal."

"I wouldn't be so sure about that one," Barb responded with a laugh. "That Ryan boy seems to have had quite an effect on her though, Lord knows, she'll fight it tooth and nail."

"You noticed that as well? Nothing gets by you, does it my old friend?" Elijah asked with an amused smile. "Even if by some miracle she were to fall in love, I cannot see her giving up her place with The

Elite. No mother has ever been a part of that group."

"Don't you go counting her out just yet. She's a strong one, our Cami. She was the first woman to join them, so who's to say she won't be the first mother? I'll leave the future-seeing to your wife, but I have a feeling that girl will surprise us all," Barb responded, her voice full of hope.

"It would be a very difficult path to take, but you are right; if anyone could manage it, it's Cami."

"Well, there goes the last patient of the day," Barb said, as they watched a young couple pass through the front door of the brick building. They continued observing as the mother loaded her infant son into the backseat of the car and the vehicle drove out of view.

Elijah closed his eyes and focused on their surroundings, listening for the unmistakably slow thump of any nearby vampire hearts. Satisfied that the area was clear, he nodded to Barb and they simultaneously pulled their door handles, stepping out of the car onto the dark asphalt of the parking lot.

As they approached the building, Elijah turned to her. "I did not realize how sad I would feel leaving this place behind."

"Don't you worry; Dr. Jameson is one of the best pediatricians in the country. You're leaving your patients in good hands, and you've got all the time in the world. Nothing's stopping you from coming back, or maybe even opening a new practice after things settle down."

"I can only hope. It does give me something to look forward to, something to fight for; working side by side with you again," he said with a smile.

"Ha, you've got a hell of a lot more to fight for than dealing with my pesky self, day in and day out!" she replied, smacking his arm. "Besides, you know that when this is over, it'll be time for me to move on so don't you go trying to charm me out of it."

Elijah let out a heavy sigh, knowing she was serious. Two hundred and fifty years was an exhaustingly long time for any human, even a witch, to live. "You cannot fault me for trying."

"I can't say I've ever been able to fault you for much of anything, Elijah. You're a good man, as good as they come and you just need to trust in that. All of this is going to work out just fine; I feel it in my bones," she said; taking his hand and giving it a reassuring squeeze. "The storm is coming, but there'll be a beautiful spring waiting on the other side of the rain."

Elijah swallowed hard, pushing down the knot that was forming in his throat as he fought back the tears which were dampening his lashes, and reached for the door.

The pair was met with an ear-piercing squeal when the receptionist, Wendy, jumped up from her chair behind the front desk and ran to greet them at the door. Wrapping her skinny arms around them both, she squeezed a little harder than was necessary.

"Oh, my God! I'm so happy to see you two!" she exclaimed, stepping back to look at them both. "We didn't know if you were going to be coming back to see us before you left. Shoot, I wish you would've called; everyone's already gone home except me, Dr. Jameson, and one of the nurses. Now, what's with you just stealing off into the night?" she asked; putting her hands on her hips and glaring sternly at Elijah.

"You must forgive me, Wendy. It has been a rough few weeks and I wasn't quite ready to say goodbye. I'm afraid this may very well be my last visit, considering the long, hard fight ahead."

Wendy's eyes grew sad. "Oh, God; I'm so sorry, Doctor. I almost forgot. To see you I would say you've never looked healthier, but I guess that's sometimes the way it is in the beginning. I'm sure they're going to take excellent care of you over there in, where was it again, Sweden?"

Elijah nodded his affirmation as Wendy stepped closer and took his hand. "Just know that we'll all be praying for you here, and when you beat that damn cancer, you come back to us, okay?" she said, pulling him into another hug as a tear slid down her freckled cheek. Elijah hugged her back, his heart squeezing tight with guilt from the lie, though he knew it was necessary to protect the people he'd grown so fond of over the years. He knew if Lucias got his way, life for the humans would never be the same, so he was willing to do whatever he could to keep them from the enduring that harsh reality.

"Elijah, so good to see you," Dr. Jameson said; stepping out into the waiting room, a big smile lighting his face as he walked over to Elijah with his hand extended. "I wasn't sure if you would be making it back for a visit before you left the country."

The two doctors moved towards the door, easily falling into a discussion about current patients and the treatment plan for Elijah's non-existent cancer; while Barb stayed behind, chatting casually with Wendy.

Suddenly feeling uneasy, Barb glanced back towards the front door. "Has anyone been in here asking questions or looking for the doctor since he's been gone?" she asked; turning back to Wendy.

"Well, of course; all his patients have been curious, but we've just been saying he's taking a leave of absence for personal reasons. Other than that, it's just been business as usual. Now tell me, Barb," Wendy said; lowering her voice to a whisper, "how bad is it really? You know we all think it's so sweet that you're taking time off to care for him while he goes through all of this. I lost my mother to breast cancer a few years back and it is such a hard thing to witness. If you ever need anything, you don't hesitate to call me, all right? I know there's not much I can do with you traveling so far away, but if you ever need to talk, or if you need any help keeping things in order over here with your house, I'm here."

Just as Barb opened her mouth to express her gratitude, the large window at the front of the lobby shattered, sending shards of glass flying into the room. The small metal object that burst through came down on the floor with a thud and rolled under a plastic yellow chair in the children's play area.

Wendy screamed, startled by the sudden noise, but her voice was drowned out by the explosion which followed, sending her and Barb flying backwards into the wall behind the welcome desk.

For Elijah, the event seemed to pass in slow motion as he tried to run to the women, knowing full well what was coming as the quiet ticking of the device pounded in his vampire ears like a jackhammer. He made it half the distance to them before being thrown back by the force of the explosion as the device detonated. Dr. Jameson, who'd been standing in the open doorway, was thrown down the hallway, away from the deadly heat of the lobby.

With ears ringing and searing burns covering the left side of his body, Elijah jumped up and covered the rest of the distance to his dearest friend as she lay lifeless against the wall, the right side of her face and most of her body burned beyond recognition.

Not wanting to leave her there to disappear in the fire that was spreading rapidly throughout the building, he scooped Barb up and flung her limp body over his shoulder, despite the pain her weight inflicted on his already-healing burns. The smell of burnt flesh filled his nostrils, as his eyes cut to Wendy whose neck was twisted at an odd angle, her mouth still agape in a silent scream. As he reached for her, gunshots rang out from the back of the building, followed by Dr. Jameson stumbling back into the lobby, gripping his chest as he fell onto a row of burning chairs.

Realizing it was too late for Dr. Jameson and the unfortunate nurse Wendy had mentioned, who'd made the deadly mistake of working late that night, Elijah leapt through the blown out window and sped towards his car. Before his preternatural speed had carried him more than a few feet, another shot rang out. With a roar of pain, Elijah fell forward, the force of his speed sending Barb's body flying on to the grass as a bullet cut through his calf. He rolled on to his back, his eyes scanning the area for the source of the attack and landing on two figures clad in black combat gear. Elijah locked eyes with one of the men, his unusually calm face smeared with camouflage paint, while he and his companion climbed through the window. With guns drawn, the pair approached Elijah as a third man rounded the building. Based on the relative slowness of their movement, Elijah knew they were human, a stroke of luck which was the sole reason he would survive.

With a heavy heart, he pushed through the pain, using every ounce of his supernatural speed to move away from the attackers and leaving Barb's broken body lying face-down in the grass. Elijah felt the breeze of bullets flying past him as several more shots resounded through the early evening air. The location of his car was well within the range of the gunman, and thus far too vulnerable, forcing Elijah to abandon it as he rushed away, saying a silent prayer for his fallen friends.

Running until his lungs felt as if they would burst, Elijah slowed and ducked into a dark alley. Typically, any vampire could have covered the same distance, exerting no more energy than a human enjoying a casual stroll but, with the extensive burns that covered his body, his system was directing nearly all of its resources to healing. His chest heaved as he dragged another ragged breath into his lungs and pulled the phone from his pocket. Miraculously, the slim device had survived the blast and appeared to be working properly. He looked down to survey his injuries and stumbled back as a sudden thirst for blood set his throat on fire. It had been a great many years since Elijah had felt the heavy pull of bloodlust and he slumped against the wall under the force of its weight. As much as it hurt, his thirst would have to wait.

Swallowing hard, Elijah tapped a few buttons on the screen, dialing the home his new in-laws were renting on the outskirts of the city. He leaned back, letting the brick wall hold him upright while he prayed that his family was safe.

After two rings, Rebecca Ryan answered, her voice cheery. "Hello, Elijah, how are —"

"Where is Chloe?" he rushed out; cutting her off.

"She's right here playing with William and Jared. Is everything all right?" she asked with concern.

"No, Rebecca; I'm sorry; please put William on the phone."

"Elijah, what's happened?" William asked instantly; taking the phone from his wife.

"My clinic was attacked, and there's no time to explain now. You need to leave immediately, get Chloe to The Elite in Boston. Barb is gone... she's dead."

"Oh, my God," William said with shock. "I understand." he said, knowing full well the implications of Barb's passing. With her gone, all of her spells were broken, including the blocking charm which hung around Chloe's neck and covered the bodies of Elijah's entire family. "Where are you Elijah? Are you injured? I'll send someone for you."

"There's no time, just take care of our granddaughter; I'll be fine. Josephine will call you shortly and we will meet you if we can manage it, but do not wait for us, just get Chloe out of here," he said; hanging up and directly dialing Ethan.

When he heard the click of his son picking up the phone, he didn't wait for a greeting. "Son, you need to get back immediately. We were ambushed at the clinic; everyone is dead," he paused; choking back his grief. "Barb is dead, we are all exposed. I have called the High Commander; they are moving Chloe to The Elite's compound. I must call your mother," he said in one labored breath.

"I have her on the other line. She had a vision; she already knows, but she needs to hear your voice. We will leave immediately for the compound; just let her know." Ethan responded quickly.

"Be safe, son," Elijah said; as Ethan ended the call.

Josephine picked up before the phone even rang on Elijah's end. "Mí vida! Gracias a Dios!" Josephine exclaimed with relief.

"My love, I am all right, but Barb—"

"I know, I have seen. Do not worry about that now, please just get home to me," she begged before he heard Cami demanding to speak to him in the background.

A second later her voice came over the line, calm and collected; the trained soldier in her taking charge. "Father, tell me what you remember. How many were there? What kinds of weapons did they use? How many bodies are in the building?"

As quickly as possible, Elijah recalled the details of the attack.

"Is there any evidence which could expose our people onsite?" Cami asked; already formulating a plan of action.

"No, I don't think so. Barb and I had already cleared out all of the patient records, which would raise questions. Everything else is probably ash by now."

"Okay; I'll contact the Indianapolis base and get a team to the scene as a precaution, but it sounds like there isn't much we can do. The humans will want to question you, but we'll be long gone before they get the chance. We've got much bigger problems now," she said; looking at her mother whose condition seemed much improved from the way it had been before she received the comfort of hearing her beloved mate's voice. "Be safe, Dad; I'll see you soon," Cami said; before she gave the phone back to her mother and rushed from the room.

"I want you to wait for me in the tunnel. Call the Ryans as soon as we hang up and then go there. Seal the door; do not open it under any circumstances and, if anything happens or I'm not there within fifteen minutes, I want you to leave and go to the Ryans'. Do not wait for me. Promise me this, my love."

"Te prometo, mí vida. Te amo."

"I love you, too. I'll be with you soon."

As satisfied as he could be that his family was safe given the circumstances, Elijah turned his focus to the problem at hand. As much as he loathed the idea of attacking an innocent human, after years of only drinking bagged blood or from the vein of his wife, he didn't have the time or the willpower to be so humanitarian. If he didn't take blood while he still had some semblance of control over the craving, he risked putting the entire race at risk of exposure.

He could hear several steady heartbeats nearby, people going about their business, enjoying a beautiful summer evening in the city. Hidden in the shadows of the alley, he didn't have to wait long before a young man wandered by, alone and vulnerable, stopping just beyond the entrance of the alley to watch as two fire trucks sped by with sirens blaring, no doubt on their way to combat the fire at the clinic. Elijah took advantage of the distraction, silently pulling the unsuspecting man back into the darkness behind a dumpster, his hand covering his mouth and effectively muffling the scream which ripped from his throat. Elijah soothed the man's overwhelming fear with his ability to influence emotions and, within seconds, the man ceased struggling while Elijah continued to whisper reassuring words into his ear.

Elijah's fangs dropped instinctually when his eyes found the steady strum of his victim's pulse at the base of his throat. He struck quickly and efficiently, taking only what he needed before smoothing his tongue over the puncture marks and gently laying the man on the ground, with his body propped up against the wall. Kneeling down in front of him, Elijah looked into his hazy eyes, completely wiping away the memory of him and the regrettable attack. It had been years since Elijah had employed memory manipulation on a human, an ability that was inherent in all mature vampires, so he lingered a moment longer than was necessary to ensure that the process was completely effective.

Satisfied, Elijah wiped his mouth on what was left of his sleeve and stepped to the edge of the alley. He peered around the red bricks of the building, sighting an escape path before he sped off down the street, moving with so much speed that he was invisible to the eyes of the humans, his passing only registering as a brisk summer breeze as he made his way home.

Josephine stood anxiously just inside the doorway to the secret tunnel, which ran beneath the home she had shared with Elijah for the last fifty years. Though its secluded location and beautiful landscape were what first attracted them to the property, it was the secret which lay beneath that sold them on it. Used as part of the Underground Railroad back in the late 1800s, the small tunnel, with its entrance concealed behind a large cabinet of shelves which housed canned fruits and vegetables from Josephine's garden, originally led back nearly one hundred yards to the edge of the property.

Shortly after moving in, Elijah secured the exit there and began systematically extending the tunnel until after several years, it linked up with Indianapolis' underground sewer network, providing access to a variety of exit points around the city. Enlisting the help of Barb and several other witches from a local coven, Elijah had concealed and secured the connecting exit, ensuring that no city employee, or enemy, would happen upon its location.

Sensing Elijah's approach through their blood bond, she reached for the handle, intending to open the silver-plated door for him, only to stop short with a startled scream when a voice cut through the still air from behind her. "I thought I told you not to open that door, my love," Elijah chided gently from a few yards away.

Josephine flashed across the short distance into his waiting arms. "Dios mío, you scared me," she whispered; as she buried her face against his chest and inhaled deeply. Even polluted with the smell of smoke and blood, his spicy masculine scent comforted her. "Why did you not tell me you were using the tunnels? I could have met you." she asked; as he hugged her close.

"When I spoke with you, I was not sure if I could get to the entrance downtown without being detected. The men at the clinic were human, but they were no doubt sent by Lucias. I feared they may have been accompanied by one of our kind and I couldn't risk leading them to you, so I traveled above ground until I reached the entrance in the forest," Elijah explained.

"Are you hurt?" Josephine asked; pulling back enough to look at Elijah's tattered clothes, though she already knew he was healed; she'd felt the force of his pain during the explosion and sensed the undercurrent of grief now pulling on him despite his calm demeanor.

As Elijah looked into her concerned eyes, his restraint snapped. He fell to his knees and began to weep without restraint or shame as he clung desperately to Josephine's waist. He cried for Barb, his dear old friend taken so abruptly, and for Wendy and Dr. Jameson. But more than that, he cried for his people as the full reality of the fate they had feared for so long, the fate he could no longer deny was upon them, engulfed him.

In that moment, Elijah's pain was consuming and Josephine could have easily drowned in it as it poured over her through their bond, but instead she chose to fight it, swallowing her pain and blocking it from her husband, not wanting to compound his despair with her own. For several minutes she stood there, murmuring words of comfort as Elijah sagged against her.

"Mi vida, there is not much time," she said gently; as his crying ebbed. "We are to meet with the Ryans at this address in twenty minutes," she said, passing him a slip of paper. Elijah stood and wiped his eyes with what was left of his sleeve. Though the tunnel was almost entirely dark, he was able to read it perfectly with his preternatural vision.

"I know this place; Barb took me there once. The witches who live there helped us save a human child whose illness was beyond the capabilities of science."

"There was no time for details. William only mentioned that they are connected with The Elite and that we will be safe there until our escort arrives to transport us to the compound," Josephine said; as she pulled a clean set of clothes from the bag she had packed.

"Before you ask," she began; as she tossed the clothes to him, "I have had no visions of Chloe, yet I can see everyone else with perfect

S. Simone Chavous

clarity. I've seen Cami at the clinic with some of the local Elite and the human authorities. Their investigation will not turn up anything of consequence and she will meet us at the home of the witches. Ethan and Alexa will board a plane for Boston, but beyond that I cannot see."

"What does that mean?" Elijah questioned; swiftly shedding his burned clothing before he pulled the fresh shirt over his head.

"It means the witches have already begun preparing blocking charms for us and I will not feel easy until they are in place. There is no doubt that Asana is already focused on us." Josephine cringed at the thought of Lucias's seer tracking her family's every move. Without the protection of Barb's magic, it would not be long before Asana discovered their location.

Slinging the bag over his shoulder, Elijah nodded to his wife, preparing to leave when a terrible realization dawned.

"Is it possible Barb was their target all along? Her death exposed us all to Asana's sight, but how could they have known she was the key?"

"Yo no sé, mi vida; but perhaps we will find answers with the witches."

CHAPTER 2 - *The Witches' Home*

"Doctor Kline, such a pleasure to see you again; though I wish our meeting could be under more pleasant circumstances," the tall witch said from the open doorway. Though her face was shrouded in a thin black veil, a symbol of mourning for the loss of a sister witch, her beauty was evident.

"Yes, Ariel; I am sorry for the circumstances as well, but it is always good to see an old friend," he replied; extending his hand. She shook it warmly, reaching up to push back a stray purple highlight which had fallen from the chignon of her mostly-black hair.

"And this must be the lovely Mrs. Kline. Barb spoke of you often," she said; regarding Josephine as she lifted the veil from her face.

"I cannot begin to express my gratitude for the hospitality you are showing our family. We all know the danger and will not soon forget your service, truly," Josephine said earnestly; while gripping both of Ariel's hands.

"Please, there is no need for such words amongst friends. Barb was our sister and thought of you as her own; we would not dishonor her memory or her sacrifice by refusing you in your time of need," Ariel responded, as she stepped away and stuck her head out the door. "Can I get either of you boys anything?" she asked two of the High Commander's guards, who were posted on the front porch. When both men declined with silent shakes of their heads, she closed the door and her eyes as she bowed her head.

With both hands raised and palms facing the door, she began to chant the words to a powerful protection spell. Elijah and Josephine watched with rapt attention as the air visibly began to swirl around her, slightly lifting the stylishly tattered black skirt which hung just below her knees. A soft white glow emanated from her palms as her voice grew louder and papers flew off a nearby desk. The glow from her hands flowed through the air and poured over the door, coming to rest around its seam as Ariel's voice fell silent.

"Now that that's taken care of, I'm guessing you are eager to reunite with our other guests. There is one in particular who I suspect will be quite thrilled to see you," Ariel said with a smile; as she led them down a dark, narrow hallway.

Josephine squeezed Elijah's hand as they followed Ariel through the old Victorian home. Despite the darkness of the day, neither she nor Elijah could help the smiles which lit their faces at the prospect of seeing their granddaughter. Though it had only been a few days since she'd left them, there was no doubt she would be much changed in that short time, given the accelerated rate of her growth.

Reaching the door to the parlor, Ariel stepped aside, allowing them to enter first.

No sooner had the brass hinges let out a low creak, than Chloe sped into Elijah's arms, her increased strength and speed surprising him and nearly knocking him into his wife.

"Grandpa, Grandma!" she exclaimed; as he wrapped his arms around her. Josephine joined in, immediately wrapping her arms around them both. Even knowing that Chloe would be bigger, the change in her appearance shocked them as they held on to the little girl who could easily pass for a seven-year-old.

Her enthusiastic greeting was succeeded by that of her living shadow, Tilly, who bounded up to the trio, with her long tail wagging hard enough to shake her entire body. The haphazard appendage swept across the coffee table in the center of the room as she walked by, sending a delicate porcelain statue flying. Mere inches from shattering on the floor, the tiny figurine featuring a mother and baby hung suspended in the air. Ariel swept her elegant hand across the space in front of her, safely returning the knick-knack to its rightful place.

Oblivious to the narrowly avoided mishap, Elijah released Chloe and Josephine and bent down to scratch the fawn Great Dane behind her ear, a spot that he'd learned shortly after meeting her was one of her favorites. "It is good to see you, too, old girl," he said; earning a lick on the cheek.

"At least some things have not changed," Josephine said; watching Tilly sidle up to Chloe, pressing her body against her as she sat down. Even sitting, Tilly was easily as tall as Chloe, who slung her arms around her companion's neck and leaned in.

"Ah, yes; Miss Tilly has made for an interesting addition to the household already," Ariel added. "Our cats are far from pleased by her presence, though I must say it's quite nice to have a pet around that actually seems to appreciate our attention. The girls barely tolerate us in all our human inferiority," she said with a laugh.

"Elijah," William said; as he walked over and pulled the other man into a friendly embrace. "It is good to see you in one piece, my friend. Our deepest condolences for your loss."

"Yes, we are so very sorry, for you both," Rebecca added; as she and Jared approached. "Barb was a truly lovely woman."

"So you have told Chloe then?" Josephine asked, her sad eyes following Chloe, who ran off with Tilly after a black cat which scurried by.

"There was really no keeping it from her," William responded, "the hazards of being a telepath. Even I have difficulty blocking her; though shielding me seems to be no trouble for her. It really is quite amazing; I've never come across another who could keep me out as effectively as she can."

"I've been working with her, trying to help her learn to control her power," Jared added; as his mother linked her arm with his.

"It's quite surprising, really that, given how close she was to Barb, she didn't seem very upset. She simply asked if she was gone, then nodded and walked away. Everything was happening so fast, we didn't push the issue further, but I have to believe she doesn't fully understand yet," Rebecca stated.

"A small blessing," Josephine added; taking Elijah's hand for comfort.

Just then, the door swung open, drawing all eyes to the short, slightly plump woman who entered carrying a small box. "Elijah, you remember my sister, Tara," Ariel said; as she approached the other witch.

"Please excuse me for not greeting you when you arrived," Tara said; addressing the room. "But we wanted be certain these were ready for you in time for your journey."

Tara walked over to Elijah and passed him the box. He lifted the lid, the scent of cedar filling the air as he discovered Chloe's four-pointed star necklace and three others like it inside. The charms were identical, except for the longer chains on the new ones intended for the rest of Elijah's family. "These should do until you get to Boston. We've already spoken with the coven there and they'll be waiting to perform the permanent spells as soon as you arrive. We would do them here, but there simply isn't enough time."

Elijah gently removed two of the charms and handed them to his wife, who placed one around her neck and carried the smallest over to Chloe, returning it to its rightful place over her heart. Barb had given Chloe the blocking charm the first time she'd met her as a toddler, only a few short weeks before, though as far as Josephine could tell, it was an unnecessary precaution, considering she found it impossible to access Chloe's future no matter how hard she focused.

Josephine's gift had always been strongest when she applied it to her own family, particularly in conjunction with physical contact, yet with Chloe, she saw nothing. Josephine knew that, if *she* was blind to Chloe's future, so was Asana, and that knowledge gave her some comfort.

"Regarding the other matter we discussed," Ariel said; turning to William. "Vivian has agreed to fly to Boston to remove the repression spell for your daughter, though it may be a few days before she arrives."

"We cannot begin to thank you enough," William responded gratefully. "If you ever have need of anything, anything at all, you know how to reach me."

"Forgive the intrusion," Captain Erikson, the head of William's personal guard, said as he approached the group. "But I have just received word that our escorts will arrive in less than five minutes."

"Thank you, Captain," William said; as Erikson rejoined the other guards against the far wall where they had been silently standing since Elijah and Josephine arrived. Much like the human Secret Service agents, who protected the President, the High Commander's personal guard remained by his side at nearly all times when he was away from the security of Red Manor, the vampire equivalent to the White House; at least as close to his side as was necessary, given their vampire speed and reflexes.

The three men waited quietly while the two witches, the High Commander, and his family exited the parlor and returned to the foyer in anticipation of their departure. As they reached the door, Erikson paused, speaking to his subordinates quietly.

"Once we are outside, I want you to stay tight to Red One. I will keep eyes on Little Red," he said; using the team's code names for William and Chloe. "The last two arrivals were exposed for nearly an hour, so there's no telling if their futures were tapped by the enemy seer and this location compromised."

They nodded in response and filed out of the room.

"I don't like this," Cami grumbled; as they turned on to the street on which the witch home was located.

Commander Claesson glanced at her sideways from the driver's seat of the black SUV. "What's to like? The house is surrounded by human residents, there's a hundred goddamn places Lucias's men could be hiding for an ambush, and odds are, we've got a mole on the inside. Seems like the only thing we have going for us is the sun, but that's only going to last a few more minutes."

"Exactly, and I still can't wrap my head around what happened at my dad's clinic. He's sure the assailants were humans, but why would Lucias send them after my father? No matter how well-armed they were, odds were good he would escape. And where the fuck did that picture of Ethan and Alexa on the lawn come from? I wish we could have investigated the scene more thoroughly," she replied; pulling one of her Glocks free to check the magazine for about the tenth time since leaving the clinic. When Cami had arrived on the scene with the local Elite cleanup team, the place was already swarming with human civilians. Luckily, Lucias's men had covered their tracks, making the explosion look like an accident caused by an electrical short too close to an oxygen tank. The fire was still burning strong by the time they'd left, destroying the three bodies that were left inside, along with all evidence of the attack.

"That's the million-dollar question, my dear," Claesson responded; as he slowed the vehicle to a stop. They waited until the other vehicles lined up behind them before exiting. Ten Elite soldiers from the Indy base quickly followed suit, all focusing their acute senses to survey the surrounding area for any signs of danger.

Satisfied that the area was clear, Claesson nodded to the High Commander's guards posted on the porch. One of them put a hand to his ear, speaking a few words into a radio device and signaling to Captain Erikson that they were clear for departure.

After hurried and heartfelt goodbyes to their hosts, the group began filing through the door. Exiting first were Elijah and Josephine, who walked quickly down the stairs to the SUV parked furthest away. On their way by, Elijah tossed Cami the necklace that Ariel and Tara had spelled for her. Catching it in one hand, she let the pendant slip from her palm and examined it as it swung from the delicate silver chain. Recognizing it as being identical to Chloe's, she quickly slid it over her head and pulled her tight ponytail through, allowing the cool metal to fall around her neck. She let out a sigh of relief at feeling the slight weight of the magic against her skin.

The sense of relief was soon replaced with another she couldn't quite describe as she lifted her gaze just in time to see Jared appear in the doorway. With Chloe in one arm and Tilly's leash wrapped around the other, his eyes found and locked on hers like magnets as he descended the stairs. Her heart began to pound even harder than it already was when he flashed a crooked grin and walked by.

Cami silently cursed the gentle summer breeze as it carried his intoxicating scent directly toward her. Its effect was immediate, causing her blood to rush and her thoughts to shift to all sorts of distracting images of him, most featuring far more skin than was decent.

Jesus Christ, Cami. Get. It. Together! she yelled within her own mind, holding her breath while she waited for Jared to move away, praying that the unwanted feelings she always experienced in his presence would pass quickly.

As he placed Chloe on the leather seat, Jared glanced back at Cami. Her unease was apparent, as she fought the urge to look at him again. He reached for her stream of consciousness and smiled wickedly at the erotic images which were fluttering through her mind. His body immediately responded, pushing the scent of his arousal into the air, a most inappropriate reaction given the current circumstances, as evidenced by the disgusted scowl he received from the Elite soldier who was holding the door open.

Jared shrugged and smiled sheepishly at the imposing man while he waited for Tilly to jump inside. "Sorry," was all he could manage as he placed his foot on the runner, not knowing what else he could offer in explanation for his current physical state. Before he cleared the door, a silenced shot cut through the air, the sound too quiet to garner the notice of the humans tucked comfortably in their homes, but as loud as an explosion to the vampires who were already on edge.

Jared spun around in a panic, his eyes searching for Cami, who was running towards the house where his parents and three guards were rushing down the stairs. She bypassed the stairs and grabbed the railing which surrounded the porch, flipping herself over it in one swift motion and landing beside the guard who was lying awkwardly on the concrete. Fragments of his skull and blood covered the wooden swing which swayed slowly behind him. The injury was absolutely fatal, even for one of their kind.

"Kline, get your ass back down here!" Commander Claesson shouted; as the last of the sun's protective rays slid behind the horizon. Though the area was still well lit by sunlight, and would remain so for at least another hour, the direct UV light, which was so hazardous to the infected, was gone. As if on cue, more than a dozen red-eyed vampires appeared in the street.

"No more blood need be spilled here. Just hand over the girl," one of them said in a voice barely above a whisper, but easily discerned by the preternatural hearing of all concerned.

Though she didn't know why, Cami's eyes instinctively shot to Jared, who was already looking back at her. Understanding the desperate plea in her eyes, he nodded in response and climbed into his assigned vehicle. Feeling easier with him and Chloe tucked safely behind a layer of bullet-proof steel and glass, Cami ran back down the stairs, flanking the High Commander and his guards as they made their way to the middle vehicle. Bullets whizzed by as they ran, some so close that their breeze could be felt on the skin of those they passed. William and Rebecca leapt into the car, the sound of bullets bouncing off of the frame around them before a guard slammed the door and rushed to the driver's seat. The already-running vehicle peeled out immediately, despite the High Commander's insistence that they wait.

"God damnit, O'Mally! Stop the damn car!" William yelled; as they moved down the street away from the danger.

"Sorry, sir; but you know I can't do that," Drake O'Mally replied remorsefully; understanding how difficult it must be for William to leave his family in the midst of danger while he fled to safety. Under any other circumstances, as a member of the High Commander's guard, O'Mally would have no choice but to obey William's orders, but in an instance where the High Commander's life was at risk, disobedience was not only permissible; it was required in service of the greater responsibility to their race William's position required.

More shots sliced through the hot summer air as Cami dove across an opening to join Commander Claesson behind the protection of the open door on his vehicle and returned fire. Her bullets expertly found their marks in the center of several of the vampire's chests, yet the men kept coming, walking at a slow, almost taunting pace, completely unfazed by the silver which should have stopped them cold.

"Fuck, they've got Kevlar," Cami said aloud; as she reloaded and two other Elite soldiers joined the fray, taking cover around the back of the car.

"Yep, going to have to aim for their heads," Claesson responded; popping off his last two rounds, catching one of the infected where it counted and decorating the pavement with a spattering of gray matter. The body crumpled to the ground and immediately began to disintegrate as the others split apart and flashed away with preternatural speed, taking cover behind parked cars and trees. Cami heard a loud thud and turned to see one of the Elite fall a few feet behind her, obviously dead, with half of his face missing.

"Kline, I'm going to lay down some cover; get back there and find out why the fuck the rest of them haven't left yet," Claesson ordered; as he reloaded.

As she turned, Cami saw four infected vampires moving in on the car which was carrying her niece and Jared.

Chloe wrapped her arms around Tilly's neck, her whole body shaking with fear as bullets bounced off the car all around them, the sound reminiscent of an intense hail storm. With each impact, the glass's protection grew weaker and weaker, having already cracked in several places. Jared knew it wouldn't be much longer before some of those shots broke through.

"It's going to be all right, squirt," Jared said; trying to reassure Chloe despite his own fear. "We're going to follow your grandmas and grandpas now," he continued, looking quickly to the cars carrying his parents, the Klines, and several of The Elite down the street. Satisfied they had made it away safely, his stare returned to Cami and it was all he could do to remain with Chloe while he watched the infected vampires inching closer and closer to her and the other soldiers.

"Erikson, what's the hold up? Let's get the hell out of here," he said; knowing that if he didn't get away soon he wouldn't be able to resist the pull in his heart telling him to go to Cami, consequences be damned.

Erikson wordlessly dropped the car into reverse and the engine died. He moved the shifter back to park and turned the key, only to be rewarded with silence as he impatiently tapped the accelerator.

"What's the problem? The engines in these things were triple-checked before we left base." The Elite soldier in the back questioned, as he popped the rear door and jumped out. He ran to the passenger door, only to find it locked as several shots struck the black metal around him. With a confused glance towards Erikson, Jared leaned forward and lifted the lock while the captain of his father's guard remained silent with his hands gripping the steering wheel tightly.

"What the fuck?" the soldier questioned; opening the door and looking at Erikson just as another shot rang out. Blood exploded across the front of the truck following the bullet which flew through the soldier's neck and found a home in the side of Erikson's seat. His hand flew to the gushing wound, only to fall away as a second shot shattered his skull, spraying his brains all over Erikson.

In all of the chaos, no one noticed that the other locks had been released until Chloe's door flew open forcefully. Before anyone else could react, Tilly let out a growl which reverberated through the car like a lion's roar, as she lunged. Everything seemed to be happening in slow motion as Jared watched the infected vampire raise a gun towards the protective dog. He dove forward, intending to absorb the shot himself, hoping the distraction would give the rest of The Elite time to save his niece.

"NO!" Chloe screamed, squeezing her eyes shut tightly before Tilly's full weight fell limp in her small lap. Everything went eerily quiet as tears spilled down her cheeks. There were no more shots, no yells, nothing except for the low purr of another engine and the slow beats of the vampire hearts which surrounded her.

After several moments passed, Chloe finally swallowed her fear, opening her eyes with surprise as she recognized the fast thump of Tilly's canine heart. Wiping away the moisture which was clouding her vision, she gazed down at her beloved dog with wonder. It appeared as if she was merely sleeping, with no signs of injury at all. Confused, Chloe's eyes shot to the open door where the infected vampire lay crumpled on the ground with his head pressed against the runner and his arm extended into the car. The gun he'd been holding was lying on the floor at her feet. Chloe gently pushed Tilly's heavy form off of her legs and turned to Jared, whose unconscious body was prone on the seat beside her.

She reached out and placed her little hand on his shoulder, shaking him hard and fast in an attempt to wake him. Her heart jumped with hope at his moaned response.

"Uncle Jared? Please wake up, Uncle Jared," Chloe begged; hearing another groan from the backseat.

"Ugh; what happened, kid?" the Elite soldier asked while he struggled to lift his heavy body.

"I, I don't know. Everyone just, stopped," she responded; her voice shaky.

Tilly let out a little whimper and her eyelids fluttered as she started to move beneath Chloe's feet.

"Chloe, are you okay?" Jared moaned; as he started to come to.

More tears began to flow down her cheeks as he sat up, but this time they were tears of relief.

"What happened?" Erikson asked groggily from the driver's seat. The Elite soldier climbed from the back of the car and stumbled to the infected vampire who remained unconscious, lying across the open door. Grabbing the back of his shirt, the soldier slid his limp body down to the asphalt.

"Who knows, but we're not waiting around to find out," the soldier replied; gripping his Glock firmly and taking aim at the vampire's head. "Turn around and close your eyes, kid," he commanded softly, looking at Chloe.

She did as requested, jumping as the quiet shot penetrated the air. Jared, now fully conscious, pulled Chloe into his arms and watched with amazement as Tilly struggled to sit up on her long, wobbly legs.

He held her close, stroking her soft hair and whispering words of comfort while the soldier walked around the vehicle and deposited silver bullets into the heads of two more of the infected. Jared's eyes darted away in a panic as he searched for Cami, whom he was relieved to find walking shakily towards him, weapon in hand. He let out a long sigh and watched her step carefully over the body of another infected. The disoriented vampire made the mistake of groaning, drawing her attention as he struggled to move. Without looking down, Cami shot twice, both bullets finding purchase in the vampire's skull.

Black wisps of smoke clouded the air surrounding the disintegrating bodies of the infected that were lying on the sidewalk and in the street; apparently another, and rather convenient, side effect of Lucias's virus which made cleaning up the messy scene in the quiet neighborhood a lot simpler.

"Get them the fuck out of here now," Cami ordered the soldier. As she locked eyes with Jared, an overwhelming sense of relief washed over her as she stared into his eyes. With a great deal of willpower, she tore her gaze away and rushed to Commander Claesson, who had managed to take out three more infected, all while leaning against the front vehicle just to keep himself upright.

"Nope, climb to the other side," the soldier said; obeying Cami's command as he pushed Erikson, who was attempting to climb down out of the vehicle, towards the passenger seat. "We're leaving."

"What about the others?" Erikson asked; moving slowly, still not fully recovered from whatever the hell had just happened.

"They're covered," the soldier replied; as he attempted to start the car. "Fuck," he said, turning to Jared. "Change of plans; we have to get everyone to the other car, like yesterday," he stated; before climbing out to help them.

They filed out of the SUV as Cami glared at the soldier. "I told you to get them out of here," she growled.

"Car's fucked. Won't start, so we're going to have to fit who we can into that one and the rest will have to hoof it," he said; indicating the last functioning vehicle.

"Shit; this mess needs to get cleaned up. We can't just leave our men out here for the humans to find," she said; holding her arms out toward the carnage that surrounded them, "But, for all we know, there could be more of those red-eyed fuckers on their way as we speak."

"Perhaps we could be of some assistance with that," Ariel said; as she and Tara stepped cautiously through their front door. "We've already ensured that all of our neighbors are safely asleep for the night, and the rest of our coven will be arriving shortly to help us protect our home. We will take your fallen inside, so send men to retrieve them and give them a proper burial when it is safe. Even if more of those creatures attempt to come here, they will not be able to find the way."

Cami looked to Claesson, who nodded. "All right; thank you," she replied; as she helped a disoriented Tilly climb into the back of the SUV.

"Yes, ladies; as always, The Elite are in your debt," Commander

Claesson said, with gratitude, before climbing into the driver's seat.

CHAPTER 3 - *Dreams & Death*

Alexa moaned and ground her hips against Ethan while she straddled him shamelessly, taking full advantage of the privacy their secluded beach paradise afforded as he tugged on the flimsy string tied at the base of her neck. He delved his tongue into her mouth, giving the string one final pull before sliding his hands to the tie at the middle of her back. Just as the second knot was coming loose, he heard a dolphin call not far off shore, and as much as he wanted to expose the hard dusty-pink nipples concealed by those thin teal triangles, he couldn't forgo the opportunity to see the look of pure joy which lit Alexa's face whenever she was near the friendly animals.

He re-tied her top without breaking the kiss and pulled back to look up at her. Her bottom lip poked out reflexively in response, as it almost always did when he moved away from her. She strained towards him with her eyes still closed, searching for his mouth again, but he slid his hands onto her shoulders and held her away.

Alexa's lids lifted, revealing stormy gray eyes full of lust as they searched Ethan's face, wondering why he was pulling away from her.

"What are you doing?" she asked, breathily.

"At the moment, I am just enjoying the magnificent view, Amor," he responded, watching her as she continued to grind in slow circles against him. Her body jerked slightly as the rotation of her hips pushed his hard cock against her engorged clit. The force of her desire never ceased to amaze and excite him, making him reconsider the break he intended to take, but before he could think better of it, a loud smack in the water behind them pulled her focus. She turned her head just in time to see a dolphin breach the water and come down on its side again.

Ethan laughed and shook his head at the resounding squeal which came from Alexa, as she leapt up and took off toward the bay their villa overlooked.

He leaned back on his elbows in the sand and watched Alexa enter the water. He considered joining her, but his erection seemed to have other ideas, so he decided to stay on the beach to enjoy watching her instead. Lucky for him, the small pod of dolphins didn't remain in the bay for long, sending Alexa back to him after only a few minutes.

He sat up for a better view as she started to come up out of the water, pausing briefly to dunk her head back and smooth her hair. Standing again, she began to strut mischievously up the beach towards him. His mouth went dry at the sight of her sun-kissed body shimmering in the sunlight against a backdrop of white sand and brilliant blue water. The scraps of material which were intended to pass for a bikini were doing a rather poor job concealing her ample curves.

His eyes raked over her body, pausing to enjoy the gentle sway of her breasts for a few steps before continuing up and locking on the bottom lip she was gripping between her teeth. Ethan groaned as her tongue appeared and swept across her already kiss-swollen mouth.

As she drew closer, the sky behind Alexa suddenly grew dark. The wind picked up and swirled violently around Ethan, throwing sand in every direction, blinding him as he tried to rush to Alexa. He struggled to his knees only to fall back into the sand as if his limbs had been bound to the ground. He laid there, paralyzed, as he started to sink into the liquid sand and was forced to watch Alexa, naked and bleeding, being pulled back into the water by an invisible force. She smiled at him sadly, with eyes full of love and understanding as she moved further and further away into waves which had turned the color of blood.

Ethan roared at the sky and suddenly found himself right in front of Alexa, standing frozen on the surface of the bloody water, watching helplessly as another vampire ravaged her neck while she continued to smile back at him. After what felt like ten excruciating lifetimes, the light disappeared from her eyes, her head falling limply onto the attacker's shoulder. The stranger carelessly dropped her lifeless body, standing with his back to Ethan as she disappeared into the ocean of red.

Ethan, too, began to sink as the strange man turned. More and more of stranger's face was revealed the further Ethan descended, until he was almost completely submerged. Just before he was swallowed by the depths, the man faced him directly, a wicked sneer plastered on his face. Ethan recognized his own red-eyed face staring back at him as he fell below the surface of the water into complete darkness.

"I hope you have good news for me, Anton," Lucias said in lieu of a greeting, as he put the phone to his ear; despite the fact that he already knew the mission had failed.

"Sire, forgive me; I don't know what happened," the man rushed out, his voice panicked. "We found them, right where the seer said they would be. Twelve men went in initially, while the rest of us hung back, exactly as you instructed. Everything was going according to plan; we took out two of their men and one of ours was about to grab the child. But then I heard her scream and the next thing I knew, we all woke up on the ground right where we'd been waiting. They were gone and the twelve were dead."

"I see," Lucias said, his tone devoid of emotion. "Are the other men with you now?"

"Yes, Sire; we returned to the safe house Kaleb arranged for us."

"Anton, put me on speaker and pass the phone to the man nearest to you," Lucias commanded calmly. After a few moments, he continued. "Anton, you are to stand completely still, precisely where you are right now; do not move or speak again. To whom has he given the phone?"

"Me, Sire; Nathan," the somewhat confused vampire holding the phone responded.

"Excellent. Nathan, you are now in charge of the unit. Take out one of your guns and place a bullet directly between Anton's incompetent eyes," he hissed.

There was no response, as Lucias listened expectantly, hearing a slight rustling, followed by a click, and finally, a single satisfying gunshot.

"Nathan, I hope you prove to be a more effective leader than your predecessor. Return home with your unit immediately. They are bringing the child to Boston," he said, and hung up.

Lucias paced the space in front of his desk, the exhilaration which always came from a demonstration of his supreme power quickly dissipating as he considered how he had just contributed to the reduction in the ranks of his army. Though thirteen out of nearly a thousand wasn't a significant blow, it was a setback, nonetheless. He had it on very good authority that his forces outnumbered The Elite nearly two to one and, thanks to his virus, they were stronger and faster. Of course, the price of the virus, the side effects which banished his men to the night and made them vulnerable to silver, closed the gap; which was precisely why he needed the child, Chloe.

Asana had been clear; she saw nothing of the child or any of the family beyond their time in the home of the witches. Of course that would be the case; he'd known the window of opportunity would be brief the moment he'd sent the human soldiers to kill the Klines' pet witch.

He scrolled back to the message he'd received moments before Anton's phone call.

From: Restricted
Men failed to acquire, flying to Boston immediately.
No access to flight info. Will contact when safe.

Lucias smiled and slipped the phone into the pocket of his blazer. His informant had proven most useful over the years, but never so much so as in the last few weeks. The spy's information had given him Ethan Kellar, along with his new bride, and the Klines' witch. Not to mention, all of the information about the child, her ever increasing abilities, her rapid growth, even her favorite blood type. Creating the forbidden blood bond all those years ago turned out to be one of his most effective strategies in his fight for power. Though his attraction to men had initially been an impulse of curiosity, things changed when he met Christopher. His feelings for him were far stronger than anything he'd ever felt for Kaleb's mother, a companion he'd taken only for appearance's sake, and he was in no doubt of Christopher's reciprocation of those feelings. Yes, the vampire loved him; so much so that he was willing to betray everything and everyone he believed in.

Lucias felt himself begin to lengthen in his pants, as he considered what it would be like to share his pet human, Molly, with his bonded mate. The circumstances being what they were, Lucias hadn't actually laid eyes on the man in many years. A separation necessary for the achievement of Lucias's goals, but it would soon be over. In the meantime, Lucias would continue to entertain himself with Molly and the humans she brought home for him.

His thoughts turning to the human woman, Lucias ran his hand lightly over his growing erection through the supple material of his expensive trousers. She was out hunting for the night, no doubt selecting the perfect little plaything for him to enjoy, the thought of which made him even harder. In just a few short hours she would return, providing a much needed release and distraction.

Like his spy, Molly had proven to be a very useful addition to his world. Her lust for pain and blood made her a nearly ideal companion, but her fragile human body had its limits. On more than one occasion, Lucias had nearly ended her life by mistake. How he wished she could be made vampire. Blessed with enhanced strength and accelerated healing, there would be almost no limit to the dangerous games they could play together.

She would make an exceptional vampire, Lucias thought to himself. Even constrained by the limitations of human strength, she'd singlehandedly captured the great Ethan Kellar, and his new bride, Alexa; an accomplishment which had eluded more than one of his vampire soldiers over the years. The brief thought of Alexa sparked a new idea, causing a wicked smile to spread across his face before he leaned over his desk and touched a button on the telephone system anchored there.

"Bring Kaleb to me at once," he said into the air.

CHAPTER 4 - *Journey to Boston*

"I don't give a fuck about your rules, Claesson! We were just attacked and I lost a damn good man, so don't try to tell me there's no danger in your precious compound! Where the High Commander goes, we go; no exceptions!" Erikson yelled, completely irate, his face mere inches away from that of the commander of The Elite, as they stood in the hangar which housed the jet they would take to Boston in less than ten minutes.

"I don't think I need to remind you that you're not the only one who lost a man tonight, considering you're still wearing half of him! My compound is the most secure facility in the country; hell, in the goddamn world! We have a leak, and you and your men are on a very short list of people who could be the source. So, as far as I'm concerned, you and your team of guards can shove your demands up your asses!" Commander Claesson retorted, equally as angry.

"Are you implying one of my men is feeding information to that filthy traitor? You've got a lot of fucking nerve! How do we know it's not one of your precious Elite? From what I hear, some of them are itching for a little action. Nothing like starting a war to combat decades of boredom, serving under an asshole like you!" Erikson responded, pushing his chest into the large vampire who had him by at least two inches and a good fifty pounds of muscle, not to mention he was several centuries older, meaning he had him on brute strength as well.

Unlike humans, a vampire's strength increased with age. But Erikson had the law on his side. Attacking one of the High Commander's personal guards was considered the same as attacking the High Commander himself, an offense punishable by imprisonment, or even death, if the High Commander deemed it so. Erikson would have liked nothing more than for Claesson to take a shot at him. With Claesson out of the way, Erikson was next in line to lead The Elite, a highly coveted position amongst their kind.

Being captain of the High Commander's personal guard was a prestigious position as well, but Erikson ached for the notoriety which came with commanding a force of hundreds of the most powerful beings in existence instead of his modest team of twenty. He was ready for it, and he had been grooming O'Mally, his first lieutenant, for years to step into his place if and when the need arose. A planner by nature, he knew he would not be allowed to leave his post with the guard without a suitable replacement in place.

"Captain Erikson, that's quite enough," the High Commander interjected; hearing the direction of his captain's thoughts. Having spent nearly a century together, William was well aware of Erikson's ambitions to lead The Elite. Hell, he even admired him for the aspiration, being a man of high goals himself.

The road to becoming High Commander had not been an easy one. A modest landowner at the time, William had clawed his way up to a position amongst the prestigious members of The Agency all those years ago, his talent for mind-reading allowing him to influence some of the highest members of vampire society and gain their support in his campaign.

When the previous High Commander was lured away from his guard and killed in a hopeless attempt to save his infected son, William pounced on the opportunity by revealing his telepathy, touting the ability as making him impervious to the kind of deception which had destroyed his predecessor. Indeed, his telepathy made him a superior leader and the other members of The Agency voted him into the position unanimously.

Now, looking at his captain, William couldn't help but see some of himself in the younger vampire. The man was driven, dedicated, focused, and unfailingly loyal, all qualities he valued and probably why, over the years, in addition to becoming captain of his personal guard, Erikson had grown to be one of his dearest friends.

"Commander, if I could have a word with you privately," William said; gesturing towards the empty room at the back of the hangar.

Reeling in his temper, Commander Claesson tore his eyes from the staring match with Erikson and flashed across the space to join the High Commander, who was already seated at the table in the sound-proof room. The airstrip was one of several like it that The Elite owned all over the world.

By sheer luck, Claesson happened to be visiting the Indianapolis base of The Elite when the High Commander's call for emergency transport came in. With someone of that level of importance under his care, Claesson was determined to oversee the mission personally.

"Alek, please sit," William said; gesturing towards an empty chair. "Of course I understand your concerns in light of what happened tonight, truly, but I can assure you, no one in this building is responsible for giving information to Lucias. We cannot be certain whether the theory of a spy is valid since, as you are aware, Lucias possesses a seer and it's entirely possible that she's the source of his information. This photograph," he said, pulling the singed paper from his pocket. "is hardly solid evidence since it could have belonged to Barb. As for the lack of contact from my daughter," he continued; stroking his thumb over her image in the picture from her wedding, "we can't yet know what it means. There has been unseasonably inclement weather down south which could have forced them to delay. It is far too soon to tell and I will not leave any of my men in the wind while we wait. Besides, if one of my men was responsible for this, I would know. It would be impossible for the most powerful amongst them to conceal his thoughts from me and I have interviewed each of them. There is no betrayal amongst my men, perhaps a little too much ambition, but no betrayal. I hope that eases some of your concerns."

"My lord, I understand, but you realize we are already making exceptions to allow the, um, other members of your family onto the compound," he said; glancing away from William's knowing gaze. The High Commander was well aware of the fear shared amongst those who knew of Chloe's existence, which was only compounded by the display outside the safe house. He heard it in their thoughts and saw it in the nervous glances they cast upon her when she walked by. They feared the unknown; vampires were no different from humans in that regard.

"You know as well as I do that war is upon us. If that wasn't already clear, it was made abundantly so tonight. The secrecy of our home base's location is vital to the safety of our entire race. You are aware of the kind of information which is hidden there; if Lucias were to gain access to those records every civilian would be in danger. Not to mention all of my men, the other compounds, our armories," Alek continued; running a rough hand over his short blonde hair.

"Yes, Alek, I am afraid that the war we have all dreaded for so long is imminent, but it is my understanding that your compound has been afforded every protection imaginable, of both the technological and magical kind. I appreciate your vigilance, as I'm sure the rest of our people do, but I give you my personal assurance that my guards are not a threat. Now, I implore you to reconsider your decision and grant my men permission to board the plane with the rest of my family," William said; looking at Alek pointedly. The Commander was aware it was within the High Commander's power to overrule him, so he was asking only as a courtesy to afford him the opportunity to save face in front of his men.

"Very well, my lord; in exchange for my acquiescence on this matter, might you grant me the privilege of restricting your men's access within the compound walls? Of course, I trust your judgment implicitly, but my men will be easier about the outsiders in their territory if you will allow this," Alek stated; his lips tight. Submission was definitely not one of the ancient vampire's strong suits.

"Of course, Commander," William said; as he reached for the door. "The compound is your home and your domain. I do not intend for us to impose upon your generosity any more than we already have. When we arrive, you can explain the rules to us all and I give you my word that every member of my party will abide by them, including me."

"I appreciate the consideration, my lord," Alek responded. "Just one more thing; back at the safe house, something happened—"

"With Chloe; yes, Captain Erikson recounted the occurrence as soon as he arrived," William replied; dropping his hand from the doorknob and pivoting to face Commander Claesson. "Alek, you realize my opinions are much changed considering that the chosen one is my only granddaughter, correct? The plans we made all those years ago… I couldn't know how I would feel."

"Yes, of course, my lord; yet with that much power, we cannot simply pretend she isn't the key to defeating Lucias and ending this war."

"No, I did not mean to say we cannot proceed; however, our approach must be delicate. Chloe is still a child, and I fully intend to allow her to remain so for as long as possible. As you mentioned, your compound is one of the most secure facilities in the world. Its protection affords us the time to delay her testing and training until she is ready. From what I have learned of my granddaughter in the short time I have had the privilege of getting to know her, she will be ready much sooner than I would like."

"I understand, my lord. I will instruct my men accordingly. Until you say otherwise, she will be treated solely as a guest."

"Alek, there is something else you should know. Chloe is a telepath; a very strong one. We have been encouraging her to control it, to block out the thoughts of others, but she is still learning. Tell your men to take care what they think in her presence. I do not want her to worry about what is coming any more than she already is," William said; finally pulling the door open.

"Consider it done," Alek replied; as they headed back to the plane.

"All right, hand 'em over. Cell phones, laptops, tablets, any electronics you brought," Matt Jesterman, better known as Jester, said as he held up a large box.

"It's nice to see you, too, Jester," Cami said to the Boston Elite's resident IT specialist as she disembarked from the jet, one of many in The Elite's top of the line fleet. He smiled and shrugged when she passed by. As a member of The Elite, she wasn't required to give up her devices. Everyone else's would be confiscated, have their GPS trackers disabled, which would then be tossed into storage until their owner's stay on the compound was at an end. Of course, as a courtesy, replacement phones would be provided once they arrived on the grounds, but everyone was made aware that all incoming and outgoing data would be monitored.

"Is this really necessary?" Erikson asked; while Jester stared at him expectantly.

"Standard protocol, Erikson. We already went over the rules of your admittance. I thought we weren't going to have any problems." Commander Claeson replied sternly from where he stood with the High Commander, "No outside devices are permitted on the compound. No exceptions."

Erikson's eyes shot to William, who nodded for him to respect the request. Reluctantly, he removed the cell phone from his pocket and dropped it in the box.

After greeting several of her fellow Elite, Cami paused near the row of vehicles set to transport them to the compound and let out a sigh of relief, though the feeling was short-lived.

"Seems like you're in a hurry to get away from me," Jared whispered right behind her ear. After the brief, but intense moments he'd shared with her during the attack, he'd hoped they had moved beyond her denial of the connection they shared. Such was not the case, as evidenced by her behavior during the flight. Even within the confines of such a small, inescapable space, she'd managed to avoid so much as making eye contact with him. If he wasn't blessed with the gift of telepathy, he would have been convinced she didn't care for him at all, but her mind told a different story. Even as she repeatedly chanted how much she wasn't interested in him and tried to distract herself by mentally running through training drills, her thoughts always returned to Jared in ways which clearly demonstrated her attraction.

Jared's intoxicating scent and warm breath on her neck made Cami shiver. She swallowed hard, trying to compose herself again before she finally replied, "Not at all; just ready to get back to base. Don't worry; Chloe will be safe from here." There was no doubt of that with the crowd of heavily armed Elite soldiers buzzing around. In addition to them, the hangar, like the compound, was protected by magic, courtesy of the local coven of witches.

Before he could say anything else, she rushed over to Commander Claesson, who was still standing with the High Commander amidst the rest of the new arrivals.

"I'm going to head back on my own if that's all right," she said; gesturing towards the row of motorcycles across the way.

"Fine by me, but you're to go straight to the compound. We won't be far behind you," he responded.

Cami walked to her parents and kneeled down on the concrete in front of Chloe and Tilly. "I'll see you in a just a bit, all right? When you get there, I'm going to take you to my very favorite place on the whole compound."

"You promise?"

"Absolutely. I just have to do one thing first, but we can go when I'm done if it's not too late. If it is, we can go first thing in the morning, okay?"

"Okay, Aunt Cami. Are you going to ride one of those?" Chloe asked with wide eyes, as she pointed at the motorcycles.

"Yep, see that one right there? That's mine," Cami responded;

pointing out her bike. "Maybe I'll teach you how to ride when you're older. Would you like that?"

Chloe nodded her head enthusiastically in response. Cami stood and smiled at her parents. Though she liked to think she didn't need anyone, she couldn't deny that she had missed them immensely over all the years that her misguided anger had kept them apart.

"Be safe," Josephine said, pulling Cami into a brief hug. Cami was a well-trained, absolutely lethal, Elite soldier, but that didn't stop her mother from worrying. In fact, her joining the group of soldiers had been another part of the rift which had kept so much distance between Cami and her family. Luckily, all of that seemed to be behind them.

"Always," Cami replied; before jogging off. Without looking back, she already knew Jared was watching her. She could feel his eyes on her skin even though most of it was fully covered by combat gear. It was a feeling which had become alarmingly familiar, since his eyes never failed to find her. And though she wouldn't admit it, especially not to herself, it felt good, comforting even.

Reaching the bikes, Cami hitched one leg over her own black and red Ducati 1098 and quickly slid on the matching helmet. It was an unnecessary precaution, given her superior reflexes and ability to heal, but it was the law in Massachusetts and the last thing she needed was a run-in with local law enforcement for not wearing it.

After adjusting the straps, she flipped down the visor and firmly pressed the starter. The engine roared to life, the sound and vibration making her feel alive with anticipation for the open road. She adjusted her mirrors and felt her heart fall into her stomach as her eyes landed on Jared's reflection strolling towards her. Knowing she just didn't have the strength to deal with him or the crazy emotions he stirred in her, she pulled in the clutch, kicked it down to first gear and sped out away without so much as a glance back at him.

Jared stood with a crooked grin, watching until she turned a corner and disappeared from sight. He'd never ridden, but damn if seeing Cami on that bike wasn't about the sexiest thing he'd ever witnessed.

Since he first laid eyes on her at his sister's wedding, he hadn't been able to stop thinking about her and, though he wished it was under more pleasant circumstances, he couldn't deny he was thrilled that they would be living under the same roof for the foreseeable future. Her resolve was weakening and he knew it was only a matter of time before she finally admitted what he'd known from the moment they met.

CHAPTER 5 - *Spells Renewed*

Cami leaned hard as she took the sharp curve, her leg hovering mere inches above the asphalt, before she straightened the bike and slowed, preparing to pass through the first gate to gain entrance The Elite's compound.

Taking a sharp right on to what appeared to be a wide shoulder adjacent to the woods which were adorned with "Private Property, No Trespassing" signs for miles, she came to a stop and looked around. Satisfied that she hadn't been followed, she slowly pulled forward through the enchanted barrier and disappeared from view.

On the other side, the long road which led to the second gate was revealed. The first barrier, a security measure added by the local coven a few years prior, was inspired by the camouflage ability of one of her fellow soldiers. The powerful spell repelled unauthorized entrants, confounding their thoughts and senses if they got too close, and completely concealing the road from view.

Rolling up to the second gate, Cami nodded to the guard posted in the booth and removed her helmet as she pulled up beside the retinal scanner. After a succession of beeps, the red light flashed green and the silver bars began to retract into the high brick wall which surrounded the compound.

As the gates closed behind her, Cami eased her Ducati onto the slope of the tunnel which housed a third gate, this one guarded by two soldiers, which led to an expansive underground parking structure.

After exchanging hellos and a quick fingerprint scan, she entered the required key code and continued her descent. Cami sped down the lane, passing rows of black vehicles as the roar of her engine echoed off the walls around her. Reaching an empty space, she parked and looked around at the variety of colorful vehicles parked nearby.

Looks like the coven is already here, she thought; before making her way to the elevator, where she entered yet another security code and hit the button for the ground floor.

"Cami, how nice to see you again," Esther, the head of the Boston coven of witches, who Cami knew was distantly related to Barb, said as she entered the sitting room.

"It's nice to see you, too, Esther. I'm very sorry for your loss," Cami replied sincerely as the short, African-American woman took both her hands. Her hair was cut extremely short, almost to the point of being bald, but the look worked for her.

"It would be more appropriate for me to offer you and your family my condolences. She was more a part of your family than mine. I never fully understood her reasoning, but she tried to keep her distance from us. I suppose it would have been hard to explain how she was still around to everyone at the annual family reunion," Esther replied with a sad chuckle.

Cami smiled sadly. Yes, a two-hundred-and-fifty-year-old human would be extremely difficult to explain. While a good number of the women in Barb's family were born with the gift and practiced witchcraft, it was kept secret from the rest of their family.

"We are expecting the others soon; why don't you step into the other room with my sister witches so they can get to work on your spell," Ester said gesturing towards the open door. "Even with all thirteen of us, we'll be here most of the night. We are in luck though, the moon is new, which is the best for banishing and blocking spells."

Stepping into the dimly lit room, the familiar scent of dragon's blood filled Cami's lungs, a byproduct of the incense which burned in each of the four corners. Though it had been nearly two centuries since Barb first perfected and cast the blocking spell which hid the futures of her entire family, Cami had been present for the ritual many times over the years as it was performed for each new member of The Elite.

Silently, one of the twelve took Cami's hand and led her to stand in the center of a circle of four witches; the number typically required to perform the spell. Only the most powerful among them could cast it with fewer; or alone, like Barb.

"Reveal your mark," one of them instructed in a whisper.

Cami unzipped her jacket and slid it off, tossing it to the floor outside the circle. She reached around her back and slid her hands under her black tank top, undoing the clasp of her bra and pulling it through the opening of each sleeve before adding it to pile on the floor. Pulling the strap of her shirt down off her shoulder, she slid her arm through and pushed the fabric down to reveal her faded tattoo, while still keeping her front modestly covered. She didn't know how long it would be before the others arrived, or who would be allowed into the room, but the last thing she needed was for Jared to walk in and see her half- naked.

The four witches surrounding her joined hands and began to chant with their eyes closed, as they slowly circled her. After repeating the incantation several times over, one of the women broke from the group and retrieved a quill made from the feather of an eagle along, with a silver inkwell filled with ink comprised of the same dragon's blood as the incense which filled the air. The remaining women continued to chant, rejoining their hands as they began to move again. The fourth witch joined Cami in the center of the circle and wordlessly pulled her down to kneel on the floor.

Setting the inkwell on the floor beside them, she placed her hands over the mark on Cami's shoulder as her voice blended with the chanting of her sister witches. Cami could feel the heat of the energy pulsing through the woman's hands as her fingers slowly traced each line of the tattoo. Though she couldn't see it, Cami knew there was a glow emanating from the witch's hands which would soon be transferred to her shoulder. Cami closed her eyes as the witch dipped the quill into the ink and placed the point against her skin. Ever so slowly, she traced each line, the burn of the ink quickly following the pressure of the quill as the magical liquid was etched into her flesh.

Cami felt a tear slide from her eye and quickly wiped it away. It wasn't from the burn; she had never cried a day in her life due to physical pain. It was the ceremony, the mark on her shoulder, the memories of Barb which filled her mind and broke loose a small piece of the grief she had been fighting to keep at bay since her mother had shared her tragic vision only hours before.

Desperate to escape the pain, Cami did something she'd been fighting so hard to avoid. She thought of Jared and, like she somehow knew it would, thinking of him dulled her pain.

After what seemed like only a few short minutes to Cami, the witch beside her began the final stroke of the tattoo as the other witches ceased their circling and knelt down beside her. With the marking complete, each woman placed a hand over Cami's shoulder, one on top of the other as they said the final words to the spell. With the end of the chant, a brilliant glow flowed again, its light filling Cami's tattoo before each witch stood and removed some laurel leaves from a nearby bowl.

One at a time, they pressed the fragrant leaves over the intricate mark as the light faded, sealing the ink and the magic which would remain intact, as long as at least one of them lived.

"The spell is complete, darling," one of them whispered; snapping Cami out of the daze she had slipped into thinking about Jared. "It's best if you go get some rest now; the magic will draw on your body for a little while as the marking heals."

"Yes, of course; thank you. Thank you all," Cami said; gathering her belongings and making her way towards the door.

She'd been so lost in her thoughts of Jared, that she hadn't noticed how much time had passed or that her parents had arrived. Glancing back, she saw each of them standing among one of the two other groups of witches. Her mother's tattoo, also located on her left shoulder, was almost entirely covered by bay laurel leaves, while the mark on her father's arm was still being retraced.

Suddenly feeling completely exhausted, Cami stepped through the doorway. She searched the room, wondering where Chloe was since she'd expected her niece to pounce on her for the little excursion she'd promised. The spell did take a rather long time to perform, so it was likely that the Ryans had taken her to get settled in for the night. With Chloe still growing, the witches would have to wait perform the permanent blocking spell for her until she reached maturity.

Grateful for the reprieve, Cami decided to heed the witch's advice and get some rest. Oddly enough, she was actually excited, almost giddy, with the prospect of lying down quietly in her bed; though not to sleep, but to continue the little fantasy she'd started in her head featuring a certain young and maddeningly charming vampire. She had no intention of changing her stance on whatever it was between them when they were back in the light of day; but for the moment, even if he couldn't ever know about it, he gave her something she needed.

While she was aching to fall into bed after an exhausting day full of tragedy, fighting, and Jared, her stomach let out an audible growl as her gums began to throb, her body's way of telling her she was overdue for a feeding. Entering the elevator, she leaned against the cool metal wall as she descended, careful to keep her shoulder from touching, though the cold surface would have been soothing to her still- burning skin. She peered at her reflection as the elevator moved, her eyes landing on her lips as an image of Jared's mouth, twisted up in that crooked grin of his, flooded her mind.

The bell dinged, signaling her arrival on the lower level and bringing her back to the task at hand. She stepped out into the darkness and sped off towards the residential wing, but bypassed the door to her suite, making her way instead to the blood storage room. While there was certainly a bag of O-negative left in the refrigerator in her room, she knew she'd need closer to three, given the strenuous nature of the day and the length of time since her last feeding.

Turning the corner, she stopped dead in her tracks, hearing the door to the cold room slide open as she was hit with a scent that was growing maddeningly familiar. Its impact on her was immediate.

Given the vast array of emotions that were already weighing on her, the extreme physical exhaustion, and the fact that she had spent the better part of the evening indulging in erotic thoughts about him, Jared's scent set her blood on fire, and it pissed her off. Somehow, her choosing to think of him as a means of escape had been an entirely different and acceptable prospect because she could at least pretend it was within her control. Actually being around him was a whole different matter.

Knowing there was absolutely no way she could conceal her body's response, or deal with Jared's unwavering efforts to get close to her,

Cami turned and rushed back to her suite praying that Jared hadn't detected her presence, or worse, the scent of her arousal.

Guess one bag will have to do, Cami thought as she quietly closed her door and breathed a sigh of relief, vowing to never again indulge in silly fantasies about something which simply couldn't be.

She flashed across the room, retrieved the sole bag of blood from the refrigerator, and tossed it onto the bed. Swiftly unbuckling all of her holsters, she dropped them, weapons and all, to the floor, feeling too tired to bother putting them in their rightful places.

She considered showering as she stripped off her clothes in record time, but quickly decided against it and fell into bed. Rolling onto her side, she lifted the thick plastic bag to her mouth and pierced the lining with fangs that had elongated the minute she'd thought of feeding.

Cami emptied the bag in a few greedy gulps, tossing it expertly into the trashcan across the room before she rolled onto her back and closed her eyes. She attempted to retract her fangs, finding the task impossible as her stomach rolled, her body's way of telling her she needed more blood. There was no way she was going to risk running into Jared again; so after tossing and turning for a while, she finally found the peace of sleep.

Cami awoke with a start, to the incessant buzzing coming from the intercom on the wall beside her door. Given the acute nature of vampire hearing, soundproofing technology was standard in most vampire households to provide some semblance of privacy. As such, each room in the residential wing of the compound was equipped with an intercom.

Unsure how long she'd been asleep, Cami lazily rolled over and glanced at the clock on the bedside table. She groaned, seeing it was after nine; she'd been out for nearly ten straight hours. A lengthy slumber was to be expected, considering the toll that the magic took on the body and the fact that she hadn't consumed enough blood in her attempt to avoid Jared the night before. Vampires required less than half the amount of sleep humans did; but if injured or blood deprived, their bodies tended to compensate with additional rest.

The intercom buzzed again, this time the high-pitched tone lasting several annoying seconds. Cami climbed out of bed, slipping her crumpled tank top over her wild hair as she ambled across the room. Standing at the door, she tapped the digital display panel, disengaging the locks and soundproofing without bothering to check who was calling. Cami could count on one hand the number of social visits she'd had in all her years living on the compound, so she had a good idea who was on the other side. She pulled on the heavy door and, as expected, was greeted by Chloe's smiling face.

"Aunt Cami," she squealed; throwing her arms around Cami's back. "You've been asleep a really long time."

"Yes, she has," Jared said with amusement, as he stepped into view.

Cami's heart fell to her stomach as she looked at him, feeling incredibly exposed standing in nothing but a tank top and panties. She made the mistake of looking him in the eye and, before she could stop herself, flashes of the fantasy she'd indulged in the night before skated across her mind.

She had never been easily embarrassed but, around Jared, she found herself falling victim to the emotion more and more frequently. Fighting the urge to close the door entirely to hide the blush she felt creeping over her cheeks, she ducked behind it to conceal as much of her body as possible. Her heart was pounding as the seconds ticked by, each feeling more like an hour as her body's response began to shift from embarrassment to something far more potent, and infuriating.

"Good morning, Mr. Ryan," she said formally from her hiding spot behind the door, careful to avoid making eye contact again as she struggled to control her growing arousal.

"A very good morning to you as well, Ms. Kline," Jared responded, mocking her formality; his eyes roaming hungrily over her exposed skin. With the cover of the door, he couldn't see much of her toned body, but he'd already gotten enough of a glimpse to make his mouth go dry.

Cami could actually hear the grin which was plastered on his face as he spoke, but refused to give him the satisfaction of meeting his gaze. She kept her eyes trained on Chloe who, looking up at her uncle, burst into a fit of giggles.

Despite her better judgment, she attempted to steal a quick glance at him, finding his attention entirely captured as he was thankfully focused on Chloe's antics. With him distracted, her quick glance became a lengthy stare with her eyes roaming freely over his lean body. A stylish black t-shirt revealed his toned biceps and met with a pair of perfectly frayed jeans hanging low on his trim hips.

Jared threw his head back with laughter as Chloe made a silly face at him, the deep rich sound causing tingly warmth to skate below the surface of Cami's skin. With her next breath, his spicy scent invaded her lungs and the warmth moved and transformed, becoming an aching fire in the pit of her stomach. Jared's laughter ceased and his body went rigid as his eyes shot to Cami's. Knowing she was caught, her breath hitched and she immediately looked away, but not before seeing the recognition in his eyes, and the desire.

What the fuck is wrong with me? she thought, knowing full well that the scent of her arousal was apparent in the small space and was no doubt the reason that Jared's demeanor had changed so quickly. Backing into her room, she tried to come up with a plausible excuse to escape before she embarrassed herself any further.

"You promised to take me to your favorite place," Chloe stated with a touch of disappointment in her soft voice.

Looking into Chloe's sad eyes, Cami let out a resigned sigh. "I suppose I did, and I would never break a promise to my favorite niece."

"But, Aunt Cami; I'm your only niece, aren't I?" Chloe asked; somewhat confused. Given how big she had gotten over the last couple of weeks, it was sometimes easy to forget how young she was.

"Yes, squirt; you are. Your aunt was making trying to make a little joke, I think," Jared interjected; giving Cami a wink that made her knees go weak.

Cami screamed at herself internally. Her body's ridiculous response to his proximity and antics seemed to be getting worse, as was her frustration. On one hand, she couldn't stop replaying a fantasy of slamming him against the wall and having him do God-knows- what to her body; on the other, she kind of felt like punching him in the face. Mentally grasping on to her feelings of irritation as a means to temper her physical reactions, Cami took a deep, cleansing breath.

Feeling as if she'd regained enough control to feel somewhat comfortable, she stepped out from behind the door.

It's just skin; flesh over blood and bone. It doesn't mean anything if he sees me, she said to herself, stepping closer to her niece. Emboldened, she cut her eyes to Jared, and raising her chin; the silent gesture almost a challenge.

Go ahead; stare all you want, she thought, still focusing on her anger as she looked at him. Jared knew better than to smile at that moment, so he did the smart thing; he looked away.

Satisfied with her perceived victory, Cami reached out and ruffled Chloe's hair. "Yep, I was just joking. You are my only niece, but don't worry; no matter how many nieces I might have someday, you'll always be my favorite."

Cami couldn't help but smile at the satisfied expression her words elicited from Chloe, who looked to Jared at make sure he'd heard as well.

"What's at the place we're going, Aunt Cami?" Chloe asked excitedly.

"Sorry; it's a surprise so you'll just have to wait and see, but I think you're going to love it. Can you give me five minutes to get ready and meet me right back here?" Cami asked; kneeling down to eye-level with her niece.

"Yep; but can Uncle Jared come, too? Pretty please?" Chloe begged. Cami inwardly cringed at the thought as the control she fought so hard to gain wavered. While she'd just made great progress with keeping her emotions towards him in check, spending the day with him would definitely test her limits.

She should have anticipated the request. It wasn't merely a coincidence that Jared had accompanied Chloe to her door; a suspicion confirmed when she looked up to see him failing miserably at trying to appear innocent. When their eyes met, he quickly looked away; obviously fighting a smile.

"If that's what you want; sure," Cami responded calmly. She wasn't one to back down from a fight, and that was exactly how she was going to look at the situation from then on.

"Yay!" Chloe squealed and grabbed Jared's hand. "Let's go tell Grandma Becca," she said, dragging him away.

I can do this; just have to stay focused and keep my mind on what's important, Cami thought as they disappeared from view.

Considering what was truly important turned her thoughts to her brother, who had been out of contact since the previous evening. Shortly after landing in Boston, Commander Claesson commissioned a civilian resource located in the Caribbean to make the trip to Eleuthera and investigate.

Due to the weather, which was likely responsible for Ethan and Alexa's delay, the resource was forced to wait until that morning to begin the journey. Barring any additional unforeseen interference, a report was expected within a few hours. Until then, all they could do was wait.

As she undressed, Cami tried to discard her worry so that she could think through the situation logically. Like a soldier.

Without the protection of Barb's blocking spell, Ethan knew their futures were vulnerable. The more time that passed, the greater the likelihood was that Asana would lock onto their future streams and determine their location; or worse, their destination. Josephine had offered some small measure of comfort on that front by sharing how she had been unable to see Ethan's or Alexa's future since seeing them board the plane for Boston.

Cami knew that Ethan had spent many years traveling and had made some useful acquaintances along the way, several of whom were witches. Because of the storms, it was likely that his plane had been forced to divert, so he would have taken refuge amongst some of those acquaintances and would have had the blocking spell recast, hiding him from his mother's, and Asana's, sight. Yes, there was a perfectly reasonable explanation as to why Ethan and Alexa hadn't arrived, but there was one question which continued to nag at her.

Why hadn't he called?

Cami stepped into her closet, hoping with everything she had that Ethan would show up soon to answer it himself.

CHAPTER 6 - *Chloe's Surprise*

Exactly five minutes later, the buzzer at Cami's door sounded.

Cami opened the door, dressed in fresh fatigues with her hair pulled back in her signature ponytail. She started to smile down at Chloe, only to find herself staring at Jared's stomach. Her eyes shot up to his and out of nervous habit, she grabbed for the strap of the holster at her shoulder, only to find it missing.

While getting dressed, she'd decided to limit her weapons to those which were easily concealed, leaving her short swords and the accompanying leather holster behind. Even though she knew that the compound was one of the most secure facilities in the country, she almost never left the comfort of her suite unarmed. Something about the weight of a weapon strapped against her body soothed her.

Realizing how silly she must look, grabbing at her shoulder that way, she dropped her hand and peered around him. "Where's Chloe?" she asked, becoming increasing flustered.

"Your parents grabbed her when we were passing by their room. Your dad needed to do a few tests on her this morning and wanted her to feed again. Chloe asked me to come meet you; she's really excited for the surprise and didn't want you to think we weren't coming," he explained.

"Oh, well just go stay with her and come get me when she's finished. I'll wait in my room until then," she responded, stepping back; not trusting herself to be alone with him for very long and already feeling her focus begin to slip.

"Dr. Kline assured me that it would only take a few minutes; they will be finished by the time we get to the medical wing if we walk slowly," Jared replied. Having anticipated Cami's reaction, he was prepared to combat her excuses and gain a precious few minutes alone with her.

"Fine; whatever," she acquiesced before stepping out and pulling her door shut.

The pair started off down the hallway, with Cami walking briskly; moving further away from Jared with each step.

"You know, it's nice to see you without swords sticking out all over the place," he said jokingly from behind her, hoping to engage her in a little harmless conversation to slow the pace.

"Don't get used to it; I only left them off for Chloe," she replied over her shoulder.

"For Chloe? What do you mean?"

Without realizing it, Cami slowed; letting Jared catch up to her as she considered his question. "I don't know. It's just, over just a few weeks her life has turned completely upside down. She's so young, but she's going to be a mature vampire soon and everyone has all of these expectations about who and what she's going to be because of that stupid fucking prophecy. Her childhood is literally going to last one lousy year. I just want to give her a little bit of peace and normalcy while I can."

"You mean as much peace and normalcy as one can have while living in hiding on a vampire military base?" he added jokingly; with a smile that didn't quite reach his eyes.

Cami stopped and glared at him, not seeing the humor in the situation.

Jared lifted his hands in surrender. "Sorry, sorry; I know it's not funny at all. I think, I don't know; I just make jokes to try to cope with all of it myself. I understand what you're saying; I feel the same way. She's such a great kid, really special, and not because of the prophecy and all the things she's supposed to do. Growing up with my parents, with my dad being who he is, I don't know; we never really felt much like a family. All these years knowing Alexa was out there somewhere, it was like they felt too guilty to let themselves be happy, but then finding her and seeing how happy she was with your brother, and then this last week having Chloe with us, somehow it all clicked."

Cami's expression softened at his words and they started to walk again.

"I wish I could take it all away for her," Jared continued as they moved. "I mean, she only got a couple of weeks with her parents together, finally having her whole family, and now it will never be the same again."

"I know. The things she had to see yesterday, and losing Barb; it's amazing how well she seems to be adjusting. Not that I have any experience with kids at all, but I'm pretty sure I would have lost it trying to deal with that kind of shit when I was her age,"

"I find it hard to imagine you ever losing it, Cami. You seem incredibly strong to me, and you are very beautiful" Jared replied; his voice low and cautious.

Cami huffed at the compliment, but smiled in her mind. It was an odd response for her; she'd always felt that beauty was a useless quality for a woman to possess, especially a soldier, but hearing Jared apply the word to her warmed her heart ever so slightly.

Jared grinned; pleased she hadn't shut down again but, not wanting to push his luck, he moved the conversation to safer territory.

"Do you expect we'll hear from Ethan and Alexa today?" he asked as they reached the door which opened into the medical wing.

"I hope so. I know everyone's trying to remain optimistic and I admit there's reason to hope everything is fine; but between us, I have a really bad feeling. Why wouldn't they have at least called? They have to know how worried we are," Cami said; entering the security code.

"I've wondered the same thing, but maybe they're just being overly careful. Anything done on a cell phone is easily tracked these days and it's practically impossible to find a pay phone. They know Chloe is safe; I doubt much else is on their minds."

Cami nodded and walked through the door, but the nagging feeling in her gut remained.

"So, you want to tell me what this little surprise is all about?" Jared asked, trying to lighten the mood before they reached Chloe.

"Nope, not really," Cami replied; shifting her head just enough to give him a satisfied smirk; her tone already sounding more cheerful.

"Fine; keep your secrets then," he replied; sounding put out, though he knew full well where they were going, having seen the images flutter through Cami's mind when he'd asked the question. When she turned, he smiled wide and followed her through the door, pleased with the progress he was making.

"She's all set to go," Elijah said; looking up from the microscope he was hovering over as he examined a sample of Chloe's blood. "Here," he said tossing a small backpack across the room. Cami easily caught it, giving her father a questioning look. "Your mother packed some snacks for Chloe. We didn't know how long you were planning on being away, but I want her eating every hour, both food and blood."

"Okay; are you ready for your surprise then, little piggy?" Cami teased.

Chloe giggled and nodded her head enthusiastically. She flashed around the rows of workstations where Elite scientists conducted research, to join Cami and Jared at the door.

The room was typically restricted to anyone but authorized Elite personnel, but Commander Claesson had given Elijah special privileges in light of his expertise and because it allowed them to track Chloe's progress without going against the High Commander's wishes. Both he and Elijah agreed that blood tests, conducted solely by Elijah, and simple observation would provide great insight into her development without being overly intrusive.

Chloe stood between Cami and Jared, taking each of their hands and tugging them into the hall.

"Bye, Grandpa," she tossed over her shoulder as she rushed away.

"Hey; slow down, little one," Cami said laughing. "You don't even know where we're going."

Chloe slowed down and peered up at Cami. "Sorry, Aunt Cami; I didn't mean to peek, but when I was waiting for you I forgot to focus and it slipped in. I saw the horses. You're not mad, are you?"

"Of course not; I guess I should have known it would be hard to surprise you. I'll have to remember to be more careful around you and your Grandpa William," Cami replied, giving Chloe's hand a reassuring squeeze. Chloe looked up at her uncle, who shook his head almost imperceptibly in answer to the question in Chloe's mind.

No, Squirt; she doesn't know I'm like you, too. Don't worry. I'll tell her, but just not yet. Until then, it's our secret, okay? Jared sent telepathically.

Okay, Uncle Jared, Chloe sent in response; feeling rather special and grown-up being trusted with a secret. *But I think Aunt Cami's going to be mad at you when she finds out. She's mad at you a lot.*

Jared stifled the laugh which threatened to break from his lips as they walked. He had to be careful, or Cami was going to discover his secret before he had the chance to tell her.

Sometimes girls only act mad at boys because they like them. You'll understand when you're older, he sent, with a wink.

Satisfied, Chloe nodded to herself and pressed forward, practically dragging them in her hurry to get to the horses. She'd never seen one in real life and was beyond excited to go riding, after seeing in her thoughts how happy the activity made Cami.

A few minutes later, the trio stood outside in the warm summer air. Chloe looked around, her eyes full of wonder as she took in the expansive property for the first time.

The mansion, which stood above the hidden compound, was titled to a Boston Brahmin; a member of the affluent and well-known Adams family, whose ancestors were some of the first humans to settle in the area. The clan's members had been some of the most influential men in history, including two presidents, an ambassador, and a Civil War general. They were also secretly included in an extremely small and select group of humans aligned with the vampire race.

The alliance was formed centuries before as both species fought their common enemies, Lucias and the black plague. As such, the family had donated the house and land to The Elite for use as their primary base of operations in exchange for protection and, when necessary, information.

Catching the scent of the stables, which she recognized from the thoughts of her aunt, Chloe giggled and sped off down a path lined with tall shrubbery.

"I'd say she's more than a little excited," Jared observed as he stared over at Cami.

"Yes; we should catch up to her," Cami replied; feeling anxious about being alone with him again. Things had started to feel different between them; she felt herself relaxing, opening up to him, and it terrified her.

As a soldier, she had conditioned herself to see fear of any kind as weakness, and there were only two ways to deal with it. Accept and face it head-on, or run. Of course, under most circumstances she would have considered running to be yet another sign of weakness; but a soldier had to learn to pick her battles and, in her heart, she knew this was one she couldn't win.

Without a word, Cami flashed away after Chloe. Jared stood there for a moment, barely seeing her move before she'd disappeared from view into the greenery. He let out a long sigh, realizing that the wall in her heart, at which he had been chipping away, had just received a new layer of bricks.

✧

"This is Pegasus," Cami said as she lifted Chloe onto the back of the chestnut-colored quarter horse, "I think he got his name because he can fly," she whispered dramatically.

Chloe looked down at her with eyes full of wonder. "Really? He can fly?"

"Let's find out," Cami challenged as she jumped onto her own horse, snapped the reins and took off out the barn door.

When they first arrived in the stables, Cami had given Chloe a quick riding lesson, showing her how to hold the reins and the basic commands to control the horses as Jared stood back and observed. Though it was Chloe's first time riding, the fact that she was a vampire with supernatural reflexes and healing removed any need for worry.

Chloe was a fast learner and quickly followed her aunt. Jared walked over to the door and leaned against the wood, watching them race off across the pasture. He smiled as the beautiful sound of their laughter floated through the air.

As much as he wanted to join them, it had quickly become obvious that Cami intended to avoid him at all costs; so he decided to keep his distance and let her enjoy the ride with their niece. He would accept defeat for the time being, giving her the space she seemed to want so desperately; but no matter how hard she fought it, he was convinced that, eventually, he would win her heart.

86

CHAPTER 7 - *Waking Up*

Ethan awoke in the dark; confused and disoriented, laying on the cold tile floor. The scent of dead blood completely saturated him as he dragged a ragged breath into his lungs. He moved to sit up, but paused as he felt the weight of the body in his arms.

Despite the darkness, his vampire vision took in the sight of the dead woman perfectly. Even in death, she was lovely. The beast which he had become wanted to toss her aside, to heed the summoning call of his master. Yet he paused; some part deep inside his mind telling him that he knew her, that he did not want to leave her like this, alone in the dark.

He looked around the small room, searching for some indication as to where he was, why he was there with this beautiful creature whose cold, lifeless form called out to the small remnant which was left of his soul. What he found was two more bodies, young women tossed haphazardly in the corner, a messy pile of torn flesh, clothing, and blood.

His focus shifted back to the woman in his arms. He studied her carefully, her nudity making him wish for something to cover her with. His eyes fell on the gaping wound in her neck and the delicate silver chain, which was miraculously still intact, hanging around it. He rolled her gently on to her back and reached out for the intricate dolphin pendant, feeling the need to move it from the cold floor and place it over her heart. When the cool metal came in contact with the skin of his fingertips, a searing pain shot through his hand and up his arm.

With the pain, flashes of images pounded through the haze in his mind; the woman alive, sitting across a table smiling at him while she gripped the pendant over her chest. Him carrying her up a flight of stairs. Their naked bodies lying together, limbs tangled in a passionate embrace. Their arms bound in red ribbon as they recited vows and became one. Her walking towards him on the beach.

He heard her name, a soft whisper in his consciousness.

Alexa.

Then the horrible truth crashed down upon him like a tsunami. This was his wife, his mate; and she was gone. The nightmare was real. He had taken her life.

The roar which erupted from his chest shook the room as he pulled her limp body closer. He held her there, in the darkness; surrounded by the carnage of his bloodlust, and wept for all he had lost.

The light of the doorway called out to her, beckoning her to pass through; yet she remained, a silent, undetectable presence witnessing her husband's, her mate's, agony as he realized what he had done.

She had lingered there in the dark room as he continued to drain her body, long after her heart stopped beating, still feeling the pull of their bond. It was not merely blood which tied her to him; he was a part of her soul. When the two frightened young women were pushed into the room, Alexa's heart cried out for them as she watched Ethan attack. She felt his guilt and torment as he drained them completely, but more powerful was the sense of need, and then satisfaction, emanating from the beast which was taking control.

As she watched the gruesome scene, the light continued to call out to her and, though its force pulled her insistently, the sensation similar to gravity, she held tightly to the love that anchored her to Ethan. In her transformed state, Alexa knew with absolute certainly that, if she left this plane, if she left Ethan, he would be lost to his beast forever; and in life or death, that was something she simply could not allow.

So she stayed, softly whispering words of comfort to Ethan with her mind, longing to wrap her arms around him and soothe his pain.

Ethan stood suddenly, abandoning her body on the floor. She instantly felt the beast rising up again, knowing Lucias was near, his faithful servant awaiting command. It was as if Ethan's soul was split in two; one part belonging to her, the other far more powerful part belonging to Lucias. With each passing second, she felt her Ethan slipping further and further into the background.

By the time the door swung open and Lucias stepped through, it felt as if she was clinging to what was left of her mate by a tiny, fragile thread.

"How are you feeling, Ethan?" Lucias questioned rather politely; without so much as a glance at any of the three bodies strewn about the room. Kaleb entered silently behind him.

"Well, Sire," he replied in an almost robotic fashion.

"Excellent; I am pleased to hear it. Kaleb, I want you to dispose of those two in the crematory," he said dismissively, flicking his hand toward the dead women in the corner, "and deliver this one as we discussed," he stated; indicating Alexa's still-naked form. "Report back to me immediately after it is done."

"Of course, Sire," Kaleb answered before he tossed the two bodies over his shoulder and carried them dutifully out the door to begin his tasks.

Though their weight was slight to one of his strength, the gravity of their deaths pressed down on him heavily as he moved. He followed his father's command without question, out of both fear and respect; but he had never agreed with Lucias's methods or philosophies. He felt no ill will towards the humans; in fact, he never took the lives of those he fed upon. Unlike his father, who not only used human females to satisfy his hunger, but also to slake his lust and desire to kill.

Kaleb found humans fascinating and often spent his free time observing them with longing.

What would it be like to act so freely, to be driven only by my own needs and desires? he often wondered.

For more decades than he cared to count, he had been bound to serve his father; bound by duty and by blood. His only divergent purpose had been to avenge the death of his brother, the brother whose life was taken by Ethan so many years ago, and now that had been taken from him as well.

For the briefest of moments, Kaleb had considered disobeying his father and ending Ethan's life before the virus took hold and Ethan's transformation was complete. He could endure the pain evoked from the sire-bond, or even death if his father's wrath demanded it, but the thought which stayed his hand was that of becoming infected, of losing what little shred of free will he had left.

His father's virus was a powerful and unforgiving weapon, stripping its victims of all prior bonds, those to mates and family, leaving a powerful and unyielding tie to Lucias in their place. His servants would cut out their own hearts if Lucias commanded it. Or worse, they could be forced to kill someone they loved.

Since his brother's death so many years ago, Lucias was the only family Kaleb had; his mother having died giving birth to him, something which was practically unheard of amongst vampires. Lucias never spoke of her, but Kaleb had been foolish enough to ask about her one evening when he was six years old, despite his older brother, David's, repeated warnings.

It was a rare occasion for Kaleb to even see his father back then, let alone speak with him. The words had come out in a quiet whisper he'd immediately regretted when Lucias's icy glare landed upon him.

"You killed her and now I am stuck with you in her place," he spat.

The words hit Kaleb like a physical blow and he couldn't help the tears which began to flow down his cheeks; a weakness which was not permitted in his father's house. He cowered in the corner as he waited for Lucias's punishing blow. Instead he only felt the soft breeze of David's movement as he sped across the room and placed himself between Kaleb and their father.

"Father, he is still a child. If you must, punish me instead. I take full responsibility for him and all of his future training. I vow he will not burden you further with questions of the past or displays of weakness."

"Very well, David; remove him from my presence at once," Lucias stated coldly. "And remember; in the future you will *both* suffer for his lack of discipline."

David immediately scooped Kaleb up in his arms and rushed from Lucias's presence.

Safely in Kaleb's room and out of range of their father's preternatural hearing, Kaleb struggled to speak as he sat on the bed and continued to sniffle. "D-did, did I kill her?" he stuttered, looking up at David with panic-filled eyes.

David ruffled his hair, as was his way, before pulling his younger sibling against his strong chest. "No, little one; you did not kill our

mother. She simply realized the fate of loving a man like our father."
He hadn't really understood what his brother meant, but he was far
too afraid to press the issue further.

Even after so many years, Kaleb felt David's loss immensely. Since
his death, Kaleb had known nothing of love. To his father, he was
merely a tool; a talented soldier with the convenient obedience
derived from the genetic blood bond.

Kaleb kept his infrequent encounters with females brief and clinical,
only doing what was necessary to satisfy his basic needs for blood
and sex. He was prohibited from taking a true mate, from creating a
bond that would sever his tie to Lucias. Not that he would have done
it anyway. In his heart, he feared that anyone he loved would be
ripped from his grasp before he could realize any true peace or
happiness. Lucias was unforgiving and cruel and Kaleb was certain
that any female he showed an attachment to would be used against
him in one way or another. But that didn't stop the longing in his
heart.

He blinked rapidly to fight the sting of tears as he pulled his thoughts
back to the job at hand and continued down the long corridor.

His body tensed involuntarily as he sensed the human woman's
presence. She was the last person he wanted to see.

"Looks like somebody had themselves a good lunch," Molly drawled
playfully; as she rounded the corner and took note of the lifeless
women Kaleb was carrying.

He did his best to keep his face impassive as he passed her silently. She was as responsible for the dead he carried over his shoulder as the vampire who had drained them. She had been more than willing, eager even, when Lucias made the request for her to lure the innocent woman to their facility; knowing very well the fate which awaited them there. And that had only been the beginning.

Kaleb quickened his pace as the hypocrisy of his thoughts washed over him. Was he really any different? He had killed countless humans along with his own kind, under the command of his father.

No, I do not take pleasure in it. I only do what is required of me; I have no choice, he thought, trying to soothe his guilt. But in his heart, he knew there was a choice, there was always a choice; he was just too weak to make the right one.

As he gently laid the women down on the sliding steel slab, he began to whisper a prayer, the light of the fire from the crematorium casting a soft glow on his face.

> *Eternal rest, grant unto them, O Lord,*
> *and let perpetual light shine upon them.*
> *May the souls of the faithful departed*
> *through the mercy of God rest in peace. Amen.*

Kaleb wasn't really sure why he did it, always praying for the dead in this manner. There was no religion in his father's house, and it was the only prayer he knew, having stumbled upon it once during a clean-up mission.

An injured human had escaped a team of his father's soldiers, only to die shortly after, but not before her body was discovered. Luckily, none of her injuries pointed to anything other than a violent assault, no evidence of the supernatural; but to be certain, Kaleb had remained close, examining the police reports, watching the girl's family, and even attending the funeral, on alert for any sign that his kind could be exposed before his father was ready.

He'd entered the church silently and had sat in the back, completely unnoticed by the other attendants as he carefully surveyed them all; paying no attention to the service in progress. Satisfied that there was no risk of exposure, he stood to leave, taking his first brief glance towards the coffin lying at the front of the long center aisle. It seemed so…small. Then his eyes fell upon the blown-up photograph to the left. The sweet face of a blonde girl smiling wide with her two front teeth missing stared back at him, hitting him like a punch in the gut. A child.

Shaking off the memory, Kaleb closed the steel door and tried to pull his thoughts back to his duties. Each day, it had been growing more and more difficult for him to block out the guilt; the pain and remorse growing and festering inside him like a cancer.

Kaleb returned to collect Alexa's body and felt his sharp hunger for vengeance dull slightly at the sight of her. David had been serving their father, intent on forcing Ethan into his service to win favor when he'd been killed. Ethan had been defending himself. Perhaps he could have escaped without killing David and his men, but if he had let them live, how could he know they wouldn't come for him again? Ethan did what was necessary for his own freedom; something Kaleb was beginning to understand. Reluctantly, he pushed aside the pain of the loss of his brother and, for the first time, acknowledged that perhaps for all those years, his anger was misdirected.

CHAPTER 8 - *Molly's Hunt*

Molly carefully spread the ruby-red lipstick over her lips before smearing them together and blowing a kiss at her own reflection. She had been on her way to see Lucias but, after seeing Kaleb carrying those bodies, she went back to her room and got dressed instead, feeling an overwhelming need to hunt. She scribbled a quick note and tucked it into her bra before she walked out the door.

A she climbed into the car, she passed the note to the vampire holding the door.

"Be a doll and give this to Lucias when you get back, will you?" she said; batting her eyelashes as he took it from her hand.

The red-eyed vampire nodded silently and closed the door.

Twenty-five minutes later, the car pulled up to one of her favorite pick-up spots downtown.

"I won't need a ride back tonight," she said; taking the vampire's offered hand as she climbed out and stepped on to the curb. "Be sure you deliver that note; I'd hate for Lucias to be worried about me. Lord

97

knows what he might do," she drawled, her words a veiled threat to ensure that the man did what she wanted. The truth was that she was just as worried about what Lucias would do to her for failing to pay him the respect of telling him what she was up to. Of course, she would be easily forgiven if she brought home an adequate gift.

Molly watched the car pull away before she strolled into the club known for its free-spirited and sexually-adventurous clientele. She was happy to find that her favorite seat at the end of the long bar was vacant. The stool provided a view of the entire place, while putting her on display for any interested parties, and she most definitely wanted to be seen in the get-up she had on. The tight black leather miniskirt, blood-red halter top, red fuck-me heels, and leather choker would attract just the kind of people she was interested in spending some time with.

Before meeting Lucias, she'd come to the club often; looking for men and women who were into the same hardcore kinky shit she was. Of course, no one she'd ever come across there could hold a candle to the fucked up shit Lucias and, as it turned out, she were into. She wasn't quite sure what it was about watching the light go out in someone's eyes, but every time she saw it happen she came like a fucking volcano.

Getting wet just from the thought, Molly shifted on the stool and shivered at the friction the motion caused on the hood piercing between her legs.

She wasn't sure if she actually loved Lucias; in all probability she wasn't capable of such a complex human emotion, but what she felt for him was likely the closest she would ever get. One day he would make her like him. She would be a vampire, his queen, and she spent most nights dreaming of all the possibilities her new life would afford.

"Hey, sweetie, haven't seen you around here in a while," the burly bartender said as he set Molly's favorite drink down on the bar in front of her. "Lookin' good tonight. This is from that couple down at the end; you can't miss the redhead," he said pointing in the direction of the smiling couple.

"Thanks, Drake; guess I better shimmy on over and thank them," she drawled with a wink.

She slung her tiny black purse over her shoulder and hopped down off the stool. Even with the four-inch heels, she was barely five-foot-five. The bag she carried was barely big enough to hold a cell phone, let alone a wallet; neither of which she carried. She had no intention of buying her own drinks and she certainly didn't want to be identified or risk losing a phone which could lead back to her or Lucias in any way. The bartender knew her face, but she never gave anyone there her real name.

No; she had the only things she needed in that small pouch. Lipstick, enough cash for a taxi if she got desperate, and two syringes of M99, a tranquilizer she chose for its use by a lovable serial killer from her favorite television show.

Drink in hand, she walked the length of the bar to the anxiously waiting couple, twirling a piece of her short blonde hair around her finger as she went. As she drew closer, the couple swiveled around on the stools, giving her a better look at them.

The woman's hair was flaming red, with a few touches of blonde highlights and she was dressed in a tight red mini-dress with cream and black stilettos. Her ample breasts were practically pouring out the top of the dress with several inches of cleavage visible. She smiled seductively as her eyes raked up and down Molly's tight body.

The man was average; almost plain, with brown hair and a nondescript face. Slightly overweight and probably below average height, he didn't appeal to Molly at all, but that was of little consequence, since she liked his companion more than enough to compensate.

"Hi y'all," she said brightly. "I just wanted to come on down here and say 'thank you' for the drink. That was awful sweet of you."

"You're just about the sweetest thing I've ever seen, next to my lovely wife, of course," the man said as he ogled Molly shamelessly, before taking her by the forearm and pulling her closer with just the right amount of force.

Mmmm, perhaps I misjudged him, she thought as he tightened his grip.

Nestled closely between them, Molly took a sip of her drink and closed her eyes as she slowly licked her lips.

Lifting her lids, she regarded the woman who was watching her with lust-filled eyes. "What's your name, sugar?" Molly asked, her voice low and sexy. "And please tell me where you got those shoes."

"I'm Violet. This is my husband, Chuck," she replied, lightly stroking Molly's arm. "The shoes are Jimmy Choos; think I bought them at Saks."

"Six-and-a-half, right?" Molly inquired as she ran her eyes down the woman's bare legs.

"That's right."

"Perfect; same as me. I'm Amber, by the way," Molly said as she turned to the man, and moved so that she was standing between his open thighs, his modest erection obvious through his khakis.

"So we could waste a bunch of time sitting here chit-chatting and drinking, pretending we're interested in getting to know each other, or we could just cut the shit and go party at my place. I've got a lot of fun toys and plenty of um, refreshments, if y'all know what I mean," she said tapping the side of her nose.

"Well, that sounds just about right to me. What do you say, Violet?" Chuck asked without looking at his wife.

"Mmm; sounds delicious. And you know, I think we might have a little bit of refreshment for the ride over," Violet responded with a wink.

Chuck settled his tab and the trio abandoned their drinks, leaving arm-in-arm to take the short walk to the couple's new Cadillac.

"Listen, Chuck. I was thinking, why don't you drive and let me and Violet here sit in back and get better acquainted," Molly suggested as she slid across the supple cream leather of the back seat, spreading her legs just enough to give them a peak at the silver piercings adorning her sex.

"Only if you let me get a little taste first," Chuck replied as Violet opened the passenger door and lifted the hatch on the center console. She reached up and turned off the overhead light then pulled out a small square mirror and bag of coke, setting it on the lid after she closed it.

"Sounds like a fair deal to me, Chuck," Molly replied sliding back further to make room for him as he climbed in, his eyes fixed on his prize as Molly slid her skirt up to her hips.

A fast snorting sound cut through the air as Violet did a line of coke. Sniffing repeatedly, she leaned over the seat to watch as Chuck inched closer to Molly; the streetlight outside casting just enough light for her to see clearly.

Chuck slid down onto his elbows and pushed his hands under Molly's bare ass, lifting her up to meet his eager mouth. He slid his tongue up over her slick flesh, the motion tugging slightly on the thin silver chain attached to the two rings piercing her left lip.

Molly moaned and tossed her head back, as he gripped the chain between his teeth and tugged ever so slightly.

"Shit, baby; you taste even sweeter than you look," Chuck groaned as he moved back, hesitantly.

"Mmm; my turn," Violet said climbing into the backseat while Chuck rounded the car and hopped in the driver's seat. She held up the mirror with four perfect white lines on top and offered it to Molly. She took it and quickly inhaled two of the lines while Violet closed the door and Chuck started the car.

"Pass that shit up here," Chuck demanded.

Violet quickly obeyed. When she set the makeshift tray on the console, Chuck grabbed her chin in one hand as crashed his mouth to hers roughly. He released her just as roughly and pushed her so hard she fell back into the seat before he leaned over and snorted back the two remaining lines.

As the drugs slid down the back of his throat, Chuck hollered, "Whoo; this is going to be one hell of a night!"

"You have no fucking idea," Molly responded with her voice low. She reached over and pulled the front of Violet's dress down, setting her large breasts free. Leaning down, she took one hard pink nipple between her teeth while Chuck turned the rearview mirror for a better view.

Thirty minutes later the car turned into the long driveway and stopped in front of the gate as Molly instructed.

"Damn; this must be one hell of a nice place," Chuck said as he put the car in park.

Violet she sat up and looked out her window while Molly pretended to rifle through her purse. Before the redhead could agree, she slumped down in the seat as the M99 Molly injected into her neck took effect.

"Well come on, sweetheart; let's get this show on the road," Chuck tossed over his shoulder, growing impatient to get on to the evening's main event.

"Sure thing, sugar; but how about a little kiss first?" she requested sweetly leaning up between the seats. Chuck obliged and turned back, the sharp needle piercing his neck the moment their lips met. He fell over instantly and Molly wiped her lips with the back of her hand before she hopped out of the car and strolled up to the gate.

"Hey, Sean," she said to one of the guards posted just inside the tall iron structure. "Can you boys give me a hand with the new toys I brought for the master? You can have the one in the front; just take the redhead to the playroom," she said sweetly as if she had merely baked too many cookies and was giving them the extras.

Without a response, the gate slid open and the two red-eyed guards walked out and gathered up their unconscious guests.

CHAPTER 9 - *Training Time*

Cami paused for a moment, her chest heaving from the exertion of the intense workout she had been punishing her body with for nearly an hour. She had been coming to the underground workout facility to work off her frustrations every day since she'd taken Chloe horseback riding.

The rest of her time was either spent in seemingly pointless strategic meetings or alone taking long rides on Pegasus. Although Chloe had asked to go riding again several times, Cami always made excuses, for fear of being forced to see Jared. Since that first day, Cami had managed to almost completely avoid him, only seeing him occasionally and from a safe distance.

She'd considered going for another ride that morning; riding had always been one of her favorite ways to pass the time, but right then she didn't need a peaceful retreat. She needed pain.

It had been nearly a week since she'd returned from the refreshing ride with Chloe and was called into a meeting that changed everything. The civilian resource who'd been sent to Eleuthera had finally reported back, having discovered the bodies of the pilot and flight attended Ethan had hired. Beyond the two dead humans, there was no information to be found nor had anyone seen or heard from Ethan. Starting that night, Commander Claesson ordered Elite security patrols in every major city in which the group had a presence. It was a long shot, but they didn't have anything else to go on.

Instead of joining those patrols, Cami was stuck on lockdown, along with the rest of her family, and it was driving her crazy. After decades of self-imposed separation, she had finally repaired things with her brother, only to have him ripped away again. The thing that infuriated her most was that while she was hopelessly worried about Ethan, her thoughts were almost constantly consumed by Jared. Knowing he was always nearby, thanks to his father's mandate prohibiting anyone connected to Chloe from leaving the compound without express permission, her mind constantly wandered to him.

More than anything, she felt guilty for indulging in some silly school-girl infatuation when she should be out looking for her brother. When she went to Commander Claesson, practically begging him to speak to the High Commander on her behalf only to be told that he saw no reason to challenge the mandate, it took every ounce of her willpower to keep her insubordination in check and not tell him to fuck off. She couldn't deny that his reasoning was solid, when he said she was too close to the situation and that her attachment could be a liability. Reasonable or not, it still pissed her off.

At least he still allowed her to attend the debriefings every evening after the patrols, and he had assured her that if any situations arose which required her expertise, he would see to it that her skills were properly utilized.

Cami swung her arms back and forth to loosen her tight muscles, and reached up to rub the knot in her left shoulder. Touching the tattooed skin reminded her of Barb and, for the second time since returning to Boston, Cami felt the sting of tears in her eyes as she thought of the kind old witch who had been like a mother to her for so many years.

Wiping her eyes, and feeling pissed at her display of weakness, Cami turned back to the workout dummy and readied her stance. Jumping up, she spun around and kicked her leg out, connecting with the rubber man's chest and sending the entire rig flying backwards to the mat as she landed silently, precisely where she'd started. The dummy smacked into the floor and bounced back up only to be met with Cami's favorite sword straight through its painted red heart. With a yell, she ripped the blade out and spun around again, this time striking the side of the neck with enough force to cut completely through the rubber to the metal rod in the center.

"I think you got him," a deep voice said from across the room. Cami sighed audibly as she looked up to see the soldier's reflection in the mirrored wall and instantly felt irritated by the amused look on his face.

Since the day she'd joined The Elite nearly two centuries ago, Dante had taken more of an interest in her than she had been comfortable with. Based on the way other women responded to him, vampire and human alike, she should have been flattered by his attention.

Standing at six feet, four inches, with well-toned muscles, spiky, jet-black hair, and piercing blue eyes, Dante was unusually attractive, even for a vampire; all members of the race being blessed with above-average good looks. Yet another positive side-effect of the genetic mutation which had spawned their race.

Cami found his advances annoying at best, especially considering the way that women rotated through his life. Not that she would have been interested otherwise; her focus having been entirely on her duty as a member of the Elite; but if she was ever going to get involved with a man, it certainly wouldn't be a womanizer like him.

If I was going to be with a man, it would be someone like Jared, she thought, immediately dismissing the idea, telling herself it could never happen. She would never let it happen.

She slid the sword into its sheath across her back and faced Dante, as he leaned in the doorway staring at her shamelessly. Cami silently cursed herself for her choice of workout attire as she stood there in skin-tight pants, a sports bra, and her weapons holster. Having planned on being back in her room before the soldiers returned, she hadn't given the ensemble too much thought.

"Hello, Dante. I was just finishing up if you want the space," she said as she grabbed her bag and moved towards him, hoping to make a quick exit.

"You know, your skills are impressive; but you might find it a bit more challenging if you faced an opponent who can actually fight back for a change," he smirked.

As intended, his little taunt struck a nerve. Up until the attack in

Indianapolis, it had been years since Cami had been in actual battle; The Elite commander keeping her occupied with recon and clean-up missions despite the fact that she was one of his best fighters. When she questioned him about it respectfully, of course, he simply said she was the most efficient team leader for those types of assignments. She knew it was bullshit, considering the other three women in The Elite always seemed to end up on her teams. It had been decades since a female was even inducted and, though no one ever spoke of it, Cami was pretty certain that since his own daughter's birth, the man just couldn't stomach the idea of putting a woman in combat.

"Screw you, Dante," she spat as he started strolling towards her.

"Well, I was only talking about a little friendly sparring; but I'm down for screwing instead," he taunted, further inciting her anger.

"God, you're an asshole. You want to fight, fine; let's go. Pick the weapon," she said, dropping her bag and strolling toward the racks lined up against the wall and ignoring the satisfied smile which spread across his annoyingly perfect face.

"Broadswords," he responded as he pulled his tight black shirt over his head, revealing perfectly formed six-pack abs and an intricate tattoo which covered one side of his bulging pectorals and ran down his side.

Seeing the dark ink of the witches' mark in that location shifted her thoughts to Ethan. She, like everyone else, whether or not any of them were willing to admit it out loud, knew Lucias had captured her brother and Alexa. There was simply no other conclusion to be drawn.

Her heart constricted as she considered the atrocities they must have endured at that monster's hands. Lucias would undoubtedly torture them for information on the location of their daughter, but Cami knew they would rather die than see their child fall into his clutches. So, after so much time had passed, they were either dead; or worse.

Again seized by her own impotent anger at the situation, Cami picked up a broadsword, letting the comfort its weight gave cover her like a warm blanket, and turned to face her opponent.

God, it's going to feel good to kick his ass! she thought as they started circling each other cautiously.

Dante watched Cami carefully as she moved gracefully, and stepped sideways into a defensive stance. He prepared to strike, expecting to be the one to initiate battle, but she beat him to it; moving in and bringing her sword down expertly, catching him off guard as the blade grazed his forearm.

He looked down at the small trickle of blood and smiled.

"I'd forgotten how good you are," he said with admiration.

Dante twirled his sword around in his palm, slicing the air to show off a bit before he lunged. Cami was unimpressed and met him blow for blow, their blades colliding in perfect synchronization over and again as they battled; their movements like those of a dance perfectly choreographed to the music of the clanging metal.

He attacked again, hoping to use his intimidating size to push Cami into the corner; but she spun away easily, jumping into the air and landing a hard elbow to the back of his head as she leapt back to the center of the floor.

Reaching back, he touched the knot at the base of his skull and brought his hand forward to reveal the smear of blood on his fingertips. Damn, she hit hard. The fight in her turned him on; he had never met a woman equal to her in his long life and he felt determined to have her, at least once. He stared at her with hunger as he licked the blood from his fingers.

She responded with a look of disgust and he laughed before gripping the hilt of his blade again. Charging at her with staggering speed that would have been nearly imperceptible to human eyes, he found she was ready for the attack. That was until a familiar scent hit her nose and she hesitated for just a moment as she realized they were no longer alone.

Dante took full advantage of her distraction and knocked the sword from her grasp as he took her to the ground, pinning her with his full weight as he lightly pressed the edge of the blade against her throat. With her lying beneath him, he couldn't help his body's response to her beauty. He stared down at her full lips, unable to think of anything but feeling them move against his own as he moved the sword away and grasped her wrists, effectively pinning them to the mat above her head. He was surprised by the way she had given in, letting him grab her arms that way when his moving the blade had given her an opportunity to escape, but he certainly wasn't going to complain.

Cami stared up at Dante, willing her body to calm down as that intoxicating scent filled her lungs and she felt a flood of moisture between her thighs. She didn't dare glance over to the door where she knew *he* was standing. She'd been learning to focus and control her emotions when he was near; but being like that, in the heat of battle with adrenaline coursing through her veins, she couldn't contain the raw sensations he stirred in her body.

A look of surprise entered Dante's eyes as he inhaled heavily, taking in the obvious scent of her arousal. The look quickly morphed to one of desire as his lids lowered and he leaned in. "Now *that* is an unexpected surprise," he whispered, so close that she could feel his warm breath against her cheek and his growing arousal pressing into her belly.

She knew what was coming, knew she needed to get away; but finding herself paralyzed by Jared's presence, she squeezed her eyes closed as Dante pressed his lips hungrily against hers.

Before her mind could even process the strange sensation, it was gone along with the pressure of Dante's large body.

Jared was powerless to stop the possessive growl that burst from his throat as he covered the distance to Cami in the blink of an eye, hurling Dante across the floor and sending the broadsword he was gripping crashing into the mirrored wall. Before the last shard of broken glass hit the mat, Dante was on his feet, stalking towards Jared.

"Watch it kid. I don't give a fuck who your daddy is; you put your hands on me again and I will end you!" he yelled, stopping just short of Jared with Cami still lying on the ground between them.

Without even acknowledging Dante, Jared knelt down beside her, looking over her body for any sign of injury. "Then you keep your filthy hands off of her," Jared said, quietly turning to face his opponent; his tone no less menacing than Dante's.

"What I do with my hands isn't up to you, sport," Dante stated, emphasizing the last word before he let his gaze roam greedily over Cami's scantily-clad form. "Besides, it's obvious she wanted everything I was giving," he said with a smirk as he glanced back at Jared, who was watching him with rage burning in his eyes.

"She may not know what she wants yet, but it sure as shit isn't you!" Jared hissed.

"I didn't see her putting up much of a fight when I kissed her, and I can still smell how turned on she was. I know you smell it, too." Dante responded feeling triumphant.

The comment which was meant to further incite Jared's anger actually served the opposite purpose. Yes; he could smell the lingering scent of her arousal but, being able to read her thoughts, he knew the response was to him and not Dante. He would have loved nothing more than to tell Dante as much, but he didn't want to reveal his advantage to his competition. That, and the fact that he was fairly certain that Cami would be less than pleased when she realized he had been reading her mind.

"As you seem keen on pointing out, I may be young, but last time I checked, you shouldn't have to hold a blade to a woman's throat just to kiss her. She may not have fought, but she didn't kiss you back, either," Jared stated, turning his attention back to Cami as he gently stroked her cheek, his eyes full of concern over her lack of response. Even her thoughts had remained silent.

The small touch finally bringing her to her senses, Cami's eyes snapped open and she jumped up and sped to the door before either man could protest.

"I'd appreciate it if you both would stay the fuck away from me. I don't need either of you speaking for me and, just so we're clear I don't want either of you or anyone for that matter," she uttered without so much as a glance back at them.

And just like that, she disappeared

CHAPTER 10 - *A Glimmer of Hope*

Back in her quarters, Cami closed the door and leaned back against it, letting her body slide down to the floor.

What the fuck just happened? she thought as she brushed her fingertips over her lips where Dante's had been only minutes before. In nearly two hundred years of living, that was the first time she had ever been kissed by a man other than her father. Even in all her fantasizing about Jared, which included a lot more than kissing, she hadn't acknowledged that somewhat pathetic fact.

She knew most people thought she was cold; the other members of The Elite referring to her as 'the ice princess' behind her back. That was probably to be expected, considering she only had one friend amongst her colleagues, and even that relationship wasn't a close one. Maybe she was a little frigid; she had always preferred to think of it as putting her duty first, but she knew deep down it was mainly her fear which kept her so closed off.

She had lost her brother for so many years because of a love he hadn't even met yet. Now that he had found her, what had it gained him? Barb was dead, he and his woman were missing, probably dead as well, and everyone else he loved was in hiding. In the end, love equaled pain and she wanted no part of it.

Cami stood and took a deep breath, the smell of cinnamon and vanilla and something inherently male filling her nostrils as she did.

This is fucking ridiculous, I can still smell him. "Snap out of it, Cami," she whispered to herself heading towards the bathroom.

She jumped slightly at the light knock against the door behind her, but stayed silent; holding her breath, knowing who it had to be on the other side.

Shit, she thought as she looked back at the digital panel, realizing she had neglected to engage the soundproofing.

"Hey, Cami; I'm really sorry about all that. I don't know what I was thinking, but I just wanted to come and make sure you're okay," Jared said through the door, unsure if she could even hear him.

He didn't know what he was thinking coming to her room now either. Since the first day on the compound, every time he got within a hundred feet of her, she would take off, but he just couldn't help himself. She was like the sun and he was pulled towards her by an invisible force akin to gravity. Every day, he secretly followed her to the training facility to watch her work out and listen to her trying to combat all of her frustrations about her brother, and him. It was an invasion, he knew that; but while a part of him was ashamed, he needed the reassurance that he was still in her thoughts as much as she was in his, even if she wasn't ready to admit it yet.

After what felt like an eternity, Cami finally responded. "I'm a soldier; not some fragile little girl, Jared. I had Dante completely under control before you showed up. I can take a few licks. I've been fighting longer than you've been alive and I don't need you or anyone else to protect me. Now if you don't mind, can you leave me alone so I can take a shower?"

Shit! Now she was thinking of being naked around Jared and had no doubt put a similar thought into his head. He hadn't made much of attempt to mask his feelings for her and she didn't know how much more she could take. The little cat and mouse game between them had been going on for far too long and the whole situation pissed her off. She was no mouse, but damned if she wasn't always running from him.

Employing the only strategy she had to combat her feelings for Jared, she grasped a hold of her anger. Anger was so much easier to deal with than whatever it was he made her feel. Anger she understood; anger she could use.

Without waiting for his answer, she went into her private bathroom, shut the door and turned the shower on full blast; silently willing him to take the hint and leave her alone. But when she looked in the mirror and touched her lips again, her heart and body ached for something entirely different. Before she could stop herself, just for a moment, she wondered what it would have been like to feel Jared's mouth there instead of Dante's.

"You seem to be in a good mood, my son," William said as he looked up from the pile of papers he was reviewing.

Jared flopped down in the chair across the desk from his father, the shit-eating grin he'd gotten when he saw Cami's vision of kissing him still plastered on his face. As irresistible as the temptation was, he blocked her stream of consciousness and walked away when she started to undress. It would have been too much of an invasion; one he guessed she would be unlikely to forgive and when he finally did see her, he wanted it to be her choice; a gift, not a stolen glance through her thoughts.

"I guess I am," he replied simply as he replayed the image in his mind.

"I see; I suppose any young man would be happy about that," William laughed, shaking his head in an attempt to clear the images from his mind. Having been concentrating on his work, William's relaxed mental shields had allowed some of Jared's thoughts to slip through.

"Is it fair to say you have made some progress with the lovely Ms. Kline?"

"Not exactly; but at least I know she was thinking about something other than being angry with me. I have a new problem though; another soldier, Dante or something," Jared said, his jealously flaring as he said the name.

"Ms. Kline is a beautiful woman; you have to know you were not the first man to pursue her, nor will you be the last. All you can truly hope for is that you are the one she accepts," William responded as he started signing papers again.

"Dad; you do realize what year it is, right? I know you're old, but you don't have to talk like it all the time."

"Old habits, my son, very old habits, but I will do my best to speak with a more modern dialect. Is that cool?" William asked sounding rather awkward in his attempt.

"Yeah, Dad; it's cool, and sure, I knew other guys would be interested, but it's a whole different thing to see it happening. That bastard kissed her, but she only let him because she sensed me and got distracted."

"And how did you respond?" William asked suspiciously.

"I know I shouldn't have interfered. I'm sorry; I just lost it for a minute."

"Jared, as a member of the High Family, you cannot afford to act so impulsively. Our people are entering very perilous times and we must set an appropriate example," William responded firmly, though he fully understood his son's impulse, possessing a rather jealous nature himself, when it came to Rebecca.

"I know; it was stupid and it just made her mad. She has feelings for me, I know it; I see glimpses of it whenever I'm around her, but she fights it so hard and I don't know if it's because she feels guilty or because she's afraid. Maybe it's both," Jared said as he ran a hand through his hair. He definitely understood her guilt. Though his parents hadn't told him about Alexa until he was nearly eight years old, he felt as though he had been waiting his whole life to find her. Yet when the time finally came, he couldn't see anything but Cami. And now his only sister was missing, and still his thoughts were consumed by another.

"Anything truly worth having is worth fighting for, my son," William said with sympathy. "I must admit that, while I am happy for you, I do envy you finding your mate at so young an age. Your mother makes me whole and I spent centuries feeling lost without her. If Ms. Kline is your true mate, I am confident you will find a way to convince her."

Jared stood and made his way to the door. "Thanks, Dad," he said receiving a knowing smile from his father before he sped off. As he passed through the corridor, his mind drifted back to Cami in the training center, remembering the fluid, graceful moves of her lithe body. He was thankful to arrive at his suite as the images sent his blood rushing south.

He flopped down on the bed, putting his arms behind his head as he laid back and let the images play, thoroughly enjoying the things she did to him until a vision he had hoped to forget jumped to the forefront of his mind. Jared felt the heat of anger rushing over his body as he relived the moment when Dante stole something which should have belonged to him; a moment which should have been his, and his alone. Cami's first kiss.

Realizing that he was literally shaking, Jared sat up in an attempt to calm down. It was the same way he'd felt before he'd foolishly attacked Dante. As much as it injured his pride to admit, the much older vampire could have easily kicked his ass and then some. More than that, interfering made it look as if he thought Cami was too weak to protect herself. Though he knew he didn't feel that way at all, his actions told her a different story; a story which made her more angry with him than ever.

The anger was a defense mechanism for Cami; that much was evident. It was her go-to emotion whenever her attraction to Jared overwhelmed her. Lying there thinking, Jared didn't know what it was going to take to get Cami to stop fighting and let him in; but he was damn certain he would wait as long as it took.

CHAPTER 11 - *Deadly Discovery*

Alexa's ethereal form followed closely behind her mate as he was led into Lucias's office. Despite the overt silence, Alexa could hear Lucias's thoughts loud and clear. She wasn't certain if the ability was something common to anyone who passed on or if it was a continuation and amplification of the power from when she was still alive. After all, vampire thoughts had been beyond the reach of her telepathy when she lived.

As they moved, she strained to keep her focus on Ethan; his stream of consciousness having remained curiously quiet since he'd wakened. It then dawned on her that she couldn't hear him because he wasn't thinking of anything; his mind functioning like a blank slate waiting to be written on by the one who held the chalk.

She was amazed by the ease with which she accepted this new state of being. Of course, before, she had expected to disappear entirely, to be forever lost in the black of nothingness while her body rotted in the ground or was reduced to ashes. Any form of continued existence felt like a gift. She rejoiced in the thought that she could stay close this way, see Chloe grow up, have a small piece of all the things she was resigned to lose. Yet somehow, deep down, she knew it could not last.

The light would call upon her again and she would eventually become powerless to resist its pull.

When the door to Lucias's office closed behind her, Alexa heard a familiar voice call out to her.

"Hello, sweet child."

Alexa turned to see a rather hazy version of a familiar face.

"Barb!" she yelled out, though she wasn't certain if the sound was only in her own mind or if Barb was really even there. Either way, if she had still been in a corporeal form, Alexa would have tried to throw her arms around the sweet woman.

"It is mighty good to see you, girl. Been a tough week," the old woman said with a touch of sadness in her voice.

"Is this real?" Alexa asked, her voice full of wonder.

"As real as anything else," Barb replied simply.

"What is this place? Where are we?" Alexa questioned; not sure if she meant in the spiritual sense or the actual location of the facility where Ethan was being held.

"You and I, we're neither here nor there at the moment. We're in the space between planes."

"What does that mean? What planes?"

"There's the plane of the living for when we're in our bodies, and then there's the plane of the dead for the soul. I'm simplifying; of course it's a little more complicated, but that's nothing for you to worry yourself with."

"What's on the other side, in the place for the dead? Why aren't we there?" Alexa pressed further.

"I reckon you already know why you didn't pass on; don't you, child? You wouldn't let him go, and you were right not to; there's still work for you to do in that life."

"But how can I go back? I died days ago and I've tried to talk to him, to touch him like this, but he can't feel me. He can't hear me."

"Ah, don't you fret about it; that'll get worked out shortly. But before then, I want you to come with me; you need to see some things here."

"I'm afraid to leave him; he's barely hanging on in there. I still feel the bond, but it's so faint. I'm not sure it can withstand any distance," Alexa said, looking back to Ethan as he sat across from Lucias, in silence.

"Distance doesn't mean anything here; you can move from one place to another with just a thought. So long as you don't pass through the light to the other side, the bond will remain and grow stronger. That's the way it is for true soul mates," Barb assured her.

"I can go anywhere?"

"Any place you can hold in your mind."

With that, Alexa's thoughts immediately turned to Chloe. "Then I can go see Chloe now," she said, her aura practically vibrating with anticipation.

"You'll be back with our sweet baby soon enough, but I need you to stay here with me a bit longer. Don't worry child, everything is going to turn out right as rain; just follow me," Barb said before her form disappeared through the closed door. Alexa hesitantly followed, having to make multiple attempts before convincing herself that she could, in fact, pass through the solid door.

Barb led Alexa on through Lucias's facility, passing by various rooms with observation windows. They paused momentarily to look in each one, revealing soldiers training with a multitude of weapons, before moving on to another wing which appeared to be a science lab. In those rooms, the views were far more disturbing.

"Take note of all of this," Barb said as she led on. "The information will be important when you go back."

"Go back? What do you mean?" Alexa asked just before she started to feel a strange tug. "Barb, what's happening to me?"

"Don't fight it, child. It's time now and don't you worry; I'll keep an eye on our boy while you're gone. Even in this form, I still have some power," she replied as Alexa's form slowly disappeared.

Cami stepped out of the shower into the fog filling the room. She had practically scalded herself in an attempt at distraction after the fiasco in the training center. As she looked in the mirror across the bathroom, her skin resembled that of a lobster, but the angry pink glow was fading quickly as her body's rapid healing kicked in.

She pulled a towel from the hook next to the shower and stepped up to the vanity for a closer look at her face. There was no denying how closely she resembled her mother, whose beauty was revered amongst their kind; but unlike her mother, Cami did nothing to accentuate it. With the exception of Ethan's wedding, she always dressed in black fatigues, kept her hair up tight, and never wore any makeup. Her only feminine indulgences were the perfume she applied sparingly, and the skimpy lingerie she wore beneath her combat gear.

Looking at her full lips, her thoughts returned to Jared. Her eyelids drifted downward as she brushed her fingertips over her moth. Stopping short, she snapped her eyes open, silently chastising herself yet again for the indulgence.

For fuck's sake; get a grip, Cami. He's just a man; like every other man, so forget him and stop acting like an idiot.

She leaned in close and stared into her own eyes as she said aloud, "I have to find my brother; that's all that matters."

Standing up a bit straighter, feeling resolved and a little more clear-headed, Cami yanked open the drawer beneath the sink with more force than intended, sending its contents scattering across the tile floor. Ignoring the mess, she grabbed a brush and pulled it roughly through her mane of curly hair as she tried to formulate a plan to persuade the commander to send her out with the next security patrol.

She returned everything to the drawer and stepped out into her bedroom. The space was much like her; functional, efficient, and relatively cold. The walls were somewhat bare, the only decor in the form of strategically-placed racks and hooks which housed her collection of ancient weapons. Against one wall stood a cabinet filled with the weapons she armed herself with daily. In the closet, there was an array of black combat fatigues and accessories.

Cami dressed quickly in her usual ensemble, carefully sheathing a set of short swords across her back and securing matching Glocks at each of her hips. As she reached for the digital panel beside her door, a familiar tone sounded, pulling her eyes to the flashing light above the door; the commander's signal summoning all The Elite on the grounds to the pit.

Seated at the long table in the central meeting room, Cami glanced around at her fellow soldiers, avoiding eye contact with Dante; though she could feel the heat of his gaze boring into her. The air was full of anticipation as they awaited the commander's appearance.

The wait was a short one; the imposing vampire stepping in moments after Cami arrived, his presence seeming to suck up most of the air in the soundproof room when he closed the door.

He leaned down and placed his mammoth hands on the table as he glanced around. "I've just received word from one of our sources at Boston PD; a human female was found with severe injuries to the neck. He thinks it was one of our kind and, whoever it was, wasn't trying to hide it."

He leveled his stare at Cami and she met his eyes without hesitation. It hadn't always been that way. Back when she'd first joined The Elite, the man had absolutely terrified her. After growing up with the kind, gentle manners of her father, it took her quite a while to adjust to the hardness of Commander Claesson. If the rumors were true, the guy had once been an actual Viking, so tact and subtlety weren't always his strongest skills; though it seemed the birth of his only daughter had softened him up a bit over the last few decades.

"Thompson has kept the crime scene quiet for now; no reporters have been tipped off as far as he can tell, but that won't keep long given the location. The body was dumped in the parking garage at Copley Place Mall. I already sent Martinez out on containment; but Cami, I want you onsite with your team to handle the rest before the shit hits the fan and the story is plastered all over the news. You know the drill. I've already spoken with the High Commander and persuaded him to release you from lockdown temporarily for this. Don't make me regret it."

Cami nodded affirmatively before he continued. "Jester, I want you on monitoring. You catch even a whiff about this on any sites, I want you to take them down."

"I'm on it, Boss," Jester replied as he pushed his wide-framed black glasses up his nose and ran a hand through his curly brown hair. The glasses were a bit of a mystery, considering vision impairment didn't exist amongst mature vampires who, on average, saw about ten times better than a human with perfect vision. Jester opened the laptop he never let out of his sight and got to work. The guy was a technical genius, even if his fashion sense was a bit out of whack.

Thank God for Jester and Martinez, Cami thought to herself. Martinez was the vampire whose ability had inspired the camouflaging protective spell which protected the grounds. Within seconds of his arrival, the scene would be covered with a heavy mist, concealing it from sight and giving any human who got too close a sudden urge to turn in the opposite direction.

As for Jester, he'd disappear into his magical little room, get a lock on every cell phone, tablet, and computer within a mile of the scene and monitor every text, email, and phone call. If he picked up anything remotely suspect, he'd have the device so bogged down with viruses, that the owner would be lucky to ever power the thing up again. On the off chance something slipped by, he'd written a handy software program he liked to call "The Bloodhound" which was always running in the background, tracking local Internet traffic. The program flagged each occurrence of a specific list of key words and analyzed them for potential security threats.

Once Cami's team arrived, it would be less than an hour before everything disappeared as if nothing ever happened. Unfortunately, for the human and her family, the situation would end up being another unsolved missing person's case. That part never sat well with Cami. She hated to think of a family spending years hoping for the impossible, never getting any type of closure; but they couldn't risk the body of a vampire victim being discovered. Not like the old days when supernatural murders were easily masked by a well-placed explosion or house fire. With the advances in modern crime scene technology, cover-ups raised too many questions and required a lot more manpower to monitor potential breaches.

Pulling out her phone, Cami sent a quick text to her father letting him know she was going out on a mission. Tucking the cell back into her fatigues, she stood and followed the flow of bodies through the door before she flashed down the corridor to her team's rendezvous point near the elevator.

"It'll be good to get out of here for a while," Cami said as she leaned against the wall next to Rachel Lehman, one of her team's memory manipulation specialists. While every vampire could erase short-term memories, Rachel and her twin brother, Jackson, could go back a lot further and even possessed the ability to fill the gaps with replacement memories.

"Yeah; I'd go fucking nuts on lockdown," Rachel responded as they waited for the rest of the team to join them. "Guess it's a good thing you only drink from the bag. The commander would lose his shit if someone brought a human onto the grounds."

"Good thing it doesn't apply to you, then," Cami responded, referring to Rachel's inability to drink stored blood. Most of their kind tolerated it fine, as long as they could get used to the stale aftertaste; but there were the rare few, like Rachel, who just couldn't keep it down.

"You must be keeping busy, though; I've barely seen you since you got back, though I did hear a little rumor about you earlier," Rachel added, her eyebrows raised in an unspoken question.

Cami gave her a look that could have frozen an ocean.

"Hey, don't shoot the messenger; just thought you would want to know," Rachel said lifting her hands in surrender. "Seriously though, is it true?" she asked, not being more specific knowing there were too many pairs of supernatural ears within range.

"I'm guessing whatever you heard was an embellished version of the truth. I assume you came by this information through Martinez," Cami replied, her tone laced with irritation.

Rachel nodded in response, giving Cami an amused smile. "Damn! I figured it was total bullshit, considering the source. That was your first time, right?" she asked cautiously.

"Technically, but in my opinion, it doesn't even count; it was nothing. He just caught me off guard; and trust me, it will not be happening again," Cami whispered, thankful it seemed that Dante had left out the part about Jared when he shared the story with Rachel's beau.

"All right, I got it. Won't mention it again. So other than that, how are you doing, really?" Rachel said with an edge of concern to her voice.

"I'm good; just needed time alone, you know?" Cami responded, hoping Rachel didn't press further. If there was anyone she could open up to about Jared, it was Rachel, but she just didn't want to get into it. The two women became friends shortly after Rachel and her brother joined the Elite in the winter of 1910 and, though the relationship wasn't a very close one, she was the only other soldier Cami considered a friend.

"Yeah; I know how hard all of this must be for your and your family. If you ever need anything or if you want to talk, you know I'm here," Rachel said, placing a hand on her arm.

"Thanks, but I'm already feeling better now that the Commander is letting me get back to work."

"So, are we ready to get this show on the road?" Jackson said sidling up to his sister with Layla Jones following close behind.

When Cami turned her eyes toward him, she had to stop herself from cringing. Dante was standing a few feet behind the new arrivals and he was staring at her. He flashed a cocky smile and moved to walk over, but stopped when his gaze fell on Layla's back. Without looking at Cami again, he turned and disappeared in the opposite direction. Cami was instantly flooded with relief, and though she'd never understood Layla and Dante's relationship, it had gotten him to leave her alone and she wasn't going to look a gift horse in the mouth.

"Where are the others?" Cami asked, feeling eager to get moving. As with most clean-up missions, time was of the essence.

"This is it; Beckett and Jasmine are meeting us upstairs," Jackson responded.

"All right, then; let's move out," Cami said a millisecond before disappearing down the hallway.

Ten minutes later, Cami was staring out the window of one of The

Elite's many black Escalades. Even with highly-evolved night vision, it was difficult to see through the layer of heavy UV prevention tinting. The feature had been added recently to allow for daytime transport of infected prisoners, just in case they were ever lucky enough to catch one alive.

The bodies recovered at Alexa's home in Fishers hadn't lasted the short drive back to the Indianapolis compound. Upon arrival, the body bags were unzipped, revealing messes of unidentifiable black goo. Even with the aid of witches and some of the world's best scientists, they couldn't obtain any viable samples for testing.

"So, Cami; what's going on with you and Dante?" Layla asked from the middle row of seats.

While she attempted to keep her tone light, there was a slight shake in her voice as she spoke. Layla and Dante had been close friends for as long as Cami had known them and it seemed obvious to everyone, with perhaps the exception of Dante, that Layla was interested in more than friendship. Their relationship was quite a mystery with Dante slaking his thirst and his desire with a slew of random strangers, while Layla, a gorgeous blonde with green eyes and ivory skin like to porcelain, waited in the wings. Of course, being well over one hundred years old, she was no innocent virgin; so while Dante remained her heart's desire, her body found comfort in those who were willing.

"Absolutely nothing is up," Cami replied cooly, keeping her gaze forward. *Fucking Dante.*

"Oh; I just thought I heard him mention something, but I guess I misunderstood. You know he really likes you, right?" Layla added wistfully.

Hearing the sadness in her voice, Cami leaned around her seat. "Listen, Layla; the only thing I'm interested in right now is getting through this mission. But trust me when I tell you, there's really nothing between me and Dante."

Layla nodded, her mouth turned up in an unconvincing half-smile. They passed the remainder of the ride to Copley Place in relative silence.

As Cami's team rolled into the parking garage, she tapped the touchscreen on the dash and locked on to the GPS in Martinez's phone. Without it they wouldn't be able to locate the crime scene through his layer of mist which not only fooled humans, but was also impervious to vampire eyes. Luckily, the mental persuasion didn't affect them or they would be driving around for hours feeling the urge to turn away every time they neared the scene. It was a damn handy trick, but it was going to be a long night for any humans who had parked in the vicinity.

"All right, Beckett; looks like were just a few yards out," Cami said to the group's newest addition, drawing his attention to the digital display.

Jacob Beckett confidently swung the vehicle into an available parking space. One of the youngest and newest members of The Elite, he'd been discovered by Jasmine Black, a fellow team member, dominating the NASCAR circuit. Given that Jasmine's special ability was persuasion coupled with the fact that she was very easy on the eyes, inducing the somewhat arrogant vampire to join their cause hadn't posed much of a challenge.

The six vampires stepped out of the vehicle and continued to the scene on foot. Seeing the telltale distortion in the air, Cami stopped just short of the invisible barrier and glanced around. The others followed suit, focusing their senses on the surrounding area. The last thing they needed was for some unsuspecting shopper to witness six people disappearing into thin air.

Satisfied that it was clear, one by one they stepped through the camouflage. Coming out on the other side, they were met by the curious stares of several uninformed officers. Martinez's mist functioned like one-way glass, allowing those inside to see and hear what was going on outside, so the new arrivals, who were clad in combat gear and armed to the teeth, stopping and looking around without acknowledging all of the activity right in front of them had to seem odd.

Detective Thompson, the civilian vampire who called in the body, had already fed the other officers a story regarding a special government task force joining the investigation in pursuit of a suspected serial killer, or terrorist, or something along those lines. It didn't really matter; they wouldn't remember any of it for very long.

Cami quickly surveyed the crime scene, noting the covered body lying in the middle of the lane.

Oh, yeah; whoever dumped her definitely wanted her to be found. As the thought crossed her mind, she got a bad feeling in the pit of her stomach, but brushed it aside. It wasn't like she should feel good while cleaning up a murder.

Noting Martinez sitting alone in his car, she started walking towards Detective Thompson. Maintaining the mist required a lot of concentration, so she knew better than to disturb him until they were ready to lift the veil.

"Hey there, Cami. It's been a while," Thompson said with a smile as he pulled her into a light embrace. He wasn't as tall as most of the men she knew, but at around six feet with broad shoulders, thick dirty blonde hair, and kind brown eyes, he was still an impressive man. Cami was always surprised by his warmth and kindness, given his line of work. As a homicide detective, he saw more than his fair share of evil and depravity.

"Damn it, Thompson; you know I hate your touchy-feely shit," she replied, only half-serious.

While it was true that she wasn't typically a fan of displays of affection, she'd grown fond of the civilian vampire over the years. He had been an invaluable source to The Elite and was something like a friend to Cami. It was unfortunate that he hadn't been born of a stronger bloodline; even having all the drive and dedication of an Elite soldier, he lacked the genetic makeup to back it up in battle, so instead he had become one of the thousands of civilians employed by The Elite to help protect the secret of their kind's existence.

"All right; so what have we got?" Cami asked getting down to business. Not that she was in any hurry to return to lockdown, but they needed to get the situation taken care of a quickly as possible.

"The husband and wife who found our victim are in my car waiting to be interviewed further. We got lucky; they waited here for the patrol car thanks to Glenda in dispatch advising them to wait in their car. Gotta love that woman; told them they would risk contaminating the crime scene and whoever did this might get off because of it."

"Jackson, you go have a little chat with our witnesses. Rachel, round up the other officers for debriefing. Make it clean; this was just a false alarm, some bored kids making crank calls. They all went home sick with food poisoning from some bad Chinese they grabbed after clearing the scene." Cami instructed making up the new memories on the fly. "Beckett, pull transport in to load her up. Layla and Jasmine, go with him and sweep the level again. Oh, and get coordinates on the nearest crematorium; I think it's Benson's, but double check me. I'm overdue for a feeding so I'm in no mood to ride very far smelling dead blood."

When the three walked away, Cami silently chastised herself for waiting so long to feed. She'd just been so distracted lately with Ethan's disappearance and...Jared. Shit; she had actually managed to go several minutes without thinking about him.

I should have made a pit stop at blood storage, Cami thought realizing she hadn't fed since the single bag she drank after the witches recast her blocking spell. She'd been so distracted by Ethan's disappearance and her efforts to avoid Jared that it had slipped her mind.

When the other soldiers passed through the mist, Cami rejoined Detective Thompson near the body. Not wanting to get too close with her growing hunger, she stood back several feet while he pulled back the heavy black plastic.

As Cami looked down at the deathly-still face of the woman, the only hint of color the dried blood smeared across her right jaw from the gaping wound in her neck, she felt the bile rising in her throat as her heart fell into her stomach.

"Fuck me."

CHAPTER 12 - *Coming Home*

Chloe giggled loudly as she sped through the hallway, looking for a place to hide while Jared counted. Seeing that the door to the training center was open, she slipped inside and made herself as small as possible behind a cabinet.

"Forty-eight, forty-nine, fifty!" Jared finished over one hundred yards away, signaling the start of his search. Since their arrival in Boston, Chloe's growth rate had increased exponentially. At ten months old, she already looked like a girl of thirteen and most of her preternatural abilities were as strong as, if not stronger than, any fully- mature vampire.

Chloe concentrated on blocking her thoughts from Jared while she continued to listen in on his. With a mind that seemed to have developed even faster than her body, Chloe had already grown bored with the childish game, but Jared had insisted that it was great practice for controlling her telepathy. Realizing he'd already picked up on her scent through his thoughts, Chloe wished she'd found a better hiding place.

Her eyes scanned the large room, the bulk of which was open space, eventually rising to the beams over her head.

I wonder if I can jump that high, she thought, looking for something she could boost herself up with, but as she thought about the space above, she felt the strangest sensation in her stomach. A second later, she panicked a little as her feet left the ground, only to immediately drop back down.

"Whoa," she said aloud as she looked at her reflection in the mirrored wall. Watching carefully, she thought about the space near the ceiling again, and sure enough, the sensation in her stomach returned, followed by her rising up. A few seconds later, she was floating horizontally against the ceiling, watching silently as Jared entered the room.

Jared looked around, certain Chloe was somewhere inside judging by the strength of her scent, a light, sweet mixture of lavender and vanilla, but as he inhaled, another more faint aroma filled his lungs and his heart squeezed. Of course that room would remind him of Cami; he'd been watching her train there every day. It was the only way he'd been able to see her, but that was over. After the mess with Dante that morning, she would likely avoid going there for a while. Turning his thoughts back to the task at hand, he closed his eyes and focused, trying to pick up the stream of Chloe's thoughts.

"It seems you are getting really good at blocking me, little one," he said aloud with pride in his tone. "I can hear your heart, but nothing from your mind."

Still listening to the steady beat, he opened his eyes and started walking towards the source of the sound. As he drew closer to the door, his eyes swept the length of the wall. His eyebrows moved inward as he realized there was no place for Chloe to hide on that side of the room.

Chloe couldn't hold back the giggle which burst forth when she saw the confused look on her uncle's face.

"What the— when did you learn to do that?" Jared questioned, his eyes wide.

"Um, about thirty seconds ago I guess. I just thought about, and it happened, kind of like when I move objects except I thought about moving me instead." Chloe said proudly as she floated back to the mat.

While Jared was beyond impressed with Chloe's new ability, he was more worried about her than ever. She had so much power and when he looked into her big, greenish-gray eyes, it wasn't the stare of a little girl looking back at him. Chloe's eyes were those of a very old soul and the deep knowledge, the weariness he saw in them, would only grow as her complicated life unfolded. With all his heart he wished she could walk a different path; that she could just be a normal carefree little girl, but such was not her fate.

"I'm sorry I'm not normal," Chloe whispered, her eyes cast downward.

Jared placed his fingers under her chin and lifted her face. "What did I tell you about listening in to other's thoughts when we're not playing games, squirt?"

"I know, I know; but sometimes I can't help it."

Jared placed his hands on Chloe's shoulders and looked into her eyes. "Normal is boring. You're a lot better than normal; you're special. You know that, right?"

She nodded and smiled, but it didn't quite reach her eyes, which suddenly looked sad. "Have you heard anything about my mom and dad?"

Jared immediately snapped his shields in place, not trusting that Chloe wasn't still listening in on him as he considered how to answer. "Not yet, but I'm sure they're doing everything they can to get back to you."

"Aunt Cami thinks they're dead. I think Grandma Rebecca does, too, but they're wrong. I know they're not; I can feel them in here," she said putting her hand to her heart.

Unable to speak, Jared pulled Chloe into a hug, squeezing her tightly as he prayed she was right.

"You all right, Cami?" Detective Thompson asked with concern as he watched her stumble back from the body he'd just revealed.

"No. Yeah. Fuck. I don't know." She replied feeling completely disoriented. The sound of a car engine turning over drew her attention. She watched in silence as the officers climbed into their cars, preparing to leave the scene and no doubt heading home to pass out. They'd wake up in the morning believing they had spent the evening hovering over the toilet. The two civilian witnesses followed suit, getting back into their sensible hybrid.

While Cami was distracted, Jackson grabbed a hold of the body, dragging it out of the driving lane to make room for the vehicles to pass through. "Be fucking careful with her!" Cami snapped, eliciting a confused look from Jackson who then scooped the body up and laid it gently beside Thompson's unmarked sedan.

"What's going on, Cami?" Thompson asked, his voice laced with concern. Though vampire killings had been few and far between over recent years, usually arising from feedings which had gotten out of hand, he'd seen Cami in action enough times to know that she wasn't easily shaken up.

"I know her." Cami stated taking a deep breath. "She's my sister-in-law. Fuck; *was* my sister-in-law," she continued quietly doing all she could to keep her emotions in check.

"Oh, shit. I'm so sorry, Cami. Just tell me what you want to do. How do you want to play this one?" Thompson asked as he put a hand on her back, trying to offer some small amount of comfort.

Cami shrugged him off and stood up without acknowledging the condolences he offered; instead choosing to focus on her anger, knowing that if she let herself feel anything, she risked completely breaking down. After standing there for a minute trying to clear her head, to think about the situation logically from a place of detachment like she would any other mission, it hit her. If Alexa was dead, what did that mean for Ethan? She immediately slammed the door on that line of thinking.

Cami turned to Detective Thompson, her face a mask of steely determination. "Jim, we've got to move now. This could be a trap."

"I don't understand; who would—?" he stopped as it dawned on him. He was old enough to know all about Lucias and the threat he posed.

Cami put her hands on his shoulders. "You know this all classified, so I can't tell you anything, but I'm guessing you have a pretty solid idea as to who is behind it," she said as he nodded in affirmation.

Hearing Jasmine giving the all clear and signaling the first vehicle to pass through mist, Cami stepped into the lane, halting the line of cars. "Nobody leaves yet. Jackson and Rachel, you're going to have to trance our friends for a few while I come up with a new plan. This location is compromised."

Jasmine smiled at Beckett as she passed by with a human couple in tow. She'd found the two window shopping in the mall, persuading them to follow her to the parking garage with a story about a flat tire. It was obvious the woman was displeased watching her boyfriend as his eyes followed the gentle sway of the beautiful vampire's hips, but like everyone else, she fell victim to Jasmine's power of persuasion and tagged along without protest.

As the threesome approached the barrier of the mist, Jackson stepped out of from behind the Escalade and walked towards them.

"Excuse me, but I think I'm lost, can any of you tell me how to get to —," his sentence trailed off when he got close and looked into each of the human's eyes. Within seconds, he'd wiped their memories replacing them with those of an armed robbery and a masked stranger.

"After I'm gone, you're going to wait three minutes, then call the police," he said to the woman in a slow, soothing tone. "A masked man pointed a gun at you, stole your purse, your jewelry, everything, and knocked your boyfriend out before he ran into the mall." She nodded compliantly.

Leading the pair around a corner and out of sight, he turned to the man. "Sorry about this," he said with a shrug before bringing the butt of his Glock down on the back of his head. Catching his weight with one arm, Jackson laid the man down on the concrete and sped off to help his sister with the memories of the humans who were still hidden behind the veil of mist.

Sounding very much like a hypnotherapist, Rachel spoke slowly and clearly. "You were leaving the scene after responding to a crank call, but before you got out, dispatch put you on an armed assault in the area. The suspect is armed and considered extremely dangerous and you're going to realize he might also be linked to a string of unsolved murders. There are a lot of innocent people in the mall right now, so you're going to call for enough back-up to surround the complex and flush him out, understood?" They all nodded affirmatively.

A moment later, Beckett pulled the Escalade through the mist, opening the rear door for Jackson who loaded Alexa's body as Layla returned from sweeping the level and gave the all clear. Leaning through the open door of his car, Cami squeezed Martinez's shoulder signaling for him to drop the camouflage.

"Do you think you can maintain cover on a moving target?" she asked as he pulled the headphones from his ears.

"Probably; but I've never tried before. How long are we talking about?"

"Just long enough for us to get out of the building and on the road. I'm pretty sure this whole mess was bait to draw us out of the compound."

"Damn; well I'd better get it right then. Wouldn't want anyone following us back to base," he responded following Cami back to the rest of the team.

As they arrived, Cami turned to Detective Thompson. "In a few minutes, there should be enough of a distraction for you to slip out of here. I doubt you'll run into any problems, but be sure to watch your six anyway, all right?"

He gave her a reassuring pat on the back before she stepped up into the passenger seat. "Always. You do the same."

With a single nod, she closed the door.

Lucias wanted them to find Alexa's body; Cami was certain he'd dumped it publicly for exactly that reason. No doubt the bastard would have loved to lay her right outside their front gate, but that was the point. After decades of searching, he still hadn't learned the location of The Elite's compound. He was using Alexa to draw them out into the open so his men could follow them, hence the moving camouflage. The witch's protection made it virtually impossible for outsiders to find the first entrance to the compound, even if they already knew its location, but she wasn't willing to risk it. The rest of her plan, the manhunt for an imaginary mugger, was to protect Detective Thompson. With half the force joining in the search, Lucias would have no way of knowing who had tipped them off about the body.

"Everybody all set?" Cami asked turning around in the seat. "All right, Beckett; as soon as the mist drops, haul ass. There's no telling how long Martinez will be able to keep it up. We just need to get out of the line of sight before he can ease up."

Taking his cue, Martinez slipped his ear buds in and cranked up the classical music he used to focus as he thought about the area he wanted to conceal.

"Beckett, get us the hell out of here." Cami ordered as she watched the hazy mist slide to the ground around them.

Sitting Indian-style on the bed in Chloe's room, Jared peered at her over his pair of aces. She grinned and laid down a pair of twos. "Sorry; I won again," she declared not sounding remotely sorry.

Jared glanced at the three cards between them, another pair of twos, and the ace of spades.

"Tell me, exactly how would you know you won without seeing my cards? You're supposed to be practicing keeping your shields up, little one, not using your ability to cheat." He chided playfully.

They'd been playing Texas hold 'em for over an hour. Like hide and seek, it was a simple way to help Chloe learn to control her telepathy, but it served another purpose providing Jared a much-needed distraction. He had been driving himself crazy worrying about his sister and everything with Cami.

"Do you love Aunt Cami?" Chloe asked innocently as she picked up the new set of cards he had dealt.

"Why do you ask that?" he responded, reinforcing his mental shields again, already knowing the answer. Chloe was getting stronger by the day and it was getting harder and harder to block her out of his mind.

"You think about her like Grandpa Elijah thinks about Grandma, and they're married. So I figured that must mean you love her."

"Love is a complicated emotion; besides, you're not supposed to be listening to my thoughts, remember?" Jared said in an attempt to change the subject.

"I know; but it's hard sometimes and I get bored. All of the soldiers avoid me; they're afraid of me. Grandpa William is always busy, and Grandma Jo is always so sad and worried about…" her voice trailed off as she looked down at her hands.

"Worried about what?" Jared asked as he strained to hear her thoughts, finding it impossible to penetrate her powerful shields.

"Lucias," she said in a whisper. "I'm sorry; I know none of you wanted me to know about him, but he wants to take me away, doesn't he? Like my parents?" Chloe looked up at Jared with tears coating her long lashes.

Jared pulled Chloe across the bed, putting a comforting arm around her shoulders. "It doesn't matter what he wants; you are safe here. He can't find you. I won't let him find you. I promise I will always protect you and I know everyone here will do whatever it takes to keep you safe." He whispered as he stroked her wavy chestnut hair.

"I know; but that's why I'm scared, Uncle Jared. I don't want anyone else to get hurt because of me."

Jared squeezed her tighter and sighed, searching for the right words to ease her fears as sounds of motion from outside drew his attention.

"You stay right here, okay? I'll come back and tuck you in a bit later," Jared said firmly as he moved towards the door.

Jared stopped as he reached the door, surprised to find Chloe smiling, considering their conversation, but he suddenly felt too anxious to ask her why.

Outside the door, Jared focused his senses searching for Cami's stream of consciousness. The instant he found it his heart hit the floor. She was frightened and sad and, though her thoughts didn't reveal the reason, he could feel the emotions as surely as if they were his own.

Cami paced the length of the pit while she waited for Commander Claesson to return. He was in the medical wing with the High Commander, Alexa's father, identifying her body. She'd split before William Ryan was summoned, in no way wanting to be present to witness the unimaginable grief he was about to experience. As it was, she was a hair's breadth from a total breakdown herself. She'd barely gotten through the team's debriefing a few minutes before and had been relieved that the commander kept it succinct. They were playing it very close to the chest, keeping the details of their mission strictly confidential. With the exception of immediate family, no one was to know of Alexa's death.

Growing increasingly anxious, Cami felt compelled to visit her mother; hoping the powerful seer could pick up something on Ethan. Finding Alexa the way she had, something inside Cami broke. She felt the wall around her heart beginning to crumble as she recognized how many years she'd wasted clinging to self-righteous anger, hiding behind her duty and need for independence, convincing herself that she didn't need anyone. But where had that gotten her? She was alone and afraid, desperate to find her brother before it was too late.

I can't lose him; he has to be alive.

Flinging the door open, Cami swayed on unsteady legs as she met with Jared's smoldering gray eyes.

"What happened, Cami? Are you hurt?" he questioned, steadying her with his hands and strong arms.

For the first time, she didn't have the will to fight her feelings for him. He'd caught her off-guard, vulnerable, afraid, and before she knew what was happening, she fell into the vortex of the two deep pools which seemed to see into her very soul. In that moment, everything changed. Outwardly, it was an almost imperceptible shift in body language, but Cami felt as if the entire earth had moved beneath her wobbly knees. Seeing the genuine concern in his eyes, and something else which, as impossible as it seemed, she could only describe as love, shattered what little remained of the wall around her heart.

And then she did something that shocked them both. Pushing up on her toes, Cami closed her eyes and tentatively pressed her lips to his. His mouth parted slightly in surprise at the unexpected contact, but the reaction was fleeting. Fearing it was all just an elaborate dream he would wake from far too quickly, Jared seized the moment. Closing his eyes, he slid his hands down Cami's arms, grabbing her waist and pulling her body flush with his own, eliciting a low moan from the back of her throat.

Cami slipped her arms around his neck and leaned into him further as she parted her lips a little, not knowing fully what she was doing or what she wanted. All she knew was that she needed to get closer to him.

Jared didn't need any more of an invitation. He dipped his tongue into her mouth, lightly stroking, teaching her, encouraging her. She was a quick study and immediately joined in moving her tongue in a similar rhythm as she pushed her hands into his hair and pulled him even closer. Her instincts took over and had her rocking her hips against him as the kiss grew hungrier; more needy. Jared couldn't help the low growl which vibrated through his chest as she pushed against his hard length.

Through sheer force of will, he reined in his desire, putting a small fraction of space between them as he slowed the pace of their kiss. Though he had never wanted anything as much as he wanted Cami, and he was beyond grateful to finally have her in his arms, he knew it wouldn't be right to take things any further. Her thoughts before she'd seen him had been full of fear and anxiety. She was vulnerable and he wouldn't take advantage of her.

Pulling back a bit further, Jared ran his tongue gently along her top lip, followed by the bottom. He pulled her bottom lip between his teeth, sucking it lightly before letting it go with a little pop. Opening his eyes, he looked down at Cami as she let out a whimper in protest to his ending the kiss.

"Now *that* should have been your first kiss," he whispered against her ear, his warm breath sending a shiver skittering across her skin.

"Mmm." Was the only response she could manage. Two hundred years of celibacy and she'd just kissed two men in one day.

Jared placed his fingertips under her chin, lifting her face slightly, but Cami kept her eyes closed, suddenly feeling embarrassed by her bold display.

Forgetting himself, Jared chuckled at her thoughts. She was such a strong woman, yet standing there in his arms, she almost looked fragile as she grew more and more self-conscious about how forward she'd been in kissing him. As far as he was concerned, she had nothing to feel bad about. He'd never experienced anything more erotic than having Cami, a woman who was always so in control, come undone beneath his touch.

"Open your eyes, babe. You have absolutely nothing to be ashamed of. That was fucking incredible," he rasped, pulling her close again, letting her feel exactly what she'd just done to him.

Biting her lip at the feel of Jared's hardness pushing against her, she slowly peeled open her eyes, meeting his lust-filled gaze. It was as it was before; penetrating, so full of emotion, and all she could think about was devouring every inch of him. Jared groaned aloud, his cock straining insistently against the denim of his jeans as he saw the images passing through her mind.

Calling upon every ounce of his restraint, Jared took a step back into the hallway as he ran a hand through his light brown hair. With the action, he realized they'd been kissing in the open doorway, so caught up in the moment that neither of them had had the presence of mind to move somewhere more private.

As the haze of the moment they'd just shared began to lift, the reality of the day's events came crashing down, seeming to fill the space between them.

With the image of Alexa's lifeless face entering her mind, Cami felt the sting of tears as she opened her mouth to speak, struggling to find the words to tell Jared that his sister, the sister he had been waiting nearly his entire life to know, was gone.

Before a word passed her lips, Jared took her hand and squeezed it gently.

"Where is she?" he asked softly.

✧

As soon as she was certain her uncle was gone, Chloe quietly opened the door and slipped into the hallway. Knowing Jared had gone to find Cami in the pit, she turned in the opposite direction and began making her way to the medical wing.

She crept along quickly, pushing up an invisible wall in her mind to block the cacophony of stray thoughts pouring in from all around her. Jared had once suggested singing, or concentrating on something visually to help her control the ability. Since her objective was to pass by undetected, she chose the latter, letting her eyes drift over the array of beautiful artwork and tapestries which lined the walls. There were pieces dating back hundreds, even thousands, of years, from all around the world spread throughout the hallway, a stark contrast to the other wings with their bare white walls and plain tile floors.

Rounding the corner, she jumped and let out a little scream, nearly crashing into the unexpected vampire standing there.

"Whoa; easy there, little one," Captain Erikson said, eyeing Chloe intently.

She took a step back, keeping her eyes locked on the leader of her grandfather's guard, whose presence made her feel increasingly uneasy as the days passed. He was always watching her with strange thoughts moving through his mind.

"I, I'm sorry," she muttered, stepping around him.

"Where are you running off to in such a hurry?" he asked, turning to follow.

"I was just looking for Grandpa William," she lied. The image of the High Commander standing over Alexa's body flashed through her mind as Erikson thought of William.

Chloe reinforced her shields, pushing Erikson's mental presence out of her mind. She didn't need to see his thoughts of her mother. She already knew what had happened, and what was to come. Every night since arriving on the compound, she'd had the same dreams and visions of her parents; glimpses of the future she hadn't mentioned to another soul.

The visions had started when her parents went missing and had given her a much-needed sense of hope. But they also terrified her. Aside from her mother's return, she'd seen only one other event. A night which always began with her father's return, yet never ended the same way. She wasn't sure how she knew, but Chloe was certain the outcome depended on her; on the choice she had to make. It was within her power to save everyone she loved, but it would come at a high cost. Standing there in all her uncertainty, the name they all feared invaded her mind.

Lucias.

Just thinking his name sent a shiver down her spine but, no matter how hard she tried, she couldn't see anything beyond his appearance in her vision. It was as if the decision she had to make was preventing her from viewing the future beyond it. Or perhaps there was no future to see until she made the choice; a proverbial fork in the road.

With all her heart, she wanted to choose the path which saved her family, but she feared what would happen once Lucias had her in his control. Though no one spoke of the prophecy in her presence, she had gleaned enough from their thoughts to understand why he wanted her; why everyone feared her and her power. What if she sacrificed herself to save her family, only to be used to hurt them, and everyone else?

"The High Commander is indisposed at the moment," Erikson said reaching for her arm. "Perhaps you should let me escort you to your room and I will bring him to you when he is finished."

Chloe moved in a flash, putting several feet between them. "No, I need to see him now," she insisted, rushing away, using every ounce of her preternatural speed. Even having not yet reached maturity, Chloe was much faster than the adult vampire, easily leaving him behind as she approached the entrance to the medical wing.

Knowing Erikson was only seconds behind her, she hurriedly entered the security code and slipped through the door, closing it behind her as he appeared on the other side. In a blur of movement, she was standing just outside the room containing her mother's broken body and her grandparents' broken hearts. The thoughts of her family slammed against her, full of grief and despair so potent that tears welled up in her eyes.

Not having the code for the high-security room, Chloe swiped at the wetness flowing down her cheeks and reached for William's mind.

"This is no place for you to be right now," Erikson said with a touch of irritation and something akin to awe as he materialized beside her.

Please let me in; I need to see her, she said directly to William, ignoring Erikson.

Little one, you should not be here. Return to your room; I will come and find you later. He ordered; his sadness evident despite his efforts to conceal it.

Grandpa, please; I can help, she sent, but sensing his resolve on the matter, she did the only thing she could to convince him.

Concentrating on the vision she had received so many times over the last few nights, she pushed the images into his mind. In an instant, the door swung open.

"My lord, I tried to stop her," Erikson stated apologetically, as William pulled his granddaughter into a warm embrace, not bothering to acknowledge the captain as Chloe wrapped her arms around his neck.

"You are truly the most remarkable little vampire," William stated with wonder, a relieved smile on his face despite the tears still staining his cheeks.

"William, no. She, she…you can't let her see this," Rebecca sobbed from her knees, still clinging to Alexa's lifeless hand.

"Come, my love; it's all right," William said taking his wife's hand. "Let us give Chloe a moment alone with her mother," he added, regarding everyone else in the room. Knowing better than to challenge him, they all lowered their heads in deference and moved towards the door. Elijah, Josephine, and Rebecca each paused, hugging Chloe briefly before they exited. Commander Claesson was the last to leave, patting Chloe's shoulder uncomfortably as he walked through the door and pulled it closed behind him.

Chloe slowly walked to Alexa's side, her eyes falling to the injury on her neck not completely covered by the sheet draping her body. She thought of her father as she pulled the white cloth back, hoping someday he could forgive himself for what he'd done.

Leaning down she placed a soft kiss on Alexa's cheek. "I love you, Mommy," she whispered as she pulled the sheet off, revealing a lovely pale pink gown. Placing one hand over Alexa's neck and the other on her wounded wrist, Chloe closed her eyes. A slow smile spread across her face as she began to hum her favorite song, 'Dream a Little Dream of Me'.

CHAPTER 13 - *Giving In*

Cami looked up at Jared, her eyes clouded with confusion.

"How did you know?" she asked a moment before the truth hit her like a blow to the stomach. "You're a telepath."

When he didn't immediately respond, she took a step back. "That explains a lot. You've been digging around in my head all this time, that's why you wouldn't give up. No matter what I said or did, you just kept at it!" she stated, her voice growing louder, angrier with each word. "And I was stupid enough to think we had some ridiculous connection for you to be so persistent; when it was just you playing me, knowing what to do and say to break me down," she said, the anger giving over to disappointment.

"No, Cami. I wasn't playing you; we do have a connection. One that I can't begin to explain and is stronger than anything I've ever imagined two people could have. Yes; at first, I listened because you intrigued me and I wanted to get closer to you, but then I could barely control it when I was around you. Something about you calls out to me, breaks down my shields, even when I don't want it to," he said, his voice almost pleading for her to believe him. He could feel her pulling away, trying to rebuild the wall which had only just fallen between them.

"Damn it, Cami! Just fucking stop and look at us; at what's happening right now! I'm here fighting for you when my only sister is dead!" he yelled, his own anger starting to flare. "I should be with my family. I should be grieving, consoling them, but I can't make myself take a single step away from you!" Jared stopped and took a deep breath. "For one time in your life, stop trying to control everything; stop fighting, stop hiding, stop being afraid of what's between us. Please."

He stepped towards her, grabbing her shoulders as she tried to move away. "Look at me," he pleaded. When she kept her eyes glued to the floor, he leaned his head down into her field of vision. "Please, Cami. Just look at me."

There was a pain in his voice, a longing she couldn't refuse. Lifting her eyes, she knew the battle was lost the instant she saw the tears freely flowing down his handsome face.

"I love you, Cami. And you fucking love me. Maybe you think I'm weak, or I'm too young, but you feel this as much as I do. It doesn't make sense; it's not the path you saw for your life, but so what? Paths change, people change and you have changed me as much as I've changed you. So just stop. Be with me. I need you and I'm not ever going to give up. If it takes a hundred fucking years, a thousand, I don't care. I will follow you around forever like a pathetic lost puppy if I have to. I don't give a shit about my pride or my position if you're not by my side."

Cami stood there silently, perhaps just shocked by everything he'd said. She knew he was right; as hard as it was for her to admit, she loved this man. She loved a vampire nearly one-hundred-and-seventy-five years her junior. Somehow he'd managed to steal her heart despite her best efforts to keep it hidden.

Not giving her the chance to respond as he saw the shift in her eyes, Jared crushed his mouth to hers; greedily drinking in everything she reluctantly gave. And then something miraculous happened. She gave in, letting herself melt into his kiss, her body saying everything he needed to hear. Perhaps it was the fresh declaration of love, maybe it was the much-needed distraction from the inevitable grief; neither of them knew, but that kiss drowned out everything else in the world. For one blissful, soul-changing moment, nothing else mattered.

Reluctantly pulling away, Jared reached out and wiped a single tear from Cami's cheek; placing a brief kiss in its place.

"Well, then," she said breathlessly.

"Yeah," Jared replied as he took her hand and led her down the hall. "Time to go and face reality," he whispered sadly.

Commander Claesson leaned against the wall, feeling awkward and intrusive standing amongst the grieving family. A glance at Captain Erikson revealed a similar level of discomfort, though his demeanor seemed more interested than anything.

The Commander couldn't fault him for being curious, given the situation, but he still didn't trust him or the other guards.

Seeing the sadness around him, he realized it had been a millennium since he'd last shed a tear, despite suffering immeasurable losses and enduring his fair share of heartache. The closest he'd come in all those year was the day his daughter, Ella, was born. His heart warmed as he thought of the little girl who had grabbed ahold of his pinkie, her tiny hand barely able to wrap around it, and turned his whole world upside down.

No; instead of tears, Alek Claesson clung to his need for vengeance. Witnessing the grief in the people he was charged with protecting, seeing Alexa, a girl younger than his Ella, laying lifeless on a cold table, he vowed to make the one responsible pay.

The sound of Jared and Cami's approach pulled his focus giving him a much-needed reprieve. An expression of confusion covered his face, quickly followed by a wide smile as the pair came into view, holding hands.

Well, I'll be damned. He never imagined he'd see the day his most dedicated, and stubborn, soldier would finally let her hair down, so to speak.

His eyes wandered over to Cami's parents and, even in their sadness, he saw the surprise on their faces as well.

"Where's Alexa?" Jared asked solemnly.

"Inside," William replied, grabbing Jared's arm and stepping in front of him. "You need to wait out here, my son."

162

"I want to see my sister. I already know what happened," he responded flatly.

"Chloe is with her now; she needs time."

"What?! Why the hell would you let her see Alexa like that? She's just a little girl; she'll never recover!" Jared yelled yanking away from his father's grip and reaching for the door, still squeezing Cami's fingers tightly in his other hand.

Before he made contact, the handle turned and the door slowly slid open.

"Hey, Uncle Jared!" Chloe said brightly, much to the surprise of everyone in the hallway, with the exception of William, who smiled proudly.

Jared released Cami's hand and dropped to his knees in front of her. "Are you all right, squirt? I'm so sorry; I shouldn't have left you." He said pulling her close as he looked passed her to Alexa. The sight was nothing like the gruesome image he'd seen in Cami's mind. If he hadn't known better, he would have believed his sister was merely asleep.

"Son," William said aloud before pushing the images Chloe had shared with him into Jared's mind.

Jared saw Chloe standing next to her mother, the injuries he'd expected still covering her neck and wrist. Chloe laid her hands over them and, miraculously, the wounds began to heal, closing completely in a matter of seconds.

His eyes shot to Chloe, then his father, and finally came to rest on Alexa as he focused his senses. The slow, steady beat of her heart flowed to his ears and he watched in stunned amazement as her chest rose and fell with each intake of breath.

"How can this be?" he asked of no one in particular. Rebecca stepped up behind her son, still unaware of the miracle which had occurred.

"She's only asleep now," Chloe said softly drawing the confused stares of the remaining adults.

Without a word, Rebecca leapt over the two in the doorway, reaching her daughter's side in an instant. Her hand shot to her mouth and she dropped to her knees as her eyes filled with tears of joy. She reached up and took Alexa's hand, feeling the warmth returning as she looked at Chloe. "This is a miracle. Truly you are our savior."

Chloe moved the short distance between them and put her arms around her grandmother. Though she kept the smile on her face, in her mind she prayed Rebecca's words were true, knowing that if she wasn't their savior, she was certain to lead them to their damnation.

"Tell me, Kaleb; how is it The Elite managed to retrieve the body and disappear without a trace with our men waiting at every entrance? They were seen going in, yet somehow were able to slip out undetected," Lucias stated from behind his desk, his voice eerily calm.

"Sire, my apologies; I have no excuse. I failed you," Kaleb replied, his head bowed low.

"Failure is not acceptable, my son. Perhaps I allow you too much freedom," Lucias said, his lips lifting into a smirk. "Yes; I think it may be time for you to fall in with the rest of my ranks. As it stands, I cannot be certain if they bested you, or if you merely decided not to follow my instructions implicitly."

"Sire, your orders were carried out exactly as you commanded," Kaleb began carefully. "If I am to be infected, there will be none left but you who can face the sun. It's too great a risk for you to travel alone, yet there will always be a need for someone you can trust to move around in the daylight. Will you leave it to the humans?" Kaleb replied quickly, trying to keep the quiver of fear from his voice. To him, there was no greater punishment than his father's virus and he was determined to take his own life before he would fall victim to such a fate.

"Yes, I suppose you are correct in that respect. However, there is still the issue of your failure. How do you propose we rectify the situation?" Lucias asked expectantly.

Kaleb was prepared for this; he'd thought long and hard as he drove back to his father's facility.

"The girl's mate has family amongst The Elite; perhaps he can explain how they could have managed such a feat." he responded, hoping it was enough to distract his ruthless father.

"Indeed; I have questioned him about the location of the compound to no avail. It is protected by a spell and no one, outside of The Elite themselves, who has seen it, can return. Perhaps he knows more; I need simply to ask the right questions," Lucias said his voice trailing off as if he was lost in thought. "Yes; retrieve Ethan. You will find him training with Mason downstairs."

"Where would you have me take him, Sire?" Kaleb asked as his eyes fell on the sunlight streaking across the floor. Ethan wouldn't be able to enter the office for some time.

"Take him to Molly's quarters. I could use a snack," he said standing.

"Of course." Kaleb bowed and quickly exited.

Entering the training area of his father's headquarters, Kaleb paused briefly to observe human soldiers sparring in one of the rooms. Given the fact that the infected couldn't go out in the sun for extended periods of time, Lucias had begun recruiting humans to carry out daytime missions.

Reaching his destination, Kaleb looked through the glass at what he had to admit was an impressive sight. Ten infected vampires surrounded Ethan, sporting a variety of close-combat weapons; short swords, daggers, nunchuks, etc. Strewn out on the mat beyond the circle were the seven vampires already bested by Ethan, each crawling away as their bodies attempted to heal.

Remaining perfectly still in the center of the circle, Ethan closed his

166

eyes and awaited the next attack. The vampires still standing looked hesitantly as Mason, one of Lucias's generals, ordered them to engage. In a blur of motion, three men lunged towards Ethan, who didn't so much as flinch until the instant he caught one of them by the throat. Breaking the assailant's wrist and catching the short sword as it fell from his hand, Ethan spun in a circle; a loud pop resounding from the dislocated shoulder as Ethan swung the vampire's body, sending it careening into one of the others.

Bringing the short sword down across the thigh of the next man, Ethan leapt over him, coming down behind his back before he slammed the hilt of the weapon into the base of his skull with a crack, knocking him out cold. After flinging his partner's weight off, the remaining vampire approached Ethan tentatively.

"Are you going to dance with him or fight?" Mason mocked, his words sending the man into action, only to be caught with a front kick to the chest, sending him flying across the room into a rack of weapons.

Mason approached the broken circle. Stepping inside, he walked around slowly, regarding each of them as the glow of their eyes cast a soft red glow over his pale skin. "Let's try this again and keep in mind, any man who disobeys another of my commands will face me. Our new addition may have been ordered to spare your lives, but I have not," he said with a sneer before moving back to observe.

Kaleb stepped through the door as Mason flicked his wrist, ordering the seven uninjured men to proceed. They moved as one, rushing upon Ethan with weapons raised. A millisecond before the first blow hit him, Ethan jumped into the air, flipping over the backs of two of the men and kicking his legs into the bases of their spines, sending them crashing to the mat and taking two of their comrades down with them. Utilizing the momentary distraction, Ethan lunged for the remaining soldiers, swiftly disarming one and using him as a shield as he engaged the others who practically tossed down their arms in defeat the moment his strong hands made contact.

Satisfied that all threats were temporarily disabled, Ethan returned to his spot in the center of the mat and closed his eyes, waiting to be released or commanded again. When Lucias had sent him to Mason, it had been with the explicit instruction to obey Mason's commands as if they were directly from Lucias himself; giving the general complete control over him until he or Lucias said otherwise.

"His abilities have not been exaggerated," Mason said quietly as Kaleb approached.

"No; indeed they have not. I saw him fight once when I was still a boy, before his powers were amplified. Even then he was a terrifying sight to behold."

"You mean when he murdered your brother and his men. I must admit, I was pleasantly surprised to find that you let him live. I am not confident I would have exercised such restraint in the absence of your father's bond."

Kaleb clamped his teeth down hard, fighting not to respond to Mason's goading. Even if the vampire general's abilities weren't heightened by Lucias's virus, Kaleb would have been hard-pressed to defeat him in direct combat. For many years, Mason had been hungry to regain the position as Lucias's second-in-command, always trying to incite Kaleb's anger and force a fight. Mason's infection ended the struggle temporarily, but over the years the virus' hold changed, allowing the infected vampire's personality and ambition to shine through. The infected remained unquestionably loyal to Lucias, yet no longer functioned as the unthinking androids they'd appeared to be in the first few weeks of their new lives.

"My only purpose is to serve my father," Kaleb recited after his anger had sufficiently dissipated.

"Of course. Can I assume that is why we are all currently graced with your presence?" Mason inquired somewhat sarcastically.

Remaining in control, Kaleb ignored Mason's tone. "Yes; my father requires an audience with Mr. Kellar."

"Very well. Soldier," he said approaching Ethan, "you are released to Kaleb's command, for now."

CHAPTER 14 - *Blood Runners*

As Dante approached Blood Runners, a vampire-owned nightclub The Elite frequented for feeding and other entertainment, he surveyed the long line which had formed leading up to the entrance. Noting several regulars decked out in goth vampire gear, complete with fangs, some having gone so far as to file down their canine incisors or get surgical implants to complete the fantasy, he flashed a seductive smile at a couple of young girls staring his way.

Bypassing the line, he approached the red velvet rope which moved aside with a nod from the imposing bouncer who, even standing over six feet, was easily several inches shorter than the handsome Elite vampire. A satisfied smirk spread across his chiseled face as he heard the groans of two human men who'd been waiting an hour for admittance to the exclusive club.

Stepping inside, he scanned the large crowd moving about surrounded by the clichéd decor of plush red velvet booths and black walls. Movie posters featuring some of the most famous, and completely made up vampires, covered the walls along with strings of garlic, wooden stakes, and ornate crucifixes. The only light in the dark room came from the strobe lights trained on the pile of bodies gyrating on the dance floor.

The intoxicating scent of blood tainted the air as he drew a breath into his lungs. Civilian vampires were openly feeding on humans as they attempted to pass off dry humping for dancing, the sensation of being bitten completely freeing them of their inhibitions, though the drugs and alcohol coursing through their veins helped as well.

The themed establishment was the perfect cover for his kind, with humans either too high or too immersed in their role-playing to notice the actual predators amongs them. As a rule, all of the real vampires wiped the memories of their chosen meals, but even if they didn't, some human patrons liked to bite one another, drawing and drinking blood with artificially sharpened teeth, making the sight of a feeding commonplace; simply chalked up to some of the more enthusiastic vampire fantasies of the truly dedicated.

Not seeing anything that interested him, Dante headed back to the VIP room reserved for The Elite and some of their race's most powerful and wealthy civilians. As he acknowledged the female bouncer guarding the room and reached for the thick black curtain, a small hand came down on his forearm. Not at all surprised, having heard the fast human heartbeat approaching along with the overpowering scent of cheap French perfume, Dante casually regarded the bold woman.

"Hiya, handsome," the petite blonde purred seductively. "I'd ask if we've met before cuz you look awful familiar, but I know that can't be true. I'd never forget you."

She lightly stroked up and down his arm, leaning in close and stretching up as high as her short legs and stiletto heels would allow. "How about you take me in back with you for a drink," she whispered running the fingertips of her free hand up the side of her neck.

Dante's gaze raked over her exposed body in a tight black miniskirt and blue halter top, complete with a black choker and fuck-me heels. Yeah, she was right; he should be familiar, having fed on and fucked her more than once in the last few months, but it was the first time she seemed to recognize him at all. He took it as a sign it was time find some fresh entertainment. The last thing he needed was some clingy human following him around his favorite retreat. Besides, he was in the mood for a brunette, preferably one with long curly hair and a lithe, muscular body. He hadn't been able to get Cami off his mind since the kiss in the training room, and he needed a woman to take the edge off. If he couldn't have her, a nameless, faceless lookalike would have to do for the time being.

"No thanks, sweetheart," he said firmly as he removed her hand from his arm. "I'm meeting someone, but thanks for the offer."

"You sure?" She asked with a smirk as she slid her hands down her sides and hiked her skirt up a couple of inches, damn near exposing herself since it was unlikely she was wearing panties beneath the strip of cloth she was trying to pass off as clothing.

"Maybe some other time," he said with a wink and passed through the doorway before she could respond. No point in completely blowing her off just in case he couldn't find someone more suited to his needs for the night. He felt completely strung out. The lust coursing through his veins had kept his cock at half-mast since the moment his lips had touched Cami's.

Inside the VIP room, things were much quieter and the decor far less clichéd. Dante had often wondered how that black curtain, thick as it may be, could drown out so much of the thumping beat from the music in the neighboring room. He assumed a touch of magic was involved in achieving the effect, but had never gotten around to asking.

He moved quickly to his regular table, happy to find it unoccupied. While he often enjoyed the company of his fellow soldiers in tossing back a few drinks, particularly Layla, things had been too weird between them before he left and right then, he only had one thing on his mind. Well, two things. He needed to feed, having gone over a month without fresh blood, and he needed to fuck.

Though they kept a healthy supply of bagged red cells on ice at the compound, he found it never fully quenched his thirst. He needed it straight from the source, warm and sweet with the soothing beat of a heart pulsing against his gums. It was almost better than sex; definitely the best when combined with sex.

No sooner did he slide his ass onto the supple leather seat, than a glass appeared on the table. Two fingers of Glen Livet with a splash of water to open up the flavor, his usual drink.

"Get you anything else tonight?" Winslow, the club's owner, inquired.

The vampire had opened the establishment back in 1934, immediately following the ratification of the Twenty-first Amendment which ended Prohibition. Things had been far more discreet back then, the club being named Winslow's after its founder, openly serving high-quality liquor, and secretly serving high-quality prostitutes to his vampire clientele. He'd changed the name to Blood Runners back in the eighties, following the release of Blade Runners, which was still one of his favorite movies, and had revamped the decor several times since to follow the trends and the newfound vampire acceptance born of popular culture's fascination with all things vampire.

"Yeah, I could go for a brunette. Thin, muscular, with long curly hair," Dante responded quietly.

"I know just the one; might take a bit to get her here, if you're okay with waiting. If not, I've got a couple in the other room who are close to that description, maybe plus a few pounds or minus a few curls," the bald vampire said, pulling his phone from his pocket.

"I'll wait. Thanks, man," Dante said taking a slow sip of his Glen Livet as Winslow hit a few buttons and disappeared into his office.

Three glasses of scotch later, Dante felt his blood quicken as the tall brunette walked through the door.

Fuck me, he thought as she moved further into the room scanning the sparse crowd, no doubt looking for him. Just a few more glasses and he could have been fooled into believing it was Cami, at least from a distance.

The human woman's eyes found Dante and immediately filled with lust, a dead giveaway it wasn't her. Cami had never looked at him that way; like a sure thing, itching to be close to him. A part of him ached for the challenge Cami presented, weary of all the easy meaningless encounters he'd had over the years. While they satisfied his baser needs, they never quenched the longing in his heart.

As the woman slid in beside him, Dante smelled her growing arousal and heard the increase in her heartbeat. She was a paid professional, but there was no doubt she wanted him; though it wasn't like he would actually be the one paying her. On the few occasions he, or any of The Elite, decided to go with more, experienced companions, Winslow covered the expense, but Dante would be sure to slip a nice tip into her purse before he wiped her memory.

"So what are you looking for tonight, sweetie," the eager working girl inquired as she inched closer and put her hand on Dante's thigh.

Her look was right, but the voice was all wrong. Where Cami's was somewhat low and smooth, hers was high and nasally. He cocked an eyebrow and half-smiled as he looked sideways at her, sporting some serious fang due to his increasing hunger.

Without waiting for his response she continued. "Biting is fine, so long as you keep it to inconspicuous areas; I have to make a living and not everyone is into that. Otherwise, anything's negotiable."

"Noted," Dante replied sliding to exit the booth on the other side. He stood and held out his hand while she looked up with confusion.

"You wanna go get a room or something?" she asked taking his hand.

"No; just want to go somewhere a little more private," he responded heading for the dark hallway which led to the back exit. Not that he was shy or overly concerned about being seen, given the nature of the establishment, but he was in a bit of a hurry having already stayed longer than he intended waiting for his Cami lookalike to arrive.

He'd gone looking for Cami after her team returned from their mission, hoping for a chance to talk about what had happened between them before the High Commander's kid interrupted, but Layla had stopped him, saying she wanted to talk to him. They were on the way to his room when he'd asked her if she knew where Cami was, seemingly pissing her off right before Commander Claesson showed up with Martinez ordering her to the pit for debriefing. The look she'd given him before she left had really thrown him. It fell somewhere between anger and hurt, and for the briefest of seconds, he saw something else, but before he could say anything, she disappeared.

Though looking back, it wasn't like he knew what to say. It wasn't the first time he'd seen that look in her pale green eyes and, like every other time, he brushed it aside and turned his attention towards safer, less complicated pursuits. Feeling as tightly-wound as a steel spring, he'd figured it was in his best interest to go blow off some steam before he attempted to do anything else.

"What's your name, honey?" the woman whispered as Dante backed her up against the wall and she stroked up and down his massive biceps.

"Doesn't matter," he replied swiping his tongue along the side of her neck, calling her vein to rise as she let out an overly-dramatic moan.

He reached down and freed his hardness from the confines of his black fatigues then grabbed her under each thigh and hoisted her up as she wrapped her long legs around his waist. He spun around and leaned back against the wall and, still holding her up with one arm, he used the other to reach between them. Fisting the wide base, he moved his cock into position and slid her moist folds down around him in one smooth motion.

She tossed her head back and let out a low moan as he stretched and filled her completely, her long dark curls spilling down her back, swaying back and forth as he rocked into her over and again. Seeing her hair moving like that, he wondered what Cami would look like with her hair all loose and wild, having only ever seen it pulled back tightly away from her face.

Just one thought of Cami and he was right on the edge. Sensing that the stranger in his arms was getting close as well, he increased the pace, pushing into her even deeper as her body started to tremble around him. He put his mouth to her neck, once again sliding his tongue over her vein, preparing it while he waited. When she found her release and cried out, he struck, hard and deep, making her climax exponentially more intense as her essence spilled into his mouth and down his throat, setting off his own orgasm.

When her body finally stilled and he had drunk his fill, he swiped his tongue over the puncture marks in her neck, capturing a few stray drops of blood and setting the rapid healing process in motion. He set her down on unsteady legs and kneeled down to look into her eyes as she opened her mouth to speak, no doubt to say something about seeing him again, or how amazing everything had been. Nothing he was interested in hearing, nor would he. Before a sound escaped her lips, he pushed into her mind extracting her memories of him and what they'd done.

"Go grab a car and head home for the night, take a nice long bath, watch a movie or something," he instructed as he moved away, not that he cared, but the memory wipe left most humans feeling disoriented and giving them simple suggestions seemed to help. With the sizable tip he'd tucked into her bra, she wouldn't need to work for the next week if she didn't want to.

Without a word, she bent down, picked up her purse from the floor and walked straight for the exit. A few steps around the corner, there were several cars lined up which Winslow kept on retainer to transport his girls and the occasional patron who overindulged in his bar.

Dante wasn't far behind, walking back to his booth only to leave a tip on the table, before slipping out the back. Right as he reached for the door, his supernatural ears perked up so to speak when he heard his name. Turning his head, he focused in on the conversation occurring on the other side of the curtain, which someone was obviously holding open slightly for him to be able to hear.

"Is Dante in there?" Layla asked the woman at the door.

"Sorry, hon; couldn't tell you. I haven't been posted here long, but haven't seen him," she lied.

One of Blood Runners' most appealing features was the discretion Winslow required from his staff.

"There's a lot of first-timers in here tonight. You in the mood for anything in particular? I'm sure we could arrange anything you have in mind, boy, girl, both," the bouncer continued, distracting Layla as Dante disappeared into the night.

CHAPTER 15 - *Hope Renewed*

Kaleb leaned against the wall outside his father's "playroom" staring across the hallway at Ethan. The newest addition to his father's army of infected soldiers stood as straight as a board with his eyes closed. He never spoke unless spoken to, even when others were talking around him and, when he did speak, his responses were short and to the point. He ate, slept, and trained according to the schedule set for him. The perfect soldier like all newly-infected vampires, but Kaleb knew better.

While Ethan was by far the best fighter, easily defeating as many as ten vampires at once during his training sessions, one look in his eyes revealed something more. Even with his irises burning red like all of the others, Kaleb recognized a sadness in them which was utterly familiar to him. It was the look of unyielding grief. Kaleb had seen the same sadness every time he looked in the mirror, the source of it having once been the loss of his brother. But over the years, the wound had slowly healed without him realizing and had been replaced with a longing for something he knew he could never have, and he grieved for the unattainable future. Luckily, his father was incapable of recognizing that type of pain. He would see it as a sign of weakness and Kaleb didn't care to imagine the punishment which would befall them if Lucias ever noticed.

Kaleb was drawn out of his thoughts by the sounds emanating from behind the closed door and his stomach lurched. He wanted to leave, to go wait for his father in his office where eventually end up anyway, but he knew it wouldn't be worth the reprimand he'd endure for not being present when expected.

Indeed, he suspected that Lucias ordered them to wait there simply because he enjoyed having an audience. While Kaleb had once felt somewhat grateful after his father found his pet human, Molly, her presence and participation in some of his unsavory activities seeming to satisfy his most repulsive urges, he realized the gratitude had been premature.

Not only did the woman no longer prevent his father's killing of innocent humans, she had become his accomplice and Lucias's appetite for murder paled in comparison to Molly's. She went out daily, hunting for new victims, like the unfortunate young woman who was currently locked in the room with them, and would lure them to their deaths with promises of any number of things. Her small stature, beautiful face, and charming accent made her seem harmless; the perfect bait.

A final bloodcurdling scream rang out, though the sound was muffled by the thick walls, signaling that playtime was coming to an end as Ethan opened his eyes and moved to stand beside Kaleb.

Several minutes later, the door swung open, the smell of fresh blood filling the air as Lucias stepped out into the hallway, naked from the waist up with exception of the blood streaking down his chin and chest. Kaleb wisely masked his disgust and remained impassive, waiting for his father to speak.

"Ah, yes; I nearly forgot I summoned you," Lucias said with a smile. The ancient vampire always seemed to be in the best of moods after one of his sessions in that room.

Molly sauntered up behind him, completely nude, and handed him a towel.

"Here you go, darlin'," she drawled sweetly as if she and Lucias were just a normal, happy couple.

Lucias took it and began wiping the blood from his face, while Molly eyed Ethan and Kaleb hungrily.

"I'm gonna go hop in the shower before I fetch a couple of boys to clean up in there. That girl put up a quite a fight; good thing I took these off of her first," she said holding up a pair of cream and black pumps. "Made sure we were the same size before I brought her home," she added winking at Kaleb as she slipped on the shoes, stood up on her toes and licked a stray drop of blood from the side of Lucias's face. Then she headed down the hallway, humming a tune none of them recognized, her naked hips swaying seductively with each click of her newly-acquired heels. Lucias stared after until she was out of sight.

"She truly is exquisite," he said in a tone akin to admiration to no one in particular.

Back in Lucias's office, Kaleb and Ethan stood in front of his desk, waiting where he'd left them while he took his time showering. That was his father's way, always making ridiculous demands to demonstrate his control.

Finally, almost an hour after they'd first started waiting, Lucias emerged, neatly dressed in a fresh gray suit and took a seat in the large wingback chair behind the desk.

"Sit," he commanded, gesturing to the two chairs across from him.

The two did as ordered, finding themselves needing to look up at Lucias from their new positions. Another demonstration of power; Lucias had built the platform for his sitting area several inches off the ground while the already short chairs in front remained at ground level, always making him the highest in the room, literally.

"Ethan, tell me what you know of the abilities of The Elite. Is there some way they could have escaped from directly under my son's nose without detection which I am as of yet unaware of, or is it more likely his failure is due to his own competence, or disobedience?" Lucias questioned turning to glare at Kaleb.

Ethan cringed inwardly, screaming in his mind not to reveal any more than he already had, but his mouth opened obediently and he began to speak.

"There are many powerful vampires amongst them, Sire. I have heard of one who has the ability to shield objects from view," Ethan replied, his voice in monotone.

Ignoring the fact that this new information relieved Kaleb from responsibility for the mission's failure, Lucias continued. "Tell me, Ethan; what other powers are amongst them?"

"Forgive me, Sire; I do not know of the others. My sister only recently started speaking to me again and the information came to me by mistake when I overheard her talking to someone else the night I met with your men in Fishers."

"You are referring to the night you slaughtered three of my soldiers."

"Yes, Sire," Ethan responded with no emotion.

"No mind," Lucias said as he stood. "I have given the matter a great deal of thought since our last discussion and it occurred to me that the only way to gain access to their compound is for one of them to let us in. So tell me, Ethan; where can we find one of these so-called soldiers? Your sister, perhaps; but any one will do. They can't possibly spend all of their time locked away behind the protection of their precious witches. They must go out to feed, at the very least."

"Blood Runners," Ethan replied over the blaring in his head. "It's a nightclub downtown."

"Ah, yes; I believe I have heard the name before," Lucias stated as he stepped down from his platform. "Kaleb, go and find Mason. I believe it is time for some of my men to partake in some of the pleasures of Boston's nightlife."

Before Kaleb reached the door, Ethan let out a loud groan and fell forward onto his knees as he gripped his head.

Kaleb's eyes shot to Lucias, assuming that his cruel father was simply using the bond to further torment Ethan for his own amusement; but he saw only confusion and interest in his eyes.

"Ethan, what is it? Do you require blood?" Lucias questioned in a tone that could almost be mistaken for concern.

"No," he replied simply as he struggled to regain control. Inside his mind, one word kept repeating over and again.

Alexa.

"Tell me what is afflicting you, then," Lucias demanded.

Powerless to deny Lucias's commands, Ethan responded.

"Alexa; my mate." In one small moment, the tiny remnant of connection he still felt to her blared to life again. "I still feel her."

Lucias laughed cruelly. "Your mate is dead; do you not recall ripping out her throat?"

In the days that had passed since Ethan awoke, he'd remembered more and more about the time he'd spent as Lucias's prisoner before his transformation was complete; the most painful piece being what he'd done to his own wife, his one true love, his soul mate. As he stood, though the feeling of it initially warmed his heart, Ethan pushed back from the connection he realized could only be meant to torture him; to remind him of what he'd lost, what he had destroyed with his own hands.

Despising the weakness he saw in his highly-prized soldier, Lucias devised a plan to free Ethan from his pointless sense of connection to his dead wife.

"Do not despair; I know precisely what you need. For now, go with Kaleb and continue your training until I call for you again

CHAPTER 16 - *A Mother Returned*

There was a blaring in her head; the swirling of a variety of voices, which, though familiar, were indistinguishable and unclear. Until one broke through, as clear and crisp as the sound of a newborn baby's first cry falling upon her anxious mother's ears.

Open your eyes, Mommy. We are waiting for you.

As if obeying the gentle command, Alexa's eyelids lifted and she found herself staring into the somewhat blurry face of a beautiful young girl. Alexa blinked rapidly, trying to focus her eyes which were already filling with tears as she struggled desperately to see the most precious sight imaginable; that of the child she had never dared to hope she'd see again.

"Your contact lenses; you won't need them anymore, my darling girl." she heard her father say from somewhere across the room.

Alexa struggled to sit upright, having existed outside her body for so long that it seemed unfamiliar, almost foreign. Attempting to raise a hand to her face, she overestimated the amount of effort the movement required, resulting in an audible thump from the self-inflicted blow to her forehead.

It appears the repression spell has been broken, William sent telepathically; the fact that she could clearly hear him and Chloe was further testament to the accuracy of his statement.

Moving with slower, more controlled motions, Alexa carefully plucked the lenses from each of her eyes.

"My God," she whispered in awe as she looked at the world for the first time as a vampire. Her breath hitched as her eyes again fell on Chloe.

Taking in the sight of her daughter with soft chestnut curls cascading over her shoulders, framing a flawless face with pouty pink lips, high cheekbones and, the only feature Alexa truly recognized, large eyes the color of a stormy sea and shaded by an awning of thick lashes, she began to sob. Instead of the bouncing toddler Alexa remembered, Chloe walked into her mother's waiting arms as a beautiful young woman.

Unable to speak, Alexa continued to weep, clinging to her tightly as Chloe whispered soft words of comfort into her mind.

You're safe now; you don't have to be afraid.

It's not that; it's just that you're so grown up and I missed it. I'm so sorry we ever left, Alexa responded, her sobbing increasing as her guilt took hold.

"Perhaps I can help," William said, stepping closer.

Alexa gasped and closed her eyes as a slideshow of images flashed through her mind; pictures of Chloe from everyone's memories. All the special little moments she'd missed which he'd been carefully gathering up for her as he clung to the hope that she would, after being lost from his life a second time, be returned to him again.

William gave Alexa the final memory, one of his from only hours before when Chloe healed her; before he pulled back from her mind. Alexa opened her eyes and released her hold on Chloe.

"I never thought I would see you again, yet here I am only because of you and how amazing you are. I am so proud of you," she said with a grateful smile, as she placed her hand on Chloe's cheek.

Chloe's face heated beneath Alexa's touch; a flush of embarrassment at her mother's praise. The response only increased her mother's adoration. With all that she was, so special and powerful, Chloe's heart remained humble and pure.

With one last smile at her daughter, Alexa moved to her father far more quickly than she'd intended; nearly knocking him back into the wall as she stumbled into his arms.

"It may take you a little while to become accustomed to your new strength," he said as he pressed his cheek against the top of her head.

"Thank you," she whispered, holding him tightly while he stroked her hair.

I would do anything for you, my darling.

Releasing her father, Alexa turned; finally seeing everyone else who'd been waiting so patiently while she'd been captivated by Chloe and the beautiful memories her father had given her.

It was all she could do not to burst into tears again as she found herself surrounded by her entire family, with the exception of Ethan. The joy she'd felt waking up and seeing Chloe had temporarily eased the dull pain which had plagued her heart since the moment Ethan had discovered she was dead.

"Ethan; we have to help him," she said desperately, turning back to William.

"He's alive then?" Josephine asked, her tone a mixture of fear and hope.

"Yes; I can still feel him," she said, taking Josephine's hand. "We have to find him; he's been infected," she added, her eyes following Elijah as he pulled Josephine into his arms. The couple clung to one another, overcome with relief knowing their son was alive; but there was pain in Elijah's eyes.

I will find a cure. The words came to her from Elijah, as an expression of determination covered his face. She recalled what he'd told her of the first infected vampires; of there being no cure but death.

"The link to Lucias is incredibly strong, but our bond remains. Before I came back, I was there with him. Our Ethan is still in there; I know we can bring him back," she said offering what little comfort she could. "I feel our connection as strongly as I did before; he feels it, too, but he doesn't believe I'm alive. The despair," she whispered swallowing hard as she allowed herself to feel the full force of Ethan's emotions through their connection. "He needs me, Father."

William sped to Alexa as her body sagged under the weight of what she was feeling. He wrapped his arms around her, holding her up as her memory of dying passed through his mind, a part of him wishing for Ethan's demise when he saw the savage way Alexa's life had been taken. Yet sensing Alexa's love and understanding, he accepted that there had been no choice for Ethan; he was not responsible. The fault lay solely with Lucias.

"We will get him back; I promise you," William whispered gently as he stroked her hair. "Your mate is safe for now. Lucias will not relinquish such a powerful weapon if he can avoid it," William added, meeting Commander Claesson's eyes over her head summoning him into the room before he looked knowingly at Elijah.

"Alexa, meet Commander Alek Claesson," William said as he released her.

"It's an honor," Commander Claesson said stepping closer, awed by the fact he was speaking to a woman who had most certainly been dead only hours before. "I'm sorry to do this now; I can't imagine what you've been through, but we need your help to find your mate. Can you tell me what you remember? How Lucias found you, where

191

you were taken, what you saw, any detail that could prove useful?"

Alexa took a deep breath as she thought back over the events of the last week, trying to remember exactly what had happened.

"We left the villa in Eleuthera right after Elijah called. When we got to the airport, there was a different crew; the flight attendant must have drugged us."

"We found the bodies of the pilot and attendant your husband hired," Commander Claesson added.

"When I woke up, I was with him; with Lucias," Alexa continued choking back her fear and sadness as she relived the memory. "He infected Ethan and waited for the bloodlust to take over before he shoved me into the room and locked us together. Ethan fought it. He wanted to die, to let the virus kill him, but I forced him to take my blood; I wouldn't let him die for me. It was my choice," she said looking to her parents, and then Ethan's, hoping they understood.

"I don't know how, but even after it was over, I was still there; I was still with him. I knew I was dead, I even saw the white light you always hear about, but the bond, our connection, kept me close."

"Remarkable," Josephine whispered with wonder. "True soul mates; bound not only by blood, but by a shared piece of your souls."

"That's what Barb called it, too," Alexa said regarding Josephine with a sad smile.

"Barb?" Elijah asked in confusion.

"Yes; she came to me, when I was, um, on the other side," Alexa replied. "She's still helping us as much as she can and she wanted you all to know that she is okay."

Elijah's eyes filled with tears as he chuckled.

"Stubborn woman; she never could walk away from a fight," he said with admiration. He took Josephine's hand, giving her a knowing look as she smiled with tears in her eyes as well.

"Before I came back, she wanted me to see things so we would be prepared," Alexa continued. "I didn't get a chance to see much; I don't know where the facility is, but I'm sure it was underground because there were no windows or daylight. Though I have no idea if it was during the day or not, I just felt like I was down in the earth. I saw Lucias's soldiers; hundreds of them, maybe more, and they were all infected. Barb told me his entire army was there, that Lucias is preparing to move against The Elite. He knows—," she paused, cutting her eyes to Chloe.

It's okay; you don't have to protect me, Chloe sent.

"He knows Chloe is here and he's trying to find a way in. He plans to make her his mate."

Josephine and Rebecca both gasped. "But she is just a child," Rebecca said with disgust.

"After I died, I could hear his thoughts. He somehow knew and about her abilities and that she would be mature soon."

Commander Claesson's eyes went to William at hearing evidence that confirmed his suspicions of a spy, but William's face remained impassive.

"Do you have any idea where you were; maybe what part of the country you were in?" Commander Claesson asked, his tone growing anxious.

"I'm not entirely sure, but when Lucias told his man to dispose of my body, he thought of the location and I sensed that it wasn't far. The other man, Kaleb; he intended to drive there," Alexa responded.

"Thank you, Alexa; you've been very helpful," Commander Claesson said as he moved to leave. "My lord, I'm sorry to take you away; but can I have a word with you in private?"

"Of course," William said. "I have monopolized enough of my daughter's time for now," he added regarding Alexa warmly.

"Yes, I agree. You've had her long enough and now it's my turn," Rebecca said, stepping around William and pulling Alexa into her arms. "My sweet, sweet girl; I thought we'd lost you again," she whispered, quietly stroking Alexa's hair.

"I thought I was lost," Alexa replied simply, before kissing her mother on the cheek.

"I will see you again soon," William said before he reluctantly walked away from his daughter and followed Commander Claesson.

"My lord," Captain Erikson began, from the spot where he'd been standing in silent observation since following Chloe to the medical wing. "With your permission, I'd like to escort you," he finished, drawing the hard gaze of Commander Claesson, who'd been typing out a message on his phone.

"That will not be necessary; you are dismissed for the night," William responded as he passed by. Though the captain had been one of his dearest friends over the years, Commander Claesson's continued suspicion of him and the other guards had sparked a seed of doubt in William's mind.

Commander Claesson's mouth turned up in a satisfied smirk before he slipped his phone in his pocket and disappeared down the long corridor with William.

"I am sorry, Alek; you were right all along. After what my daughter has shared, there is no denying someone has been giving Lucias information about my family," William said, taking a seat in Commander Claesson's office.

"I would have been happy to learn I was mistaken, my lord," he responded graciously.

"I am not a man easily deceived. I will defer to your experience in the matter. How do you suggest we proceed?"

"Going forward, our meetings need to be completely private. None of your guards and or my men can be involved. I'm going to contact the other bases and get as many soldiers here as our facility can accommodate."

"Yes; I agree," William said with a nod.

"There is also the matter of Ethan. You are well aware of his strength. Lucias keeps him alive for that reason and he will use him against us. I cannot begin to imagine the power he possesses now that he is infected. It would have taken several of my men to take him down before; now, who knows how many he will kill if given the chance. We have to be prepared to—"

"Alek," William said putting his hand up, "Ethan's death, at least by the hand of anyone in my domain, is out of the question. I won't do that to my daughter; not after what she has already suffered for our people. If we cannot find a cure before we find him, we will tranquilize him and hold him in a cell until one is found."

"My lord, we don't know if a cure is even possible. You remember what it was like before."

"Yes, but this virus is different; you have seen it with your own eyes. These men are in control; nothing like the infected we faced before. If Lucias were to be killed and the bond broken, it is possible Ethan could live with the disease."

"Perhaps, but Lucias is not going to be easy to get to."

"No; he has quite a talent for self-preservation."

"Security patrols will continue, daylight shifts targeting rural areas, scouting only until we get more men. Lucias isn't hiding a thousand infected vampires in the city, and *we* still have the advantage. As far as he knows, Alexa is dead and we don't know anything about his plans. Not to mention that his men can't move in the daylight and we still have Chloe. He won't risk open war until he has her or—"

"I know," William interrupted, already picking up the commander's thought; not needing the possibility of his granddaughter's death vocalized further.

"One other thing," Commander Claesson continued, "the lockdown needs to apply to everyone on the compound with the exception of the soldiers on patrol. I know some of my men are off the grounds on personal leave already tonight, but none of them knows anything about what's happened here over the last couple of hours. All other access to the outside needs to be restricted; meaning no Internet and no cell phones. If Lucias's informant is on the grounds, we need to make sure they can't get to him."

"Then we need to move now, before anyone else learns about Alexa's return," William said standing in a panic.

"Not to worry, my lord; before we left Alexa, I told Jester to take care of it," he said, slipping his cell from the pocket of his fatigues.

He tapped his fingers over the screen, and then turned the device towards the High Commander.

"He's jamming the signal on the entire compound right now as a precaution and I informed the soldiers on guard duty that no one is to leave without express permission from me. If we need to send anything out electronically, we'll have to go through Jester and there's a monitored landline for calls. I'm going to head down to the IT cave now and start contacting the other bases. We should have at least three hundred men here within a week."

"Oh, Alexa; if only I had been able to see. How different things may have been for you," Josephine said, her voice full of regret as she drew closer to her daughter-in-law.

"Everything has happened as it must," Alexa replied, using the comforting words Josephine had given Ethan, as she let go of Rebecca and pulled her mother-in-law into a warm embrace.

"Very wise words," Elijah said, joining in on the hug. "It is so good to have you back, Alexa."

You sure are taking your sweet time over there.

Alexa pulled away from Elijah and Josephine and turned to her little brother standing next to Cami. In a blur, she was in front of Jared as he stood there with his customary crooked grin and messy hair. She started to reach for him but stopped short when she noticed his hand linked with Cami's. Her mouth actually fell open before she snapped it shut and glanced quickly at a rather embarrassed-looking Cami, then looked back at her brother.

Um, when did that happen? she asked him silently.

For me, the first moment I saw her. It took her a bit longer to come around, he replied, his smile widening.

"I think we need some rules against telepathic conversation in mixed company," Cami said, feigning annoyance.

"I don't know what you're talking about," Jared said with a wink as he pulled Cami's hand up to his mouth and kissed her knuckles. Her response was a somewhat uncomfortable looking smile.

I don't think she's really into PDA, Alexa sent.

Yeah, I know; but she'll have to get used to it. I can't keep my hands off of her.

"Ugh; too much information, Jared," Alexa joked, finally hugging him and Cami. To her surprise, Cami returned the hug easily.

"I'm really happy you're back," Cami said.

As she stepped back from them, Alexa suddenly felt unsteady on her feet and wobbled back slightly as an overwhelming thirst came over her. Elijah was immediately behind her, helping her to stay upright. She reached for her throat and struggled to swallow against the sudden burn.

"I need some water," she croaked out.

"No, you need blood," Elijah responded as Josephine appeared with the two chilled bags of O-negative that Elijah had brought in anticipation of Alexa's revival.

"No; I can't drink that," Alexa protested, repulsed by the thought of drinking a stranger's blood. Mentally she may not have wanted it, but her body had other ideas as her mouth began to water and her fangs punched sharply through her gums.

"Just think of it like one of those juice pouches kids drink. Trust me; you'll like it when you try it," Jared encouraged.

Josephine offered one of the bags to Alexa, who began to turn away; but then she caught the scent through the heavy plastic. Just like that, raw instinct and need took over as she grabbed the offered blood and plunged her fangs through the soft barrier. The taste was like nothing she had ever eaten before; not even the blood she had sampled as part of the bonding ceremony with Ethan. This was sweeter and oh, so satisfying, though there was a hint of something that could only be likened to the staleness of a cracker from a box which had been left open too long.

As she reached greedily for the second bag, her thoughts again turned to Ethan. She focused on the pull of their bond and took comfort in its strength; knowing with certainty that Ethan was alive and believing with everything she had that she would be able to reach him and bring him back from anything Lucias had done to him.

Jared tugged on Cami's arm, gesturing towards the door. She didn't budge as she watched Alexa feeding, with a variety of questions burning in her mind.

There has to be more she remembers, Cami thought as Jared stepped in front of her and took her face in his hands.

"There will be time for that," he whispered.

Reluctantly, Cami backed into the hallway with him as Elijah began to speak.

"Alexa, you should rest. Your body has been through an unimaginable amount of stress and the transition itself takes quite a toll. As quickly as your body is changing, you are going to feel very tired for a while."

"Yes; he's right," Rebecca added. "Chloe and I can show you to your room; we've kept it ready for you," she said fondly, taking Alexa's hand.

Still standing in the hallway, Jared squeezed Cami's hand. "You seem exhausted; why don't you let me show you my room," he whispered against her ear. "There's nothing more we can do tonight so just let me take care of you."

Not wanting to give her a chance to fight him, Jared nudged her a little further down the hall and kissed her lips softly.

"No one wants Ethan back more than my sister, Cami. Not even you; he is her bonded mate. She will think of nothing else until he is returned to her. I hear it in her thoughts and I know that, if it was you out there, I would stop at nothing to get you back; and we're not even bonded yet," he said in all seriousness.

Speechless at the implication of his words, Cami simply nodded and let him lead her away.

"I feel fine, better than fine; maybe there's more I can do," Alexa said as her mother pulled her towards the door. "What about the bond? Is it affected by distance?" she asked, her eyes darting to the three mated vampires still there.

"Yes; it grows stronger as mates draw nearer to one another," Elijah responded.

"Then I should go out. If I drive around—,"

"Alexa," Elijah interrupted, "you know I want to find my son as badly as you do, but it is too dangerous right now. Even if we found where Ethan is being held, Lucias's numbers are far too great. We need time to devise a plan as I'm sure your father and Commander Claesson are already doing," he said stepping closer to her. "And there is the matter of his infection. Lucias will force him to fight against us and—"

"But if he sees me; when he sees I'm still alive, he'll fight it. He'll come back to me," Alexa said with desperation.

"And if he can't?" Elijah asked. "Would you risk him killing one of us, or being killed himself, if you're wrong?"

Alexa shook her head, a fresh set of tears welling up in her eyes. "I can't just sit by and do nothing while he suffers," she whispered.

"Give me time; I will not rest until I find a cure," Elijah promised.

Sensing that her mother would continue to argue, Chloe sent an image into Alexa's mind. Alexa's eyes slid closed as a vision of Ethan standing in a room, which was obviously part of the compound, ignited her hope.

He will come back to us, Chloe reassured; careful to keep the rest of the vision shielded from Alexa's view. As much as she wished she could tell her mother what was coming, she knew the truth would drive her crazy with worry over something she could not change. It was her choice and her burden; no one else's.

"Okay," Alexa finally acquiesced as she took Chloe's hand.

"Show me again," Alexa said anxiously as she closed the door to her new room, after she'd convinced her reluctant mother that she needed some time alone with Chloe.

Wordlessly, Chloe pushed the image of her father into her mother's mind as Alexa closed her eyes and sighed.

"How long have you been having visions?" Alexa inquired after reveling in the brief glimpse of her husband.

"They started right after we came here," Chloe said climbing on to the bed, "but I haven't seen very much. Just flashes of you and Dad coming back," she lied.

"My darling girl, I'm so sorry; for all of this, for everything that's happened to you," Alexa said joining Chloe on the firm mattress. "It's so strange seeing you like this; so grown up. It's easy to forget how young you truly are," Alexa said placing her hands on the sides of Chloe's face.

"I wish everyone would forget. They all treat me like a child, but I don't feel young; not anymore," Chloe replied flopping back on to a pillow.

"No; I imagine you wouldn't. I can understand some of what you're going through. Even though I was much older when my gift developed, it changed me very quickly. I practically grew up overnight. Hearing the deepest, darkest thoughts of those around you has a way of doing that," Alexa replied, her voice wistful as she wished that things could be different for her child.

"It's not just my telepathy, Mom. Before I could talk, I understood so much more than anyone gave me credit for and, even when I was able to speak, I couldn't make my words keep up with my thoughts; with what was in my heart. I have been growing so fast physically, but what no one seems to understand is that, inside I have been growing even faster," Chloe responded, her voice almost pleading as she hoped her mother would understand; that she could see her for who she truly was and not for what everyone hoped she would be.

Looking into her daughter's eyes, seeing the old soul behind them; for the first time Alexa recognized just how wise Chloe had become.

"As hard as it is for me to accept, I think I understand, and I promise you I will do my best to treat you like the young woman you are. As for everyone else, they will come around. Elijah tells me it won't be long before you're fully mature, physically," Alexa corrected quickly, "then I'm sure it will be easier for us all."

"I've really missed you," Chloe said quickly moving into Alexa's arms.

"Oh, Chloe; I don't think there are words to describe how much I've missed you," Alexa replied feeling the sting of tears in her eyes. "I'm afraid to ever let you go again."

"We're safe here, and you'll have Daddy back soon," Chloe said attempting to ease Alexa's fear.

"We'll both have him back," Alexa responded laying them back as she started to feel the pull of exhaustion Elijah had warned her of.

"Yes; of course," Chloe replied trying to cover the sadness in her voice. While she wanted her father back more than anything, to see his handsome face again, and feel his strong arms around her, she knew that the next time she saw him could very well be the last.

"I feel so tired," Alexa said groggily, her lids growing impossibly heavy as she fought to stay awake, having hoped to spend hours talking with Chloe. She had missed so much in the past weeks and she wanted to hear every detail, but her transitioning body had other ideas.

"Don't fight it, Mom. Here," Chloe said flashing across the room to retrieve two bags of blood from the refrigerator and immediately returning to Alexa's side, "drink this, and then sleep. Grandpa Elijah said you're going to need to feed often for the next few days, just like I do."

Chloe willed her fangs to drop from her gums and bit into the plastic as she had done many times before. The scent of blood hit the air and called Alexa's own fangs to appear as she sat up. She took the other bag from Chloe's outstretched hand and drank it down.

Chloe took both empty containers and walked them to the trashcan as she licked a stray drop of blood from her lip.

Walking back to the bed, she couldn't help but smile. In the short time it took her to throw the bags away, Alexa had already fallen fast asleep.

Quietly, Chloe slid onto the bed next to her mother. She cuddled into the warmth of Alexa's body, savoring the comfort of having her mother near once again, though she knew it wouldn't last for long. Pushing back the dread over what was yet to come, Chloe closed her eyes and let the slow beat of her mother's heart and steady sound of her breathing comfort her to sleep.

CHAPTER 17 - *Love Expressed*

Jared secured the door to his room and turned to let his eyes roam hungrily over Cami's lithe body, following her as she slowly walked around pretending to take in her surroundings.

Her eyes scanned the room, but none of what saw registered over the sound of her own heart pounding in her ears.

Jared breezed across the space, stopping mere inches behind Cami as she stared through one of the many paintings which adorned the walls.

"Are you nervous?" Jared asked leaning in close to inhale the sweet scent of her hair. A wicked grin spread across his face as the fragrance of her arousal filled the surrounding air.

"You know that I am," she replied sharply. "I don't like you digging around in my head all the time."

"Then keep me out," he challenged, knowing that Cami had learned how to shield her thoughts like most of their kind; it was just something many grew lazy about because they weren't often in the presence of telepaths. There were those, like William, whose ability was too powerful to be blocked by most, but Jared's talent wasn't nearly as strong.

"Do you like art?" she asked with a shaky voice as she focused on building her mental shields. "This is a lovely painting," she continued, still staring straight ahead at the pastoral image, trying to use the vibrant colors of the wildflowers portrayed in the rolling landscape to anchor the wall in her mind.

"Did you know that a lot of the pieces here are the originals and the famous exhibits on display for the public are actually replicas?" she continued, anxiously tugging at the leather strap at her shoulder.

"Very good; I only heard the words you said," he praised. "But I'm not particularly interested in art at the moment," he continued against her ear, sending a delicious chill skittering down her spine.

"What *are* you interested in?" she asked closing her eyes as she let herself lean back into his warmth.

"Turn around and I'll show you," he replied, his lips so close to her neck she could feel a whisper of their soft touch against her skin.

Trying to relax, Cami took her first deep breath since entering the room. The moment the mixture of Jared's spicy masculine scent and her potent arousal filled her lungs, her anxiety was shoved to the background by an intense, almost painful, hunger.

Before Jared could even register the movement, she spun around and pushed her hands into his hair; fisting it roughly as she yanked him down to her mouth. Jared growled in response as her soft tongue plunged demandingly into his mouth. Without warning, she swung them around, pushing him against the wall, barely missing the painting she'd been admiring, and practically knocking the wind out of him.

Without breaking their frenzied kiss, Cami released Jared's hair and with both hands began tugging up on his shirt but, realizing that she would be forced to give up the spicy sweetness of his mouth to get it off, she grabbed it at the neckline and cleanly ripped it apart and off with one pull.

"God; I want you," Jared groaned into her mouth as her hands slid across the bare skin of his chest and perfectly-chiseled abs, causing his already-hard cock to lengthen even further.

Her hands continued on their journey south and she reached for the front of his frayed jeans, her fingertips grazing his erection through the thick fabric as it strained for release. Impatient to get closer to him, she started to rip those off as well, but he grabbed her wrists, forcing her back ever so slightly as he flicked his tongue wickedly across her top lip, catching the tip of one of her fangs as he did.

The taste of his own blood hit his tongue and Cami's eyes snapped open as the scent hit the air. Jared eyed her carefully as they both panted and she strained to get back to what she was doing.

"Fuck, Cami; when was the last time you fed?" he asked, his hooded eyes trained on her elongated fangs, the sight of which kicked his arousal to a new level and caused his own to slide down from his gums.

"I don't know; too long," she panted pulling one hand free and pushing it into Jared's hair as she tried to force his mouth back down to hers. Jared fought against her a little, grasping her forearm as he flashed r a crooked, fang-revealing grin which flooded her panties with moisture.

In a blur, he spun them around, pinning her hands against the wall above her head as he pressed his body against her.

"You need to feed," he whispered against her neck before he ran his tongue slowly across her sensitive skin. Keeping her arms restrained with one hand, he used the other to reach between them and unbuckle the leather holster which crisscrossed her chest.

"You expect me to go down to the blood room feeling like this?" she rasped, pushing her hips forward in an attempt to temper the ache building in her core.

"No; I'm going to feed you," he whispered before he crushed his mouth to hers again. "But first I'm going to undress you," he continued, releasing her wrists and sliding the straps off of her shoulders. The whole contraption fell to the floor with a loud clang as the short swords knocked together.

"Oh," she replied, swallowing hard as the thought of taking his blood kicked her hunger and her arousal up another notch. Jared swiftly unfastened the buckle of her belt and added it and the twin Glocks it held to the pile on the floor before he dropped down to his knees and starting working on the laces of her boots.

Standing, he scooped her up and placed one arm beneath her knees as she wrapped her arms around his neck. He sat her down on the black comforter which covered his king-sized bed and pulled off her boots and socks, tossing them aside.

Jared stood upright, grabbing her hands and pulling her up with him. As she slid up against his body, he groaned at the feel of his hardness running between her breasts and down her stomach through the denim and spandex layers still between them. Gripping the hem of her shirt, he slowly pulled it up as she raised her arms in assistance. His breath caught as he looked down at her twin peaks unexpectedly covered by feminine black lace, her hard nipples jutting out under the delicate fabric.

Cami reached back and pulled out the tight band which held back her hair, letting the long raven curls tumble over her shoulders. Jared grasped a long tendril in his hand, inhaling the delicate scent of her shampoo and then rubbing it between his fingers.

When he reached for the button of her fatigues, she reciprocated, grabbing a hold of the waist of his jeans and quickly releasing the copper-colored button. Just as she got the zipper all the way down, he dropped back down to his knees and slowly began tugging her pants down over her smooth, muscular legs while he kissed his way along her well-toned stomach.

She giggled as he dipped his tongue into her bellybutton, discovering for the first time that she was ticklish there. Looking up at her with a wicked glint in his eye, he slid his tongue down from there to the top of her lacy black thong. He nibbled the skin there before pressing a kiss over her most sensitive flesh through the thin material. He inhaled deeply as a fresh wave of arousal poured from her skin. Realizing that she needed blood more than she needed the pleasure he intended to give her with his mouth, he reluctantly stood, with his open jeans hanging delectably low on his trim hips.

The smallest push from Cami and they crumpled to the floor around his already-bare feet. She felt her stomach do a somersault as she looked down at his exposed flesh. Apparently, Jared wasn't a fan of underwear because there was nothing left to conceal the sheer size of him.

Sensing her nerves, Jared pulled her against him and pressed his mouth down upon hers, sliding his tongue achingly slowly along the seam of her lips.

Tentatively, Cami reached between them and gripped the stalk of his erect manhood, surprised by how silky and soft the skin was against her palm.

Jared groaned as she started to move her hand up and down and greedily deepened their kiss. He pressed forward into her touch as he placed his hands on her shoulders and eased her back on the bed. Covering her body with his, he slid an arm around and under her back before rolling them both over.

Lying on top of him, Cami stared down into his stormy gray eyes; her breath catching as she took in all of the emotion swimming in their depths.

"I love you, Cami," he whispered as they continued to stare at one another. "Drink from me; I want to give you everything you need and more," he continued as he tilted his head back and to the side.

Cami's eyes widened as she took in the deliciously slow thrum of his pulse beating in the vein there. Her fangs, which had retracted slightly from earlier, dropped back down to their full length as she leaned down and swiped her tongue along his carotid artery.

Jared gripped her hips tightly as she struck, her fangs cutting through the soft flesh with ease. He growled his approval as her first long pull sent a jolt through his body and straight to his achingly-hard length. Running on pure instinct, Cami's hips began to thrust involuntarily; grinding her hot flesh against him through the thin fabric barrier of her panties.

He responded in kind, grinding his hips upward to meet each of her thrusts, feeling her incredible heat against his tender flesh and striving to get even closer; his cock throbbing with the need to be inside her. As she continued to drink, Jared pulled on the thin straps of her thong, the material snapping free easily before he gripped under her thighs, lifted her and positioned his wide tip between her wet folds. He held her there, suspending her as he rocked her back and forth so the head of his cock slid over the tender flesh, skating over her engorged clit before returning to her tight opening. With each pass more of her sweet moisture coated him as he pressed a little harder; testing, teasing, torturing them both.

Her body began to quiver as an orgasm built and she struggled against Jared's grip while she remained attached to his neck, trying desperately to push her body down onto his, aching to feel him inside her. Sensing that she was close, and feeling precariously close the edge himself, Jared eased his hold slightly, letting her slick heat sink a little further down onto his throbbing cock. When he met with the delicate barrier there, he stopped, squeezing his eyes shut from the sweet torture.

"Fuck, Cami; you're so tight," he husked, "I can't, I can't hold back much longer."

She released her grip on his vein and slid her tongue over the marks there as she lifted her head, feeling slightly drunk and on fire with need. "Please, Jared. God; please fuck me," she begged.

Hearing those words, his body took over with his hips thrusting upward forcefully as he released his hold on her legs and she sunk down onto his cock, the thin barrier of flesh giving way with a slight pop. She cried out from the pain, her nails digging into Jared's shoulders hard enough to draw blood as she buried her face against his chest. With great struggle, he remained motionless waiting for the pain to subside; his body trembling from the effort as he fought the urge to move inside her. She was so tight; her body surrounding him so completely, drowning him in her sweet juices. Every little movement she made, every breath she took seemed to squeeze him tighter, pushing him closer and closer to the edge until finally she began to relax against him.

Lifting her head and pressing up with her arms, she began to move her hips against him as the pain gave way to pleasure. Jared moaned as she moved forward and her hot flesh stroked up his length before she slid back down again. With him buried to the hilt, Cami swiveled her hips in small circles, drinking in the feel of him as a tingling sensation spread across her body.

Unable to hold back any longer, Jared rolled them over and pressed himself even deeper, sending her over the edge as she called out his name in ecstasy. Her body pulsed around him, squeezing his cock like a wet fist, which quickly set of his own exquisite climax as he continued to thrust inside her.

When their bodies finally stilled, Jared lifted up on his elbows and looked down at Cami as she stroked his back lazily, her eyes closed and a small satisfied smile on her face.

"What are you thinking?" he asked as he started to roll away from her, but she gripped on to him and held him in place.

"Don't move yet; I like this, feeling you all over me," she said opening her eyes. "I was just thinking I can't believe I waited so long for this. If I had known…" Her voice trailed off.

"If you had known what?" he pressed

"Just, wow; I never realized it would be like this. If I had known I don't think I would have—"

"Don't even say it," he said cutting her off. "You were made for me.

This experience, this incredible experience wasn't just sex, it was us; soul mates coming together for the first time. It wouldn't be like this with anyone else; that is why you waited. You were waiting for me."

Cami smiled and started stroking his hair where it fell forward onto his forehead, but her smile quickly faded into a frown.

"That's a nice sentiment, but you've clearly been with other women," she said bitterly as she turned her head away from him. As soon as the words left her lips, she was angry with herself for acting so childishly; but her jealously was stronger than her sense of reason.

Jared lifted his hand and gently turned her back to face him. "Are you jealous?" he said with a slight chuckle, which only pissed her off further. She pushed him off of her and jumped from the bed, gathering up her clothes as she moved towards the bathroom.

"Cami; wait," he demanded speeding across the room to block her escape.

"Move out of my way," she commanded as she regarded him angrily.

He just stood there completely naked, staring at her standing there with her arms full of her things, her eyes blazing, her black curly hair crazily framing her beautifully-flushed face.

"There's been no one else, Cami; only you. This was my first time as well," he stated stepping towards her to take the clothes from her arms. Seeing the truth in his eyes, she relented, letting him drop everything to the floor and pull her against him. He kissed her lips softly and started moving them back towards the bed. "Come on; I want to hold you."

Jared sat on the bed, turning her and pulling her with him. He slid them to the middle and wrapped his body around hers, her back to his front. She snuggled into him and started to relax, suddenly feeling very tired. She turned her head back towards him. "Well, at least now we'll save some time," she stated with a yawn.

"What do you mean?" he asked, puzzled by her statement.

"If you'd been with other women it would have taken me a while to hunt them down and kill them," she replied sounding completely serious.

Jared just laughed, unsure if she was being sincere; but judging by the way the thought of another man touching her made him feel, he was pretty certain she was.

CHAPTER 18 - *Comrades Lost*

Layla stepped through the thick curtain to the VIP room at Blood Runners, her sharp green eyes immediately cutting to their usual table, the one she'd shared with Dante more times than she could count over the years. A wave of disappointment washed over her when she didn't see his muscular frame occupying a seat.

Taking a breath, she immediately picked up on his intoxicatingly masculine scent as she continued to survey the room. It was a typical crowd of rich civilians sprinkled with an occasional human brought in from the other room.

"Looks like you missed him," Jasmine said over Layla's shoulder. "I don't know why you bother asking anything here," she continued referring to the tight-lipped bouncer. They all knew the deal at Blood Runners. You could ask, but they wouldn't tell.

"Sorry, Layla; but we're here now. Might as well make the most of it," Rachel said stepping around her two companions on her way to the booth.

As Rachel slid onto the seat, her eyes went wide, shooting to Jasmine as she shook her head. No sooner than her ass made contact with the bench, she was back on her feet and in front of Layla.

"We should grab another table," she said trying to move her friends towards the other side of the room.

"What the hell, Rachel, we always—," Layla swallowed the rest of her words as Rachel's motivation for moving became apparent.

"Maybe it wasn't him," Jasmine said trying to ease the hurt which flashed across Layla's eyes as she picked up the scent of a human woman. And sex.

"I'm fine," Layla said in a tone of agitation. "We're just friends; he can do as he pleases," she added attempting to school her features into a mask of disinterest as she sat down.

Jasmine gave Rachel a knowing look as both women reluctantly followed suit and joined Layla.

"You two can stop looking at each other like that," she said, glaring at her friends.

"Sorry, Layla; but it's just us. You don't have to try and act so tough about it; we know how you feel about him. What we don't get is how you can spend so much time with him, letting him talk about all those other women, and not just tell him."

Layla let out a heavy sigh. "I'm going to tell him; I tried to back on the compound, but everything got all fucked up."

"Really?" Rachel asked with surprise. "What the hell finally changed your mind?"

Layla looked at her with uncertainty. "I heard him talking to Martinez about kissing Cami. I know you're friends with her and she said nothing is going on, but he likes her; I think he always has and I don't know," she paused leaning back against the seat, "I guess before, with the other women, they were all just strangers; mostly humans, so I know it never really meant anything. But with Cami it's more. I think if she wanted, they would be together, as a real couple."

"If Cami says nothing is going on, then nothing is going on," Rachel responded. "In all the years I've known her, she's never once talked about any man, or woman, for that matter, romantically. She cares about her duty, about the war. Look at everything that's happened to her family. And that poor girl we found tonight; I've never seen her so shaken up. You know as well as I do that finding a mate is the last thing on her mind."

Rachel was right. She knew Cami wasn't interested in Dante, but it didn't change the fact that Dante was interested in Cami. And she knew him; he was a stubborn, persistent man. When he really wanted something, he didn't give up easily. Cami might not be looking for a mate, but she couldn't imagine anyone resisting Dante's overwhelming charm forever.

Even after seeing Dante with other women for decades, watching him disappear into the dark to take their veins and their bodies, there was one thing she knew she couldn't bear to watch. She couldn't watch him fall in love with someone else.

And if it was Cami, there would be no escaping it. Living on the compound, she'd have to see them together every day. Layla swallowed hard as she tried to choke back the bile that was rising in her throat at the thought.

"Layla; hey, earth to Layla," Jasmine said waving her hand in front of her friend's face.

Layla blinked a couple of times and looked at Jasmine. "What's up, Jas?" she asked.

"Where the hell were you just now? I asked you if you wanted to head back into the other room with us to find a little, uh, entertainment," she said winking. "It will help you take your mind off of things."

"A little later; I'm going to grab a drink first," Layla said as they started walking away.

"Suit yourself, but be warned; if I find anything particularly delicious I'm going to bring him back here for you. You could use the distraction," Jasmine teased giving Layla a sympathetic smile.

"Yeah; all right," Layla said as she watched her friends disappear through the entrance.

Catching a waitress's eye, she waved her over and ordered a double shot of tequila and a tequila sunrise. When the waitress returned, Layla held up a one-hundred-dollar-bill.

S. Simone Chavous

"This is yours as long as I don't see the bottom of this glass tonight," she said pointing to the colorful drink in front of her.

"Sure thing," the cute young vampire said with a smile.

Without hesitation, Layla tossed back the shot and immediately started in on the mixed drink, knowing it would take at least one more round before her supernatural body would start to feel the effects, and she *definitely* wanted to feel it.

After polishing off a second round, and feeling sufficiently buzzed, Layla's eyes wandered toward the back where the private rooms were located. Feeling a flare of jealousy as she imagined what Dante had been doing there, she realized Jasmine was right. She needed to get her mind off of him. She needed a distraction. Downing the rest of her third drink as the waitress brought her a fourth, Layla decided she was going to go find someone to drink, maybe more if she didn't slow down with the alcohol.

Standing, she looked towards the door and had to sit back down as her mouth practically fell open. She watched with rapt attention as four male vampires strolled into the room. To say they were impressive would have been an understatement.

Her eyes followed the four men as they made their way to a booth directly across the room, giving her a perfect view. So intent on watching the newcomers, Layla didn't notice Jasmine and Rachel approach.

"Holy shit, Layla. I was going to ask if you saw them, but clearly you've already gotten a better look at them than we have," Jasmine whispered though the other patrons were far enough away and the music loud enough to keep anyone from overhearing their conversation.

"Commander Claesson must be calling in the other bases after what happened today," Rachel added assuming the four men were Elite, based on their size and apparel.

"Text Martinez and see if he's heard anything on base about the new arrivals," Jasmine said sliding in next to Layla to enjoy the view. "They have to be from up north; look at how pale they are, and what's with the sunglasses?"

Rachel pulled the cell from her pocket and quickly sent off the requested message.

"They're probably just trying to fit in with the human crowd in the other room. Half of them have shades on even though they can barely see in the dark as it is," Layla added as she finished her fourth drink.

"Hmm; that's strange. My text doesn't seem to be going through," Rachel said as she hit the first number in her speed dial.

After several rings, she gave up and slipped the phone back into her pocket. "He's probably asleep; throwing camouflage wears him out."

"Oh, yeah; I bet that's not all he's recovering from right now," Jasmine teased as she signaled their waitress. "I could smell him all over you as soon as you got in the car."

"It wasn't like that," Rachel replied as her cheeks flushed. Even after being married and bonded for nearly a year, she still got shy when her friends talked about, or even hinted at, sex. Lucky for Martinez, behind closed doors was a whole different story. "He just wanted me to feed before we went out."

"I'm surprised he lets you come here at all anymore; you know how possessive bonded men get. I'm guessing that's why he made you feed first; he wanted to make sure you weren't hungry enough to be tempted."

Rachel and Martinez had been pretty much inseparable for the last ten years since he joined The Elite, but only as friends until about a year ago when they finally realized they were in love with each other. Since then, Rachel filled the bulk of her blood needs with her mate; but as with any vampire couple, they needed to feed from humans occasionally to keep their blood strong.

Rachel had never been able to stomach the taste of bagged blood, so she had to drink it straight from the source. To keep Martinez from going absolutely crazy with jealousy, she promised to feed only from women, and since it had only been a couple of months since she'd last had human blood, this particular night out was only about unwinding after the mess they'd dealt with on their last mission. Still, with her going to a club where fresh blood would be flowing all around, Martinez insisted she go on a full stomach.

"Well, looking at those four, I don't need to be all that hungry to be tempted," Layla said with a mischievous grin.

"Damn, Layla; how many drinks did you suck down already?" Jasmine asked just as the waitress reached their table. "Never mind; you still need at least one more," she added gesturing to their empty glasses.

When the young vampire returned with their drinks, Jasmine pushed Layla's glass forward in encouragement. "Drink this fast; you're going to need it in a minute."

Layla eyeballed her suspiciously for a moment, but then shrugged her shoulders and drained her glass.

"All right; let's go," Jasmine said pulling Layla up from her seat. "We need to go welcome our new guests to Boston."

"Good luck with that," Rachel responded watching her friends make their way across the room while she nursed her drink.

Even in her intoxicated state, and being dragged by Jasmine, Layla glided effortlessly across the room, her blonde hair swaying across her back in sharp contrast to the black tank top she was wearing, drawing the eyes of the four mystery men and every other being in the room with a pulse.

"Good evening, fellas," Jasmine purred, sauntering up the edge of the table and placing her hands on the smooth surface. "I was hoping you could settle something for me and my friends," she said cutting her eyes to Layla, who though she was smiling and a little drunk, looked uncomfortable. "We were wondering which compound you boys were in town from?"

"Compound? Not sure what you mean," responded one of the men on her left. She drank him in as he smiled up at her with shaded eyes and neatly-trimmed, honey-blonde hair. Peeking out from the collar of his fitted black t-shirt was the top of what had the potential to be a pretty badass tattoo which she definitely wanted to see more of.

"Oh, come on; it's cool. You're Elite, from out of town, right? My friends and I are stationed here in Boston."

"So you're Elite?" a black-haired soldier sitting next to the wall asked casually as all four men eyed them carefully, though it was difficult to tell through their dark shades.

Jasmine nodded, never taking her eyes off the blonde vampire who'd initially caught her eye.

"Well, why don't you let us buy you a drink then," he asked moving his legs from under the table to stand. Taking advantage of the opportunity, Jasmine slipped onto his lap before he could get up, flashing him a bright smile.

"A drink sounds perfect," she responded simply as she looked at Layla and gave her a hard stare as she inclined her head towards the two men on the other side of the table.

Layla shrugged and dropped down into the lap of the dark-haired man closest to her. Between all the alcohol she'd basically chugged and her frustrations over Dante, she felt like doing something crazy. All she had to do was follow Jasmine's lead. The visitors would no doubt be staying on the compound, so a little voice in her head even whispered something about using them to make Dante jealous. That voice was quickly followed by another which reminded her he had to care to get jealous. She'd been with other men before and he hadn't seemed to notice.

"So, guess we should introduce ourselves. I'm Layla," she said trying to relax as the muscular vampire slid his hands around her waist. Jasmine would have been fine skipping the names, but Layla hadn't mastered the art of casual sex as well as her friend. "I'm Vic," he replied with a smile which revealed his fangs. "That's Dillon, Tony, and your friend is with Mason," he said pointing to each of the other men in turn.

Across the table, Jasmine leaned into Mason's neck and inhaled deeply, her fangs elongating as she took in his scent and zeroed in on the steady beat of his pulse. She kissed him softly on the thin skin covering his vein, then grazed one sharp fang over the surface gently. Mason pushed his hand into her thick hair roughly, turning her head and capturing her mouth in a rough and demanding kiss.

Jasmine tried to pull back, wanting to tell him to take it easy, but he held her tightly as she struggled. Suddenly feeling a sharp pinch in her upper thigh, her hand shot down to the source of the pain and met with the syringe jammed into her leg as she finally broke away from Mason's mouth. "What the fuck," she tried to yell, but it only came out as a whisper.

Already feeling as if her hand weighed a thousand pounds, she yanked the needle free and reached for the silver blade strapped to her inner thigh. As her fingertips grasped the handle, Mason's strong hand wrapped around her wrist, holding it in place.

"There'll be none of that, lovely," he whispered as she used her free hand in an attempt to strike his face, but as the tranquilizer took effect she only managed a weak swipe which knocked his shades down revealing his glowing, blood-red irises.

Hearing the eerie tone of Mason's voice, Layla turned her head to see Jasmine slumping down in his arms and reached for her dagger, but was met with Vic's strong grasp as he jammed a needle into her arm. Unable to pull it out, she received the full dose and went out immediately.

Observing from across the room, Rachel noticed Jasmine struggling and jumped up from her seat, yanking her trusty Glock from the holster hidden under her jacket as she moved forward and took aim. Somewhat shy in all other areas of life, Rachel excelled as a soldier; moving with grace and surety as she sped across the space separating her from her friends.

The four men stood, rushing for the door with Layla and Jasmine in tow, unaware of Rachel's fast approach. Uncertain of what was happening, Rachel aimed low with her first shot, clipping Mason's thigh. He fell forward to his knees, dropping an unconscious Jasmine to the ground with a loud thud. He roared out as the path left by the silver bullet seared with pain. The loud pop of the gunshot had already sent civilians and humans alike screaming with panic as they scattered towards the exits and away from the danger.

Vic jumped over Mason and Jasmine, making his escape with Layla slung over his shoulder as Rachel took aim again, but the other two men fired back, forcing her to roll to the ground as she squeezed the trigger, sending her second shot wide while Vic disappeared down the dark hallway. Rachel's third bullet found its mark, hitting Dillon in the chest and sending him flying into the wall. While the shot wasn't enough to kill him, he was out cold and the silver would keep his infected body from healing until the bullet was removed. A rush of terrified patrons passed, blocking her shot and her view. She leapt up as they passed, prepared to fire again only to find that the four men and Layla were gone.

In an instant, she passed Jasmine lying prone on the dirty floor; assured by her acute senses that her friend was alive as she sped down the hallway to the backdoor and kicked it open. Cautiously stepping out into the alley, she focused her senses, drowning out the chaos inside the club as she zeroed in on her targets. Hearing a car door slam, she rushed down the alley to the street as the dark-blue SUV peeled away. She fired several rounds at the driver's window, each bouncing ineffectually off the bulletproof glass.

Rachel took off after the fleeing vehicle on foot, gaining ground until the back window slid open and bullets sprayed out at her, the light from each shot like the flash of a firework in the dark. Unable to effectively return fire running at that speed, she ducked behind a parked car and took aim, hoping to blow out one of the tires, but the vehicle took a hard right and disappeared from view.

Heart pounding in her chest, she slid her cell from her pocket and tried to dial the compound but, like before, the call wouldn't go through.

Running back into Blood Runners, she sped around the bar to the hallway there, slamming into Winslow as she rounded the corner on her way to his office.

"I need your landline now," she said offering no further explanation. None was necessary since he'd witnessed most of what had occurred through the surveillance footage which was fed to the monitors in his office.

Winslow entered the security code and pushed the door open, letting her inside his private space.

Picking up the phone on his desk, she dialed the central number for the compound.

"This is Rachel Lehman. I need the commander now," she said without greeting the operator on the other end. Rose, one of the two women who took turns manning The Elite switchboard, immediately put her through.

Several seconds later, Commander Claesson came on the line.

"Sir, we've got a big fucking problem."

"Winslow, my man; you've got to give us something here," Dante pressed as he stared down the bald vampire.

"Come on, Dante, you know the drill; my policies are half the reason you even come here. We don't ask, and we damn sure don't tell. You guys in here like this, asking people all these questions, is really going to fuck up business for a while," he said pointing to where several Elite soldiers were interviewing civilian vampire customers.

Humans were being questioned in the other room, in a far more discreet manner, though most of them were too drugged up to know their own names let alone notice that they had likely just been caught in the midst of a vampire war.

"Like I told Rachel, all I can tell you is no one's ever seen them here before."

Dealing in the trade of blood and women, Winslow's clientele expected a certain level of anonymity and confidentiality when they visited his establishment. While most civilians would be trembling under the interrogation of a vampire like Dante, Winslow took it in stride. He'd been in the business way too long and had seen way too much shit to fold under a little intimidation.

"What about those?" Dante asked pointing to one of the surveillance cameras mounted in the corner near the ceiling.

"Surveillance only; they don't record."

"Fuck," Dante spat.

"I'm sorry, man. I really wish I could help you out, but I just don't see what else I can do," Winslow said genuinely.

"Yeah, all right, Winslow. Thanks," Dante said placing a hand on his shoulder before walking off to go tell the rest of the team to pack up.

Before he moved, Winslow stepped closer and whispered, "So is it true then? This all have something to do with Lucias?" Dante raised an eyebrow at him curiously. "Come on, you know word gets around; especially in my business. People are scared, like before. I've even heard talk about the child, you know, the one Lucias has been after all these years."

"Rachel is pretty sure their eyes were red which explains the shades and from what I know, irises that color mean one thing, but you can draw your own conclusion. As far as the rest of it goes, I honestly don't know. The only thing I'm concerned with right now is getting one of ours back in one piece," Dante replied walking away.

Motherfucker. Why didn't I just stay? Dante thought to himself angrily, but he knew why and in that moment, he hated himself for it. He was a coward and when he'd heard Layla asking for him earlier, he hadn't thought he could get away fast enough. Just thinking her name, he suddenly found it hard to breathe.

"Hey; you all right, Dante?" Rachel asked, walking over to where he was hunched over with his hands on his knees.

"Yeah, just overdue for some blood," he lied, standing upright and trying to shake off the feelings threatening to overwhelm him.

"You want me to take over so you can deal with that?" Rachel asked eyeing him suspiciously. She knew he was lying. When she'd arrived there with Layla and Jasmine earlier, it had been almost impossible to miss the evidence of Dante's feeding and there was no way he wouldn't have taken enough of the human's blood if he'd been so blood-starved that it was still affecting him.

"No; I've got it," he responded. "What did the doctor say? How long before she wakes up?" he inquired about Jasmine; having sent Rachel to speak with the medical team before they transported her back to the compound.

"Best guess was within a couple of hours, but the doc said he'd know more once they got her blood to the lab."

"All right; I want to be there when she comes around. She might be our only shot at finding," he swallowed hard, finding it hard to even say her name, "Layla," he finally forced out, feeling as if his heart was being squeezed by a vise.

"We're going to get her back, Dante," Rachel said trying to offer some comfort.

"Yeah; I know," he replied, unable to let himself even consider any other possibility.

Finally reining in his emotions, he addressed the soldiers who were still interrogating a small group of witnesses who hadn't fled the scene before The Elite arrived.

"I think we've got all we're going to get in here. You can let all these people go home."

He watched for a few seconds as the civilians started to file towards the doors then turned to Rachel. "Walk me through what happened after they got outside again. Probably a long shot, but it's all we've got to go on right now," he said knowing he needed to focus on his mission, on getting Layla back, to stave off the growing ache in his chest.

Standing in the street outside, Rachel recalled the events as they'd happened up until the car turned out of sight. As she spoke, Dante's eyes shot around looking for something, anything that could help. Just as he was about to give up and head back to base to wait for Jasmine to wake up, he spotted an ATM across the way.

"Come on," he said speeding over to the machine. Locating he camera, Dante leaned in and looked in the direction it was pointing. "Where'd you say the car was parked?"

"Right over there; at the curb on the corner," she replied pointing to the spot.

"Think we might have just caught a break," he said with relief as he pulled out the satellite phone Jester had given him to bypass the block that was in place on the compound. "Hey, Jester; I need you to pull footage from the First City Bank across the street from Blood Runners."

"What is your name?" Lucias asked coldly from his seat, where he seemed perfectly comfortable in the dim light of the exam room.

Layla spat loudly on the ground at his feet, but didn't utter a word in response. Knowing the menacing man sitting across from her was Lucias, she was utterly terrified, but refused to let them see it.

The kick Mason threw to the back of her legs sent her to her knees with a loud thud against the hard floor.

"When the master asks you a question, you answer," he hissed.

"Fuck you," she replied defiantly, earning a blow to the side of her face. Her cheek exploded with pain as she fell over sideways into the wall. With her hands tethered behind her back, she had no way to catch herself, but immediately sat back up when she regained her balance. The cut which had opened up over her cheekbone had almost completely healed by the time she was upright again.

Mason raised his arm to strike her once more, since she had yet to offer her name, but Lucias lifted his hand signaling him to stop.

"Her name is of little consequence," he said quietly as he stood. "Place her on the table."

Mason grabbed Layla by her armpits and hoisted her up onto the cold steel slab. Between the handcuffs and the lingering effects of the tranquilizer, there was little she could do against his manhandling.

She kept her eyes locked on Lucias; following him as he approached the small table and picked up the syringe. Lucias smirked as he saw the fear flash in her eyes as she realized what he intended to do to her.

"Yes, my dear; in a short time you will tell me your name and anything else I want to know."

She opened her mouth to protest, trying desperately to stall for more time, praying her fellow soldiers would find her; but before a sound escaped her lips, Lucias covered the short distance between them and plunged the needle into her chest.

Layla cried out in pain as he depressed the plunger and released the virus into her heart. The poisonous liquid spread like fire through her veins with each slow beat of her pulse, but she clenched her mouth shut, refusing to cry out further as she tried to accept her fate. As she struggled, a lone tear slid from the corner of her eye.

Lucias reached out and stroked her cheek almost lovingly. Layla squeezed her eyes shut to hide her pain and fear as he collected her tear on his finger and placed the salty liquid on his tongue.

"I want her fed immediately," Lucias said, instructing Mason. "At least two humans, as I want her transformation to be swift. I have great plans for our lovely little soldier," he continued before moving to the door. "Oh, and Mason; after she is fed you are to clean her and take her to my playroom to complete her transformation. Alert me the moment it is done," he said and disappeared from view.

CHAPTER 19 - *Finding Cami*

"Here's what we've got; picture quality wasn't great, but I've cleaned it up as much as I can," Jester said as he spun around in his chair and wheeled across the floor; back to his workstation in the room full of computers, monitors and all sorts of other gadgets neither Dante, Martinez or Rachel could accurately identify.

They watched as the video started on screen with the dark SUV pulling up to the corner across the street facing away from the alley behind Blood Runners. Shortly after, four very large vampires exited and walked out of view.

"Fuck; that doesn't tell us anything we don't already know," Dante said; his disappointment apparent.

"I'm not done," Jester said with a smile. "We got lucky; the State of Massachusetts gives the option of plating vehicles on the front or the rear. Just so happens, our mystery guests chose the former." He reached up and tapped the screen pointing to the plate which was too small to read. Punching a few keys, he blew up the image, clearly revealing the numbers.

"I already ran it; comes back registered to a Sean Taylor. I cross-referenced the RMV records against ours and, as far as I can tell, the registrant's human. Lives alone just outside of the city," he said, handing Dante the address, "There haven't been any reports filed for a missing person yet, though Taylor *does* has one hell of a long rap sheet; lots of violent offenses, mainly assaults, but nothing too major. I'm guessing these boys probably paid Taylor a visit right before they showed up at Blood Runners. Odds are the only thing you're going to find out there is his body, but at least it'll save us from the hassle of trying to get in a clean-up after humans show up on the scene. And who knows; we could get lucky."

"Thanks, Jester. Can you get us satellite images of the area around the address?" Dante asked.

"On it," Jester replied simply.

"Rachel, head to the commander's office and fill him in on what Jester found and tell him we'll meet up with him in the pit. Martinez, you're with me. We need to find Cami; I want her there to run her team in case we do need the clean-up."

"You mind if I swing by the medical wing and get Jasmine? The doctor said she'd be clear as soon as she fed, and I know she's going to want to go. Layla is her best friend," Rachel said, making her way out.

Jasmine had woken up before they'd even gotten her back to the compound; but, unfortunately, she didn't remember anything more than what they already knew with the exception of the vampire's names, which they assumed were aliases.

"Yeah, of course; just clear it with the commander."

Dante and Martinez flashed through the hallways from Jester's cave to Cami's room. Dante knocked hard several times before trying the handle and finding it locked.

"Where the hell is she? In all these years, has she ever ignored a call?" Dante wondered.

"Hell, no; not since I've been here. Did you notice the commander didn't even ask where she was and, you know damn well, he noticed she didn't respond to his signal. You think maybe he ordered her to hang back because of her family?" Martinez asked in response.

Both men, knowing Cami fairly well, had expected her to show up on- scene, with or without permission, considering that Layla and Jasmine were both members of her team and she was the kind of leader who put her people and the job first.

Besides, after working with her for so many years, everyone knew that her job was really all she cared about. She never took leave, and she damn sure never went out to feed. As far as anyone knew, she fed exclusively from the bag.

"Who the fuck knows? One minute her whole family is on lockdown; the next she's out on clean-up and hauling body bags back," Dante replied. "If it was up to me I'd keep all of the females on lockdown until this whole mess is over with. Lucias is after the girl; he doesn't know what she looks like, so they're all potential targets. Besides, that whole scene tonight would have gone down a lot differently if it had been us instead of Layla and Jasmine."

Martinez laughed. "I would hope so; not sure about you, but I've never really been a fan of sitting on other guys' laps. And really, I'm disappointed with your antiquated ideas about the softer sex. I always took you for more of a feminist," he said sarcastically.

In a blur, Dante had his hand around Martinez's throat, pinning him to the wall and knocking down one of Van Gogh's early works in the process. "You think this is fucking funny, Martinez?" Dante growled.

"Jesus Christ, Dante; I was just kidding," Martinez choked out, shoving his friend back.

Dante didn't respond as he took off for the training room. Martinez's remark shouldn't have bothered him. His best friend had always been a bit of a smart-ass; it was part of his charm, but it had been hard enough schooling his temper the first time he had to hear about Layla cuddling up on the lap of some stranger.

With each passing minute, he drew closer and closer to the edge realizing that that same stranger and his cronies now had Layla and could be doing God-knows-what to her. The sting of his own nails cutting into his palms drew him out of his thoughts. Taking the opportunity before he sunk back into despair over the unknown, he shoved the darkness to the back of his mind as blood filled his hands.

"Listen, man; we're all worried about Layla and I know you've been feeling strung-out on Cami since that little workout thing you told me about earlier but, if you were asking me for advice, I'd tell you to dial it back a few notches. If you go at her, trying to tell her what to do and getting all alpha male on her, she's going to put your nuts in a jar," Martinez said as they reached the training room. "And the way it sounds, you're going to have some serious competition from that kid.

"You think this is about Cami?" Dante asked, stopping to face Martinez.

"Well, yeah; you've seemed pretty amped up since this morning, and then with—" Martinez stopped, eyeing Dante as he started to pace. "Oh, shit; wait, is it Layla?"

Dante stopped walking and ran his hand through his hair as he regarded his friend; his eyes revealing the answers his mouth didn't seem able to say.

"It's about fucking time. You know, I think she's been in love with you since her first day here," Martinez responded, grabbing Dante by the shoulders.

Dante pulled away, lowering his head; his voice barely above a whisper. "She wanted to tell me earlier. I think I knew what it was about. I think I've known for a long time; I saw it in her eyes, but I just did what I always do. I used another woman to push her away. I don't know what the fuck is wrong with me; all these years, I just couldn't, and now—"

"Hey, Dante," Martinez said stepping closer to his friend and looking him in the eyes. "We *are* going to find her. Layla is a good soldier, and she's fucking stubborn. She has to be to keep putting up with your shit all this time. She never gave up on you, so don't you give up on her."

Unable to speak, Dante nodded.

"There's no one here," Martinez observed as he peered through the glass into the training room. "Let's head back to the pit; Cami might already be there."

Silently, Dante turned and Martinez followed.

Stopping suddenly, Dante inhaled deeply. "You smell that?" he asked looking behind his friend.

Martinez took a breath. "Yeah; Cami's close by, or she was."

Dante pointed at the door behind his friend. "No fucking way," Martinez responded as he realized they were standing outside the guest quarters Jared had been occupying for the last week. "You really think she's in there?"

"Only one way to find out," Dante replied as he pressed his finger to the button beside the door.

Having lost track of the number of times she and Jared had made love in the last few hours, Cami rolled away from his embrace, feeling deliciously sore.

"Where do you think you're going?" Jared asked as he anchored his arm around her waist and dragged her naked body back against his.

"Just coming up for some air. I need a shower and I should check in. Guest suites don't have call signals, but I'm guessing just about everyone would know where to find me now."

"I'll join you," Jared said, sliding them both to the edge of the bed. Cami swung her legs over as Jared sat up behind her, putting his much larger feet down on the floor on the outside of hers so that she was snuggled between his thighs. He pushed her thick mane of hair to one side and nibbled softly at the tender flesh at the base of her neck; eliciting a low moan from the back of her throat.

"That might be a bad idea. If you get in there with me, we may never make it back out," Cami said, her tone half-teasing.

Jared kissed her shoulder before moving back just a little and letting her hair fall back into place. "I'll behave; scout's honor," he said making a cross over his heart with his hand as she stood and he flashed her that crooked grin of his.

"You weren't a boy scout," she responded as more of a question than a statement. While many vampire families integrated with humans and participated in their activities, it seemed unlikely that the High Commander's family would have done so, given the demanding nature of his position amongst their kind.

"Actually, I was. My mom liked to get away as much as she could when I was younger, said she got sick of always being on display, being watched. Spending time around humans was an escape from the expectations that come with being a member of the High family. She liked to take classes, yoga, painting, dance, all kinds of stuff; so she had to find something to keep me occupied, too."

"A real-life boy scout. Is there a merit badge for what we just did? Because, if so, you would have my highest endorsement." Cami said playfully, as she turned and sped into the bathroom.

Jared was right on her heels, but he stopped and leaned against the doorjamb as he watched her move around the space.

Cami threw two white towels on to the hook on the wall, slid open the glass door and moved her fingers over the digital touchscreen to set the temperature and turn on the shower. She looked over her shoulder at Jared, as she closed the door and smiled as he had to pull his eyes from her naked ass to meet her gaze. Turning to face him, her eyes moved over his chiseled form, drinking in his masculine perfection as she licked her lips.

In a breath, Jared was up against her, pushing her back against the frosted glass. "You can't look at me like that if you expect me to behave," he whispered against her mouth, his lips barely brushing over hers as they moved.

"Mmmm; I may have changed my mind about that," she said before capturing his bottom lip between her teeth and sucking it into her mouth. She released it with a pop as she gripped his hard stalk and backed them into the warm streams of water.

Jared cupped Cami's tight ass with his hands and hoisted her up as he covered her mouth with his own. With a moan, Cami wrapped her long legs around his waist and slid her arms around his neck as the water cascaded over them. Taking advantage of the bench seat behind him, Jared sat back bringing Cami down with him, the contact between their mouths never breaking as she slid her wet body down over his hard length.

As she rocked back and forth, Jared moved his hands up over the slick skin of her back and into her thick hair. He tugged just hard enough to pull her head back, getting her full attention as their mouths separated and she looked down at him with lust-filled eyes.

Jared stared up into her eyes as she continued to move against him; the delicious friction between their bodies bringing her close to orgasm and making it difficult for her to maintain her rhythm. As the first waves of her climax started to crest and her eyes slid closed, Jared released her hair and cupped her face in his hands.

"Look at me, Cami. I want to see your eyes when you come," he commanded.

With some difficulty, she obeyed and immediately came apart when her eyes found his again. Seeing the pleasure flood Cami's eyes, and feeling her body tighten around him, sent Jared over the edge right behind her. He growled lowly and his hands shot down to the bench as he thrust upward with the surges of his orgasm while she gripped his shoulders to ride out her own release.

Cami collapsed against him, their bodies still joined as Jared reached for the shampoo. With Cami nuzzled against his chest as the water ran down her back, he squeezed a small amount of shampoo into his hand and began massaging it into her scalp. She let out a satisfied moan as his fingertips circled, applying the perfect amount of pressure.

"Stand up and rinse your hair," he said easing her off of his lap. As she obeyed, he grabbed his loofa and began to wash her body, taking his time appreciating every gentle curve and line of her toned figure.

"You are so beautiful," he whispered standing up straight and pulling her thoroughly-cleansed body into his arms.

"An overrated quality," Cami replied before placing a soft peck on his lips. "Now I really need to go. You should check on your sister and Chloe when you're done showering."

Jared groaned as he pulled her even closer. "Now that I finally have you in my arms, I don't want to let go."

Despite her first instinct to pull away as she felt her fear starting to creep back in, she stayed still and let Jared hold onto her.

"Cami, you don't have to be afraid with me. I will never hurt you. You are everything to me," Jared promised in reply to her dark thoughts.

"You're going to have to stop reading my mind," Cami said trying to sound annoyed; but in truth, she needed his comfort just then and was grateful for his gift. It wouldn't be the last time she'd need reassurance as they navigated this new territory together. She didn't know the first thing about being in a relationship, let alone being in one with the threat of war pressing down on them harder and harder each day.

After several minutes holding each other under the streams of warm water, Jared loosened his grip and kissed Cami firmly on the lips before stepping back and starting to wash himself.

"You just going to stand there and gawk at me the rest of the night? Thought you had work to do," he teased, trying his best to lighten the mood despite the anxiety he felt about letting her out of his sight.

As much as he wanted to keep her with him always, he knew she wasn't the kind of woman who would put up with a possessive man. She was strong, independent, a soldier; and if he wanted to keep her, he would have to give her the room to continue to be those things.

Cami took one last long deliberate look at him, letting her eyes travel thoroughly over his body before she winked at him, turned, and flashed to the other room to get dressed. Jared shook his head and chuckled as he lathered up his body.

God, I love that woman.

Cami dressed quickly in her fatigues before strapping on her holsters and securing various weapons to her body. Just as she was finishing up with tying the lace of her combat boot, the buzzer at the door sounded.

Cami hurriedly pulled her hair back into a ponytail and rushed to answer. She groaned as she looked back into the room, seeing the bed in complete disarray with Jared's clothes piled haphazardly on the floor. She considered taking a moment to straighten the mess.

Fuck it; not like it's a secret, she thought, realizing that the whole family, and the commander, had seen them together.

Her stomach dropped as she considered the possibility that it was the commander on the other side of the door coming to look for her because she wasn't in her room where he could signal for her. Despite the fact that she was nearly two hundred years old and one of the toughest soldiers in The Elite forces, somehow she still felt the rush of blood in her face which outwardly showed the awkward feeling she had in the pit of her stomach, like a teenage girl being caught with a boy in her bedroom for the first time.

Taking a deep breath, as she silently berated herself for succumbing to such foolish emotions; she disengaged the lock and yanked the door open. She couldn't hide her surprise at finding Dante there.

Dante's eyes moved over her head, scanning the room behind her and prompting her to pull the door shut; a vain attempt to maintain some semblance of privacy and prevent another altercation between him and Jared. She hadn't disengaged the soundproofing, so once the door was shut she wouldn't have to worry about Jared overhearing and there being a repeat of the scene in the training room.

Cami watched Dante closely as he took a step back; seeing him at Jared's door, she expected some ridiculous display of anger or jealousy.

"Is Jared here?" Dante asked simply.

"It's really none of your business; but yes, he's in the shower," she responded, eyeing him suspiciously.

"One of ours was abducted by four infected from Blood Runners tonight. It was Layla."

"What?! When? What the fuck happened?" Cami inquired, her voice laced with concern.

"She was grabbed a couple of hours ago. Layla, Jasmine, and Rachel all went out after you got back from Copley Place. The fuckers almost got Jasmine, too, but Rachel managed to take one of them down before they could get away."

"Did he die; the one she took down?" Cami asked, immediately thinking of Ethan. Getting ahold of a live infected vampire could help her father find a cure.

"I'm guessing he didn't, but who knows? His buddies got him out."

"Shit. Do we have any leads?" Cami asked.

"Yeah, we happened to get a shot of the plates on their vehicle from an ATM security camera across the street. Jester did his magic and got us an address. The place is out in the sticks and the owner is human, so I expect we're only going to find pieces of him lying around. That's why I was hoping you'd come along."

"Of course. Are you doing okay? I know you and Layla are close," Cami asked, growing anxious. The abductors were infected, which meant they worked for Lucias, and whatever they found while searching for Layla could lead them to Ethan as well.

"I'll be doing a lot better when we get her back. Hey, about that; earlier when we were sparring—"

"Dante, can we just forget it? I'm sorry if you got the wrong message, but Jared and I—"

"No, I get it; you and the kid are together now. I just wanted to say I'm sorry; kissing you was a mistake. I've been confused about a lot of shit for a long time now, but I think I finally see things clearly," he said sincerely.

"Uh, oh, okay then," Cami replied, a little confused, but relieved that Dante seemed to finally understand that she wasn't interested.

"So, listen; can you give me a minute with Martinez? The rest of your team should already be waiting in the pit. We'll be right behind you."

Cami eyed Dante and glanced back at Jared's door. Opening her mouth to protest, he beat her to it.

"Nah; it's not like that. I don't have any beef with the kid, not anymore. If the situation had been reversed, I probably wouldn't have handled it half as well as he did and I swear I won't come between the two of you again."

Cami looked at Martinez, who shrugged. "I would believe him, Cami. Turns out he's finally realized he's in love with Layla."

"You should learn how to keep your mouth shut, my man," Dante responded, though hearing someone else acknowledge the feelings he had yet to give a voice to felt good.

"Hey, just trying to expedite the process so we can go find your woman," Martinez replied with a smile.

"Okay, I'll meet you in the pit; but hurry, you know the trail only gets colder as time passes," Cami said before disappearing down the corridor.

"So, you want to tell me what you're up to?" Martinez asked as soon as Cami was gone.

"I had an idea," Dante said as he strolled towards Jared's room.

"Hold on, my man; what the fuck do you think you're doing? Cami will castrate you if you mess with the kid, and don't forget who he is. You could get booted from The Elite, or worse," Martinez said, trying to get between his friend and Jared's door.

"I appreciate the concern, Martinez. I just have a couple of things I need to say to him; to apologize."

Martinez's mouth fell open.

"I know; apologies aren't usually my thing, but I owe him one. All this time we've been calling him kid, but I've been the one acting like a newbie fresh out of transition, chasing a bunch of random women because I was too much of a coward to recognize what was right in front of me.

"Glad you came around; but can't this wait?" Martinez asked, confused as to why Dante would delay anything that could help find Layla.

"No, it can't. I think he might be able to help us find her," he said, taking a deep breath before hitting the buzzer for a second time.

CHAPTER 20 - *Jared's Help*

Jared hopped out of the shower and stepped to the mirror; unable to stop smiling as he swiped his hand over the fogged up glass to clear a spot.

He rubbed his fingers roughly through his damp hair then surveyed his reflection in the mirror. Having achieved the desired un-styled effect, he walked into the bedroom and pulled on a pair of black pajama pants.

It was late, or early, depending on how you looked at it, so he hoped that once he was done checking on his sister and niece, Cami would be back and waiting for him in bed. He couldn't think of anything better than spending the rest of the night sleeping with her in his arms.

Just as he was about to head to the door, he heard the buzz of the intercom and smiled, thinking that Cami must have forgotten something and didn't have the code to get back in.

The smile dropped from his face when he opened the door to find Dante and Martinez standing there, fully-clad in combat gear, and his relaxed stance immediately became defensive.

"Hey; sorry to disturb you so late," Dante began, putting his hands up in a gesture of surrender. "I just need to talk to you for a minute."

Jared eyed Dante carefully before stepping aside to allow the two men into his suite.

"I know we got off on the wrong foot," Dante started, eliciting a huff from Jared as he crossed his arms over his chest. "I want to make amends. I realize now that I was out of line with Cami. Obviously there is something between you two, and I want to let you know that I won't be interfering with that from now on. It was a mistake and I'm sure you'll be happy to hear that Cami made it pretty clear where she stands, and that's with you."

"Okay; thanks for that, I guess," Jared responded, with a touch of uncertainty as he looked at Dante and Martinez and started to relax.

"That's not really why we're here now, though," Dante continued. "One of our soldiers was taken tonight; a woman. The attackers were Lucias's men, infected; and we've only got a small lead to go on. We're going out now to check it out and I want you to go. I think you might be our best shot at getting her back."

"You want me to go with you on a mission? Why?" Jared asked, stepping closer with interest.

"Telepathy runs in your family, right? You're one, too, aren't you?" Dante questioned, though he already knew the answer. It was a rather subtle gift, but Dante had the ability to detect the powers of others with a single touch and, with prolonged contact and focus, could even manifest those abilities for short periods of time.

Jared responded with a nod.

"The vehicle the attackers were in belongs to a human. We assume he's already dead; but if he's alive, or if one of the infected is still there, you could get into their heads, maybe get a bead on where they took Layla."

Jared considered for a second; he wasn't sure if he trusted Dante, but he couldn't argue his point. His gift could help them find the missing soldier and, in turn, his brother-in-law. He knew how worried his family was, how worried Cami was, and he would do anything in his power to get Ethan back for them.

"Yeah, of course I'll help, but I don't know how we'll get my father to clear me to leave. He's ordered the whole family to remain on the compound indefinitely," Jared replied, already trying to think of what he could say to persuade the High Commander to release him.

Dante looked to Martinez, then back to Jared. "Did your father actually order you to stay? Did he say the words?"

Jared smiled as he realized what Dante was thinking. "No; as a matter of fact, he didn't."

"Well, then he doesn't have to know about this little excursion. We'll have you back in bed before dawn."

"Just one problem with that, Dante," Martinez chimed in. "Commander Claesson isn't just going to watch us walk out with Jared without hearing the High Commander actually give permission. And that's not even your biggest problem."

"So, what's the biggest problem?" Jared asked.

"Cami. No offense, but you're just a civilian. This is just speculation, but based on what I know about her and what I've seen and heard today, Cami must have some pretty strong feelings for you. I can't really see her happily letting you stroll out on a potentially dangerous mission while disobeying a direct order from the High Commander."

Dante placed a hand on his friend's shoulder. "Guess it's a good thing we have you, then."

"Dante, you can't be serious. You know what kind of trouble we could get in if something happens to him? And what if the High Commander is down there right now? You think you can keep your mind clear of it, because my heart is already pounding just thinking about trying to not think about it," Martinez said, his voice laced with anxiety as he and Dante made their way to the pit.

They left Jared behind to get dressed, but he would be meeting them in the garage before they left the compound.

"That's why we're going to make damn sure nothing does happen. He won't even have to get out of the car, and if his father is in the meeting, you can hang back and head to the garage; I can handle it," Dante said as he stopped and turned towards Martinez. "Look, I know it's a big risk, and I'm sorry for asking this of you, but I'm going to do whatever it takes to get her back. What would you do if it was Rachel?"

"Shit; yeah, all right."

Martinez felt ill as he considered Dante's words. Rachel had been in Blood Runners with Layla; it could have easily been her who was taken, or worse. As he thought, they covered the rest of the distance to the pit in record time. Dante peered through the glass and quickly scanned the room, while Martinez stayed out of view.

"It's clear," he said as he reached for the handle.

When they stepped through the door, all eyes turned towards them. Martinez's immediately locked on Rachel and he couldn't help but feel overwhelmingly grateful. It was all he could do not to rush to her, scoop her up in his arms and carry her off to their bed to spend the rest of the night showing her just how much he loved and needed her.

"I love you," he mouthed to her silently, causing a light blush to steal over her cheeks as she smiled back at him.

"Nice of you to join us, gentlemen," Commander Claesson said as Dante and Martinez slid into the two closest chairs.

"I've been in touch with our civilian contacts in the area; everyone is keeping their eyes open for any sign of Layla. As far as they know, they're looking for a civilian tourist, but that won't stick for long given the number of civilians who witnessed the attack tonight," he continued, running a hand over his drawn face. As with all of their kind, the millennia-old vampire normally didn't look a day over thirty-five, but the stress of the last few weeks was beginning to take its toll.

"I'd hoped to avoid this, but we cannot put off alerting the civilian population to the danger much longer. A few hours ago, I received word that two civilian males were also grabbed downtown and, according to Thompson, there have been some suspicious human disappearances over the last few months. If word gets out that Elite were taken, we'll have widespread panic. I'm going to meet with the High Commander in the morning to discuss a communication strategy and, I think it goes without saying, breaking the news will be a lot smoother if you come back with something positive tonight," he continued. "I also want to put you all on notice; for the time being, we're going into full lockdown, meaning that no personnel leave from the base. No exceptions."

A low murmur of groans filled the room. "I don't like it any more than you do, but we can't take any chances. One more thing; reinforcements are going to be arriving over the next few days, so those of you in suites need to be prepared for company."

"But sir, there are enough single rooms for at least a hundred and fifty," Dante interjected, knowing the size of the entire Elite force and that no outlying base would send so many men as to leave their homes unprotected.

"I am aware how much room we have. It won't be enough. Unmated soldiers in double rooms and suites are going to have to share. You can choose to bunk with your local brothers and sisters, or you can wait and be assigned roommates from among the new arrivals; your choice, but figure it out soon," he said, eyeing the soldiers seated around the long table.

"Dante," he said to the soldier, who stood and followed the commander to the door. "you run into any problems out there tonight, you call me directly on the satellite phone. Regular cell service on the compound is going to be down indefinitely. I'm sending two other teams to the city to pick up rations, so they won't be far off if you need back-up."

Dante nodded as the commander clapped him on the shoulder and disappeared through the door.

"So, what's with the communication blackout? Any idea what's really going down?" Jackson asked as Dante stepped over to the large flat screen which covered the back wall of the pit.

"Your guess is as good as mine, but I don't give a shit at the moment. When we get Layla back, I'll start worrying about when you'll get a chance to call your mommy," Dante retorted. Speaking Layla's name was like throwing gasoline on the fire that was the ache in his heart; so while other soldiers burst into laughter and Jackson flipped him off, Dante couldn't even muster a half-smile.

Swallowing the pain that threatened to engulf him, Dante turned his focus to the only hope he had of finding Layla.

"All right, I want four vehicles rolling in from the south side, here," he said pointing to a long stretch of road about half a mile from the house on the satellite image which covered the screen. "You two will bring up the rear in the fourth vehicle with the medical supplies," he said, pointing to a couple of mid-level soldiers on his team who were trained for medical detail. "I don't know what we're going to find, but I want to be prepared for anything and, with any luck, we'll need the room to transport at least three back with us. Seeing as how the two civilians were grabbed around the same time as Layla, it's likely they're being kept together. Cami, your team will fall in third, and mine will split between the front two vehicles. From there, all of you will continue on foot and I'll drive the lead vehicle up to the house with Martinez, so he can work his magic and lay down our cover. Is everyone clear?"

After getting affirmation from everyone, Dante continued. "Chances are we won't find much out there, but remember what we're up against. These vampires are confirmed infected, which means they're faster and stronger than all of us so no one take any chances. Stay in pairs at all times and remember: your guns are your best friends. You do not want to go head-to-head with one of these guys with blades and, for God's sake, don't let one of those fuckers bite you." Dante pulled his side arm, popped the magazine out and held it up.

"This new silver ammunition is tipped with a tranquilizer, courtesy of the boys down in the lab; so no matter where you hit, the targets will go down." He replaced the magazine and slid the gun back into its holster. "Let's move out."

Jared hung back in the shadows a good distance away from the entrance to the garage where The Elite soldiers were filing through and loading into their black SUVs. Dante had instructed him to stay out far enough to keep anyone from detecting his scent, especially Cami. With all of the other bodies milling around and the adrenaline of the impending mission coursing through her veins, he felt pretty confident that she wouldn't notice him. He watched in silent admiration as she climbed into one of the trucks and closed the door.

"We're going to have to walk back," Martinez said, appearing out of nowhere.

"Fuck; you scared the shit out of me!" Jared exclaimed in a loud whisper, having been so focused on Cami that he didn't see Martinez approach.

"Sorry, my man; but we've got to go now. I'll have to concentrate to keep the mist down over you once we start moving. It will cover everything; your scent, heartbeat, breathing, so even I won't be able to see or hear you when you're inside. Since I won't be in there with you, you have to stay directly on my right and keep pace with me. I'll make it big enough that you'll have some room, but don't push it or someone might see you. We're riding in the first vehicle. Dante left the door open, so when we get up to it, I'm going to toss this bag in," Martinez said, raising the bag in his left hand, "and you need to jump in right behind it and lay down on the seat. The windows are heavily tinted; but just to be safe, stay down until we're out of the building."

"Ok, I've got it. I'm ready when you are," Jared replied feeling unexpectedly excited. After a lifetime living under his father's overprotective thumb, going out on a mission with The Elite was empowering.

The two covered the distance as quickly as Martinez could walk without breaking his concentration, and Jared leapt in after the bag just as the other vehicles started to pull away.

"We all good?" Dante asked as Martinez slammed his door shut.

"Piece of cake," Martinez replied. "That was a hell of a lot easier than trying to cover a moving vehicle."

"So, kid; uh, Jared," Dante said shifting his eyes to the rearview mirror as he adjusted it to see Jared lying across the seat. "When we get to the location, you're going to hang back in here with Martinez. He's going to throw mist over the whole house, so none of the other soldiers will approach unless it's absolutely necessary, which means life or death; in which case, if they see you, we'll deal with it. No matter what goes down, you stay in this car. Are we clear?"

"Yeah, man. I've got it," Jared said awkwardly from his supine position, as he met Dante's eyes in the mirror.

"I'm serious; no matter what you see or hear, especially when it comes to Cami, you've got to keep your shit reined in. She can take care of herself, trust me; but you being out there would distract her, like it did in the training room with me."

Jared felt the heat of anger and jealously skating over his body as he recalled the sight of Dante lying over Cami and pressing his lips to hers. The anger was compounded as he lost focus and his shields weakened, allowing Dante's remembrance of the event to leak through in infuriating detail. He couldn't stop the growl that burst from his throat and it was all he could do to stay down on the seat as they drove through the garage.

"If you expect me to be helpful out there, it would be best if you don't think about kissing my mate again. When I drop my shields completely, I'm going to be getting the thoughts of everyone within range and that will distract me from anything useful," Jared said through gritted teeth.

"My mistake; won't happen again," Dante responded, feeling guilty for even thinking about the moment he'd had with Cami.

Jared relaxed as the brief image of Cami was replaced with flurry of Dante's memories of Layla. The reason for Dante's sudden change of heart became abundantly clear as Jared sensed the love and pain that followed in the wake of the images.

"Martinez, get the radio ready," Dante said pulling himself back into the present.

Martinez reached for the bag he'd tossed in the backseat. Quickly unzipping it, he pulled out a handset radio and two earpieces.

"We're good now; you can sit up," Martinez said passing the radio and an earpiece back to Jared.

"This radio is set to feed only to Dante's second earpiece," he explained, as Dante popped the tiny electronic device into his ear. "You'll be able to tell him if you pick up anything, and if he needs to respond he can do it on the same channel which only feeds to you. Everyone else will be on another frequency."

Jared silently inserted the earpiece and leaned back against the seat. He took a deep breath and thought over the last few hours he'd spent with Cami, trying to distract himself from the nerves that were bundling into a tight knot in the pit of his stomach. As the son of the High Commander, he'd been formally trained in combat and self-defense starting at young age, but he'd never once had to apply those skills living his life under the constant protection of the High Commander's guard. As he pictured Cami lying next to him, with her wild hair falling over the flawless skin of her shoulders, he realized his fear wasn't for himself; not at all. The only thing he truly feared was losing her.

CHAPTER 21 - *A Sudden Change*

"Ethan!" Alexa shouted as she shot up in bed, waking suddenly from the deep sleep her body needed as it attempted to adjust to her rapid transition. She gripped her chest, trying to calm the pounding of her heart as the effects of her nightmare dissipated. Her vampire eyes adjusted quickly to the darkness surrounding her, as she struggled to remember where she was. A wave of relief washed over her as her gaze landed on Chloe curled up next to her on the bed.

Feeling abnormally warm, she kicked the covers off and swung her feet over to the edge of the bed seeking the cool relief of the wood floor. After a brief reprieve, she still felt as if there was a fire burning behind her.

She turned and reached for Chloe's hand, finding her daughter's skin so hot she nearly dropped the appendage the instant she made contact.

"Chloe! Oh, my God; Chloe, wake up!" Alexa yelled, shaking Chloe furiously.

Alexa closed her eyes, reaching desperately for Chloe's stream of consciousness as she stroked her daughter's sweat-soaked hair, but she was met with an impenetrable barrier much like what she had encountered when Chloe first began her transition.

Her body moving on autopilot, Alexa sped across the hallway to Elijah and Josephine's suite. She pressed the buzzer several times in rapid succession, her motions so fast she was pounding on the door before the sound even registered inside.

The door swung open and Alexa grabbed a rather groggy Elijah's arm, dragging him the short distance back to her room so fast there was no time or need for an explanation.

"My God; Chloe," Elijah whispered, suddenly fully alert, as he kneeled beside Chloe's unconscious form.

"What happened to her?" Josephine asked appearing next to Alexa.

"I, I don't know. I woke up and she was like this," Alexa choked out as she swiped at the tears pouring down her cheeks.

I can't lose her again. Please, God; don't take my baby from me, Alexa prayed as she moved to the bed and took Chloe's burning hand.

"I've never seen anything like this," Elijah said with his hand on Chloe's forehead. "Our people are not susceptible to fever or illness in this way."

"What can we do? Tell me what to do," Alexa pleaded.

"We must get her to the lab so I can draw blood," Elijah replied, scooping Chloe up into his arms and flashing from the room.

Alexa and Josephine were right behind him as they reached the door to the medical wing. Luckily, most of the soldiers were either sleeping or away from the compound, so there was no one around to see Alexa. The family and the few members of The Elite who knew of her miraculous return had agreed to keep the event secret for the time being.

Josephine entered the security code to access the restricted area. The door slid open and Elijah carried Chloe across the threshold to the area where she had brought Alexa back from the dead only hours before.

Inside the laboratory, Elijah moved about the space with familiarity as he drew several samples of Chloe's blood and began the process of analyzing them for the source of her rampant fever. While the samples were spinning in the centrifuge, Elijah returned to Chloe's side and began adhering sensors to several areas of her body. Though vampires didn't typically suffer from fever or illness, the fully-stocked lab contained a digital thermometer which was indicating that Chloe's temperature had reached nearly one hundred and twenty degrees.

Alexa gasped when her eyes landed on the high reading.

"Remember Alexa; she is not human, so this will not affect her the same way. Our bodies can withstand extreme heat and cold in comparison," Elijah said calmly as he continued to attend to Chloe. "Her heart rate and breathing are still normal, so just try to stay calm."

As Alexa nodded, an alarm sounded indicating the completion of the cycle on the centrifuge.

The breeze from Elijah's swift movements sent some unsecured papers flying off of a countertop and onto the floor. In a matter of seconds, he was placing a slide of Chloe's blood beneath the lens of a microscope. Before he even took a glimpse, Josephine exclaimed, "Dios mío!"

Elijah's eyes shot to his wife, whose gaze was locked on Chloe; her mouth agape as she inched forward towards their granddaughter. In a blink, Elijah was beside her. All three watched in stunned silence as Chloe transformed before their eyes.

Her once-loose nightgown began to mold to emerging curves, the hem sliding up slowly from below her knees as her feet inched closer to the end of the table. Everything was changing; her hair, her face, her body, all morphing like a movie on fast forward.

So mesmerized was she by what was happening, Alexa didn't realize how hard she was clutching the edge of her chair until the crack of the hard plastic breaking resounded throughout the room. The sudden sound startled them all, finally snapping them out of the trance they'd been in as they watched Chloe in amazement.

Alexa regarded Elijah and Josephine, opening her mouth to speak, but stopped as she heard movement behind her.

"I'm all right, Mom," Chloe said, placing her hand on Alexa's shoulder, the sound of her voice as different as the rest of her.

Alexa closed her eyes and let out a sigh of relief as she placed her hand over Chloe's. Turning to face her, Alexa's eyes took in the fully-mature vampire who was her daughter.

"Oh, Chloe; I was so worried," she whispered as she wrapped her arms around Chloe, who was suddenly taller than her.

"Corazón," Josephine said as she held out a robe to Chloe. Alexa couldn't help but laugh as she looked down at the cartoon character nightgown which barely covered Chloe's now rather womanly curves. Chloe's cheeks heated, realizing how exposed her new body was as her eyes shot to Elijah who, thankfully, had already averted his gaze.

"I suppose this finally answers the question of when your growth would be complete," Elijah said, sitting down in the chair behind the microscope he'd already prepared to confirm in Chloe's blood what was already obvious in her physical appearance.

"How do you feel?" he asked, approaching Chloe as she fastened the belt on the robe.

"Great; amazing really, but thirsty," she replied brightly with a smile, which revealed fully-extended fangs behind her plump pink lips.

"Of course," Elijah said nodding to Josephine who, understanding her husband's silent request, disappeared through the door only to return a few moments later with several bags of stored blood.

"Perhaps it would be best if we returned to our rooms now that we know that Chloe is safe," Josephine said, passing the bags to Alexa and Chloe. Given the small amount of sleep required by advanced vampire metabolisms, she knew that, despite the hour, many of the compounds residents would be moving throughout the hallways at any moment.

"Yes; that would be wise until William and Commander Claesson determine how to proceed," Elijah agreed gesturing towards the door.

"We'll see you in a few hours," Josephine said as she released Chloe from a hug and moved to follow Elijah across the hallway to their suite.

"Despite everything that has happened to me in the last couple of years, I have to say today just may have been the strangest day ever," Alexa said, smiling as she closed the door.

"Really? I would say it was just like any other day," Chloe responded with a smirk. Dodging the pillow Alexa tossed at her, she stood in front of the dresser and pulled open the top drawer. "I guess I'm going to have to borrow some of the clothes we brought here for you until I can get some of my own," she said, pulling out the camisole and shorts of a pair of dark gray pajamas.

Stepping over to the full-length mirror, Chloe undid the belt and let her robe drop to the floor around her feet as she gazed at her new reflection. She turned to each side slowly taking in each new curve and muscle.

"Your father is going to have a meltdown when he sees how beautiful you are," Alexa said with a proud smile as she joined her daughter in front of the mirror. "Be prepared for him to try to lock you in a cell to keep you away from all of the soldiers around here."

"I look like you," Chloe said smiling at her mother's reflection.

After staring at Chloe for a moment, the smile melted from Alexa's face.

"How do you feel; about this, I mean?" she said gesturing towards the mirror. "I can't imagine what it must be like for you; to look at your own reflection and not recognize yourself."

Alexa's words brought an image to the front of Chloe's mind. "That's not entirely true; I've seen myself like this before," she said turning to face her mother. "In my vision when Daddy comes back, I was like this."

A smile lit Alexa's face again. "Do you think that means he will be back soon?" she asked hopefully.

Chloe thought for a moment, recalling the details of her vision, but careful to shield her mind from Alexa's telepathy.

"Yes; I was wearing some of your clothes. I imagine Grandma Jo will send someone out shopping as soon as possible, so it must be in the next few days," she replied, doing her best to seem cheerful and optimistic despite the implications of the revelation.

Alexa hugged Chloe tightly, unable to control her excitement about Ethan's return despite the anxiety she sensed in her daughter. Chloe could shield her thoughts, but Alexa still perceived underlying emotions.

"Is there anything else you want to tell me, Chloe? Anything I should know about your visions?" Alexa asked releasing her and walking towards the bed, as Chloe peeled off her tight, child-sized nightgown and slipped into the borrowed pajamas.

"No, I'm sorry. I feel a little anxious. This is just a big adjustment and I'm really tired; that's all," she replied giving Alexa the response her thoughts revealed she was hoping for. As much as it pained her to lie to her mother, Chloe knew there was no other way.

Without another word, the two slid under the soft comforter, both so exhausted from the day's events, and the tolls their transitions had taken on their bodies, they were asleep in a matter of seconds.

CHAPTER 22 - *Sean Taylor's House*

Four SUVs loaded with Elite soldiers, weapons, and medical gear pulled off the side of the road in the spot Dante had designated, along the way to the house owned by Sean Taylor.

"Everyone hang back and wait for my signal," Dante said over the radio, before he killed the headlights and continued driving towards the target.

He carefully eased the vehicle off the road just at the edge of the field adjacent to the property. The place was completely dark, the moon tucked safely behind a cloud and not so much as a security light to illuminate the yard. Any human would be completely blind, but the darkness provided perfect cover for the band of vampires who could see as clearly as if they were standing under the noon-day sun.

Jared closed his eyes and lowered his shields as Dante opened the windows and he and Martinez focused their acute senses on the surrounding area, searching for any signs of life.

"I'm not getting anything human or vampire, just a couple of animals; raccoons from the smell," Dante said.

As if on cue, there was a rustling in the neighboring woods, followed by the telltale chirping of a pair of raccoons.

"There's no one any closer than your men back at the cars. Someone is a really loud broadcaster; Rachel, I think," Jared said stifling a laugh. "Didn't realize you two were mated," he said cutting his eyes to Martinez.

"What; is she thinking about me?" he asked cautiously.

"More like visualizing," he replied unable to contain his laughter anymore. "Dante, the house is clear; I don't think you need me right now and I'd really like to block these images before I see more of Martinez than I can forget," Jared said with a smirk as he looked at Dante.

Dante shook his head and chuckled, "Yeah, we're good for now." He signaled the rest of the team that it was all clear. Several seconds later, the other soldiers appeared a few yards away.

"All right Martinez, do your thing. Jared, just sit tight while we sweep the place. We don't have to worry about anyone getting close once the mist is in place, but I'll want you to check things out again before he lifts it," Dante said before hopping out of the car.

Martinez popped a set of buds into his ears, leaned his seat back, and focused on the area around the house. Jared watched in amazement as the misty veil seemed to melt down out of the night sky, slowly pouring out all around them until it reached the ground and disappeared.

Jared's eyes scanned the group standing a few yards away, immediately finding and locking on to Cami. Seeing her standing out there in her element, poised for battle, was more of a turn on than he expected. He closed his eyes and focused on her stream of consciousness.

Perimeter's down; teams get into position at the three entrance points. Go on Dante's signal; sweep to center of the house. No traces of blood in the air; adjust directive to information sweep only.

She was planning the mission out, talking through the steps in her mind; something he'd heard her doing numerous times as she trained, mentally mapping out her attack before each move. It was truly fascinating hearing the way her mind worked.

"Anyone scenting blood?" Cami asked, receiving unanimous head shakes confirming her assessment. "I think it's safe to say there won't be a need for clean-up then."

"Agreed," Dante responded, his disappointment evident. "They must have grabbed the car from another location. Your team can hang back; we'll do the initial sweep, but this is probably a dead end. We'll head back to base and see what else Jester can dig up on Sean Taylor."

Jared's eyes remained locked on Cami, while Dante's team approached the house.

What a fucking waste of time, she thought as she paced the front lawn a few yards from Jared. *We need to talk to Alexa; she's the only one who's seen that son of a bitch. She's got to remember something about the location that can help us. Even if she can't, I'd rather be...*

Jared's pulse quickened as Cami's thoughts moved from her internal monologue to flashes of images and he closed his eyes, melting back against the seat as the images took over. Her looking up at him as he moved inside her, looking down at him as she slid down over his cock, watching his pulse move under his skin before she struck his vein.

With each image he felt himself growing harder and shifted on the seat to adjust his pants. Luckily, Martinez was so lost in his own thoughts and keeping the veil down around the house, that he didn't notice the change in Jared's heartbeat or the scent of his arousal which was filling the small space.

I better knock this off or it's going to be an awkward-ass ride back, Jared thought as he started to reinforce his mental shields and reached down to move his uncomfortable erection to the side. Just before Cami's visions faded from his mind, he heard a whisper of her voice and stopped.

Fuck; there's another vampire here, she thought as she casually moved closer to the car with her eyes scanning the area around the vehicle. Her mind was immediately back to soldier mode as she assessed the potential danger. As her thoughts had wandered and her arousal kicked in, she'd put a little space between herself and the other team members on the lawn who remained closer to the house. Since Jared was behind her in the car with Martinez, his increase in heartbeat caught her attention and alerted her to his presence.

Martinez's mist is still in play so they've got to be on the outside, she thought, with Jared watching helplessly as she raised her wrist towards her mouth preparing to signal the others. He didn't know if the other soldiers would keep quiet if they found out about his little ride-along, but it wasn't a chance he was willing to take. If his father learned of this little excursion, the word lockdown wouldn't begin to describe the level of restriction which would be placed on him. It had been a struggle convincing William that he didn't need a member of the High Commander's guard with him at all times on the compound in the first place; not to mention the punishment that would fall upon Dante and Martinez.

Knowing it was his only option, Jared reached over and hit the button to lower the window. Luckily the other soldiers were still watching the house and engaged in conversation amongst themselves, knowing that they were under the protection of the mist, so they didn't notice the sound.

Cami froze when Jared's face came into view through the window. Jared grinned sheepishly as she slowly lowered her arm. His grin disappeared almost instantly as he sensed the anger washing over her. The physical indicators were subtle; the clenching of her fists, the tightness of her lips, but Jared could feel the emotion rolling off of her like a blast of hot air as she silently covered the few yards between them in an instant.

Without a word, she calmly pulled the door open and climbed inside while Jared slid to the far side of the bench to stay out of view. One of the other soldiers noticed Cami's movement and watched curiously as she closed the door.

Silently, Cami pointed to her forehead, then to Jared's, knowing that if she spoke, the vampires outside might be able to hear since they had undoubtedly noticed her entering the truck. The bulletproof frame of the SUV would certainly conceal any whispers, but she was far too angry to keep her voice at such a low level.

Jared's eyebrows pinched together in confusion for a moment before he realized she was telling him to read her mind. He nodded once and lowered his mental shields.

What the fuck are you doing here? What, did you talk Dante into letting you come because you don't think I can handle myself? Just because I love you doesn't mean I'm going to change who I am, so you better get that through your thick skull now! Do you know what will happen if the commander finds out about this, or your father? I can't believe Dante would be so stupid, and Martinez; how the fuck did you get him to go along with this?

Jared tried to take her hand which she immediately snatched away. He opened his mouth to speak and was caught completely off guard as Cami crushed her mouth to his; demandingly sweeping her tongue over his lips as they fell open. She shoved her hands into his hair and grabbed it tightly, tilting his head back forcefully to gain better access to his mouth as she pushed her tongue into his mouth. Jared groaned his approval as she pulled him closer, conquering his mouth with her tongue. The kiss was an assertion of her power, her way of putting him in his place; showing him she wouldn't be controlled or protected

278

and, God help him, he loved her more for it.

Cami loosened her grip and broke the kiss, pulling back to look into Jared's eyes as they both panted with desire. When his breathing slowed, Jared leaned in close. "I fucking love you," he whispered against her ear.

We'll finish this discussion at home. I have to get back out there before one of them gets too curious, she sent before placing a quick peck on his lips. She looked down at Martinez's bag lying on the floor and reached in before jumping out of the car.

While the other soldiers watched, she popped the receiver from her ear and tucked it into her pocket, replacing it with the one she'd taken from the bag.

"Busted piece," she said as she walked towards the group on the lawn. Her explanation seemed to satisfy their curiosity as they all turned back towards the house and resumed their conversations.

"We've got a security system in play," Dante said, pointing to a panel through the window in the back door of the human residence.

"I'm on it," Beckett said from behind him. In addition to being one of the resident wheelmen for The Elite, Jacob Beckett was pretty handy with alarm systems having spent a few years boosting cars as a teenager. His career as a criminal was short-lived after word got around about a few run-ins he had with police, resulting in legendary high-speed chases and him being scouted to drive professionally.

Dante made quick work of picking the locks and stepped away, letting Beckett take the lead through the door. In less than thirty seconds, Beckett had the system disarmed and the team proceeded through the house, clearing each room systematically.

Dante put his hand on the handle to the basement door, when a soldier called out. "We've got something over here."

The entire team swarmed to the entrance to the garage. "What does this mean?" Beckett asked.

"Fuck if I know," Dante responded.

"Silver team two, we need you to join us in the garage," Dante sent out over the radio; calling the clean-up team, including Cami and Rachel, into the house.

In a matter of seconds, the six soldiers filled the space behind Dante. "Rachel, that the vehicle you saw leaving the scene?" Dante asked moving aside to give her a better view into the garage that was dimly lit by an overhead motion-detecting light.

Rachel stepped through the open doorway to get a closer look. "It's the same make and model," she said running her hand over the cool glass of the rear door, as she examined it more closely. "This is definitely it; I bounced a few rounds off this window," she said pointing to the cracks in the glass above the driver's door.

"What the hell does this mean?" Cami asked stepping down onto the concrete floor. "There's no way four infected vamps came out here, stole this car, used it to snatch one of our people and take them to a separate location, then kindly returned the vehicle to its rightful owner."

"Yeah; I could maybe buy this Sean Taylor being gone when it went down, but that doesn't explain the car getting dropped back here. And there's the question of why an average human would have bulletproof glass installed on their car," Dante interjected.

"So, what's the move then?" Becket asked.

Dante tried one of the doors and, finding it locked, he breezed around to the remaining three with the same result.

"We tag it, finish sweeping the house, and get the hell out of here. Maybe we'll get lucky," he said pulling a small magnetic GPS device from a side pocket in his fatigues.

With incredible grace, he rolled down under the SUV and affixed the device to the undercarriage inconspicuously.

"Remind me to thank Jester for making us carry those damn things around. Silver team two, head back out and secure the perimeter; we'll clear the basement and attic and meet you out front in five," he said as he stood and dusted off his pants. "I want everything in this house exactly as we found it; not a dust particle out of place. If this is some kind of safe house or outpost for the enemy, they'll be back and they can't know we were here."

While Cami's team exited to check the perimeter, Dante's split into two groups of three to cover the sections of the house left to be cleared. In less than five minutes, all twelve soldiers were gathered on the lawn.

"Perimeter is clear for us to move. You find anything else inside?" Cami asked as they walked towards their vehicle.

"Yeah; there was some interesting stuff in the basement. We got photos of all of it to analyze back on the compound, but I think we may have just found one of Lucias's humans," Dante responded.

"Great. I'll ride back with you and take a look on the way," Cami said reaching for the door while the other soldiers sped off on foot.

"You should stay with your team," Dante said stepping in front of her.

"I'm sure they can find their way home without me," she responded as she crossed her arms, waiting for Dante to move aside.

"Look Cami; with everything that went down earlier, I just think it would be better if you rode back in the same car you came in, you know?"

"Really? So I guess you think it will be awkward riding with me and Jared, whom you snuck out here without the High Commander's permission?" Cami retorted before speeding to the other side and climbing in beside a rather amused Jared.

Dante stood there, shaking his head for a moment, then walked around and climbed into the driver's seat.

"I assume we can trust that you won't say anything about this," Dante said to Cami as he reached over and shook Martinez, who was still concentrating on maintaining the camouflage around the property. She responded with a nod he could see in the rearview mirror.

"We rolling out, man," he said as Martinez groggily pulled an ear bud out. To maintain his mist on a large scale for extended periods of time, he had to completely zone out; going into a trancelike state, which meant he was often a little out of it for a few seconds after lifting the veil.

Martinez looked over to Dante, and then turned to the backseat. "Well, shit," he said at seeing Cami. "You know what? I don't even want to know," he said turning back around and relaxing into the seat.

"Fair enough. Since you insisted on riding back with us, Cami, I'm sure I speak for both myself and Martinez when I say we'd appreciate it if you two could keep your hands off each other for the duration."

"I don't think you're in any position to make requests, but I'll take it under advisement. Can't make any promises, though," Cami responded jokingly as she moved closer to Jared and laid her head on his shoulder.

Dante looked back at them in the mirror and couldn't help but smile. Cami had never been much for joking around, but he'd said before that something was different about her lately; that was part of what he had found so irresistible. Seeing her with Jared that way, he knew what the change was. She was in love, and it looked good on her.

He watched her for just a moment too long as she stared up at Jared with eyes full of love and adoration and felt a knot forming in his throat, realizing he'd seen that look before; many, many times. It was in Layla's eyes every time she saw him, yet he had pushed her aside again and again, forcing her to watch as he warmed his bed with woman after woman. Dante gripped the steering wheel tightly as he silently berated himself for being such a fool.

He had to get her back; no matter what it took. Layla was his to save.

"I'm locked on to the signal from the device you planted. If that car moves more than a few feet, we'll know about it," Jester spun around in his chair and smiled. "While you were gone, I tapped into the NSA's system and got this footage rolling back over the last few days." He looked up at Dante and Commander Claesson expectantly. "You know, the National Security Agency; like, the human's most sophisticated intelligence organization?"

"What, Jester, are you waiting for a cookie or something?" Dante responded sarcastically. He knew it was an impressive feat, but he was so damn irritated knowing Layla was out there somewhere at the mercy of his enemies.

Dante's foul mood suddenly seemed to be fogging up the room, so Jester wisely decided to drop the issue. "I can go back further, but it's going to take some time to sift through all of it." He continued to scroll through the various satellite images of Sean Taylor's property.

"It just so happens that the eye in the sky was pointed in the right direction. This is from earlier tonight, right before sundown. A second vehicle pulls into the garage and a few minutes later the vehicle in question pulls out. Unfortunately, the sunlight runs out before they return."

"Is there any way to see inside the cars?" Commander Claesson inquired.

"Unfortunately, no; the closest satellite is nearly two hundred miles away, so we're stuck with a straight view; think line of sight, but assuming those infected vamps were inside is a pretty safe bet. I also found some interesting shots from a couple of days ago. Two other vehicles show up, but the occupants don't go up to the house. See this over here?" Jester said pointing to a small area of the screen, "They take off into the field on what seems to be a hidden trail."

"Where the hell does it go?" Dante asked, leaning in toward the screen of one of the large monitors.

"Not sure yet; the area is off the grid of images captured during that time, but I'm working on getting into the system to shift the view. We can't go back, but once I get in we'll be able to see whatever goes down going forward. I'll have to keep the shift subtle to be sure the humans don't realize they've been hacked, but I shouldn't have to move it very far since they went on foot. It's probably safe to assume the visitors are human, since the sun was still out."

"We should get a team back out there now to check it out," Dante said already moving toward the door.

"No; that is too great a risk," Commander Claesson said stopping Dante before he reached the door.

"But one of ours is out there; every minute that goes by the chances of finding her intact get slimmer. You just want us to stay here and wait to find her body dumped somewhere?" Dante responded, his agitation beyond apparent as he stood with his mouth tight and his hands clenched into tight fists. He had to hold on to his anger; it was the only thing keeping him from falling apart as he thought of the horrible fate which Layla could be enduring at any moment.

"If we go storming out there completely blind, we could be signing her death warrant," Claesson responded in a surprisingly calm tone.

He wasn't usually one to stand for any kind of disrespect or insubordination, but he was giving Dante a wide berth in light of the current circumstances. They'd never had one of their own taken like this, and he'd always suspected there was something between him and Layla.

"Think about it, Dante; if Lucias wanted her dead, she would be already. His men would have done the deed right there in Blood Runners because it's clear that, after all these years, he's done with hiding. Killing a couple of Elite soldiers while surrounded by civilian witnesses would have been a good way to start scaring people into falling in line, but he obviously has other plans." Claesson walked over to Dante and laid a hand on his shoulder. "For now, Lucias doesn't know we've found this place and you know as well as I do that he is not keeping her there, but it's our only lead. We can't risk tipping our hand because our emotions got the best of us. His men returned that car for a reason and they just might come back. We find them; we use them to find Layla."

Dante merely nodded in response as the tension in his body relaxed ever so slightly.

"Great work, Jester. Keep at it; but make sure you keep yourself fed, especially if you're not going to sleep. I know how you get," Commander Claesson said, turning away from Dante to look at the young vampire who nodded and started typing away.

Even though they kept the refrigerator in Jester's cave stocked with food and blood, when he got zoned in on a project, he barely left the chair in front of his keyboard for anything if someone didn't remind him.

"First thing tomorrow, the High Commander and I will need your help getting a message to the civilian leaders. Have you heard anything back from the other compounds?"

"Yeah; we've received confirmation from each base," Jester replied without looking up. "They've all agreed to run on skeleton crews and send every soldier they can spare. The first wave should be arriving tomorrow, but it will be close to a week before they're all here."

"Good; I think it will be best to send a team from another base to check out the property as soon as you figure out where that trail leads," Claesson responded, raising his hand to silence Dante who was preparing to protest.

"Don't go getting all worked up; you can still lead the team but, other than that, as the guards have already been informed, none of the soldiers who call this compound home are to leave the grounds without my permission. Lucias is growing bolder and we can't risk having any more men captured or worse. The visiting Elite are going to be on very tight leashes as well."

Satisfied that he would still be leading the investigation to find Layla, Dante remained silent.

"You want me to get everything set up in the pit to meet with the High Commander tomorrow then?" Jester asked swiveling around.

"Dante, go get some rest; I need a minute with Jester," Claesson said, waiting for Dante to exit before responding.

"No, stay here for tonight. In the morning take whatever you need to my office. I want to avoid using the pit for the time being. With it being in the center of the compound, it gives too much visibility to our guests when something is going on. One other thing; before you set up, I want you to sweep the room for transmitters."

"I don't understand; you think someone bugged your office?" Jester asked as his eyebrows pinched together.

"This must remain between us, but as you know, Lucias not only learned the location of the High Commander's daughter and her new husband, but also knew enough to intercept their flight home. That information was only shared with a select few people and almost all of them are on this compound as we speak. I hope that I am wrong, but there is too much at risk to ignore the possibility of a traitor amongs us."

"Shit," was all Jester could manage.

"If possible, I want you to do the same in the pit, but only if you can be certain no one will discover what you are doing there. If the spy is here, I don't want him or her to know of our continued suspicion. The High Commander himself admits that someone must have betrayed us to our enemy. Though it is difficult to believe, considering his ability, whoever it is must have found some way to deceive him."

"I understand; I'll get to work on it within the hour. Most of the compound is still asleep and this is probably the last chance I'll have to do it what with sifting through satellite feed and dealing with all the soldiers pouring in over the next few days."

CHAPTER 23 - *What the Mirror Reveals*

Chloe stepped out of the shower; not bothering to grab a towel as she slowly approached the mirror. Her eyes slid over her new body, taking in each dip and swell of the womanly curves which had literally appeared overnight. Though she was slightly thinner than her mother, she was definitely just a voluptuous. Her cheeks heated slightly when her eyes landed on one dusty pink nipple which began to pucker against the cool air as she continued to move away from the heat of the shower.

Her eyes traveled lower and she felt a strange new sensation beginning in the pit of her stomach as she took in her own naked beauty for the very first time. Having gotten glimpses of lust and sexuality in the thoughts of the adults around her, Chloe knew that what had happened to her body the night before changed much more than her appearance, and the realization both excited and scared her.

"Chloe, are you all right in there?" Alexa asked from just beyond the door.

Chloe moved in a flash, grabbing her robe from the hook, and securing it around her damp body before she opened the door.

Alexa smiled warmly as she passed Chloe a bag of blood. She turned and walked slowly towards the trash, tossing in the empty bag she had finished while Chloe was in the shower.

"You know, if you have questions, about anything, you know boys, or sex, or whatever—"

"Mom, please don't; I already know, at least as much as I need to know," Chloe interrupted, her voice somewhat sad as she considered how unlikely it would ever be for her to have a true mate. While Lucias intended to complete the blood bond with her, she knew that even if that happened, she could never love him; just like he could never love her. He wanted her power, not her.

"You never know, someday you could meet a nice young man, or maybe not so young," Alexa said cringing at the thought, but with their kind living for centuries, extremely large age differences were common.

What wasn't common was a fully-mature and extremely beautiful female vampire who was less than a year old. That particular fact was what was going to be incredibly difficult for Alexa, and everyone, else to adjust to.

Chloe felt sick as she picked up on the concerns running through her mother's mind, and her thoughts again turned to Lucias and what was to come. While she hoped with everything she had that Lucias would never get what he wanted, a part of her knew that she may not have a choice in the matter. As much as she had tried, she still could not see beyond the vision of Ethan's return.

Chloe was grateful for the buzz of the intercom which pulled her from the dark thoughts. Focusing for a moment, she smiled and sped across the room, pulling a set of her mother's clothes from the closet and throwing them on.

"Uncle Jared and Cami," she said as Alexa moved towards the door.

"How do you know?" Alexa asked, looking at the digital screen which indicated that the soundproofing, about which Chloe had explained to her the night before, was still engaged.

Curious about the technology's impact on her telepathy, she had tested it while Chloe was in the shower, lowering her shields to listen for the thoughts of the other residents. She was met with complete silence; even from Chloe, who it seemed had been being very guarded with her thoughts since Alexa's arrival.

"If I focus, I can still read thoughts through the soundproofing," Chloe responded, approaching the door.

"Is there anything you can't do?" Alexa asked proudly, as she glanced at Chloe. Her hand shot to her mouth to cover her smile as she took in her daughter's appearance. "Well, I guess you haven't figured out the importance of a bra just yet; but I suppose that's to be expected, since you only started needing one a few hours ago."

Chloe looked down and felt her cheeks heat as she realized her mistake. Like her mother, she was well-endowed and the shirt she had picked out was rather tight, revealing far more of her new body than she was prepared to show her waiting relatives; or anyone else, for that matter.

Alexa breezed across the room to the dresser and pulled out a pretty pink bra with an adjustable clasp. "Here," she said tossing the light material to Chloe. "I'm bigger than you, but you should be able to tighten this one enough to do the job."

Chloe plucked the bra from the air and rushed in to the closet to change; this time taking a moment to check her appearance before she emerged to greet her aunt and uncle.

Unaware of the change Chloe had undergone during the night, both Cami and Jared looked at the young woman who stepped into the room with complete confusion. The couple looked at each other, then at Alexa, then back at Chloe.

Oh, come on, Uncle Jared. I know I look different, but not so much that my own family wouldn't recognize me, she sent to her uncle before she erased the distance between them and pulled him and Cami into a hug.

"Chloe? How, when, why didn't, um…?" Jared stammered as he pulled back to take another look at his niece.

"It happened in the middle of the night; practically right before our eyes," Alexa began. "I woke up to find her unresponsive with the hottest fever I've ever felt. Elijah rushed her to the lab for tests, but she was awake and like this," she said gesturing to Chloe with a smile, "before he could even view the samples."

"Wow; we always knew she would grow up too fast, but this is, well, crazy," Jared said hugging Chloe again.

"Perhaps this is a good thing," Cami added from behind him.

Alexa looked at her curiously, waiting for her to explain. Cami looked at Jared, then at Chloe who nodded, with eyes full of understanding.

"Jared and I were coming to talk to you, Alexa. You probably haven't heard, but one of our soldiers was abducted by some of Lucias's men last night. His moves are getting bolder and, after talking to your father and Commander Claesson, we've all agreed you should both be trained to fight. As much as I hope it never comes to it, we must prepare for the possibility of open war and—"

"And, since I am the one he wants, I need to know how to defend myself," Chloe interrupted.

"Yes," Cami continued. "I'm sorry, Chloe; I wish we could be more optimistic, and I can't begin to understand how hard and confusing all of this is for you. I'm still having a hard time accepting the fact that I'm talking to my little niece," she said with a hint of sadness in her tone, "but now that you have reached maturity, your training will be simpler and far more effective."

"It's all right, Aunt Cami," Chloe said stepping forward and taking her aunt's hand. "I can handle it," she whispered before she closed her eyes and pushed a flurry of thoughts and images into Cami's mind to ease her concern over Chloe's age.

When Chloe released her hand, Cami looked at her with awe. Sliding his hands around her waist, Jared kissed the side of Cami's neck as she leaned back into him, not realizing she had needed the support until it was offered. He winked at his niece and gave her a crooked grin. No words were necessary between them. He had viewed all that Chloe had shared through Cami's mind; just as Alexa did and, with the strength of his niece's telepathy, he was certain she was reading all of their thoughts despite their shields.

"So, I guess we're all caught up then," Jared said breaking the silence.

"I think that's a fair statement," Chloe replied with a laugh. "So when do we start training, anyway? I have to admit, I think it might be kind of fun."

"We can start today if you like, but I'll need a little time to set up an area. We can't use the training room, since no one is supposed to know about Alexa," Cami responded.

"Who will be training us? Will it be you two?" Alexa asked regarding her brother and sister-in-law.

Cami chuckled and cut her gaze to Jared, who responded with a scowl; feigning irritation as he listened to the thoughts his lover didn't bother trying to shield.

"Jared will be participating in the training, but as another student. I will be in charge of your lessons, along with a fellow soldier named

Dante, who typically runs training on the compound. You haven't met him, Alexa, but he's been brought up to speed on the situation and can be trusted to be discreet."

"Yeah, just be careful with him thoug; he can get a little grabby," Jared teased spinning Cami around in his arms. She struggled momentarily, still not fully comfortable with public affection, but quickly melted into his embrace when he pressed his lips against hers.

"This is just too weird," Jared said readying his stance in front Chloe. "At least tell me I can still call you 'Squirt'," he teased as he watched her pull her wavy chestnut hair up into a ponytail.

"Sure, Uncle Jared," she replied raising her hands up defensively like Cami and Dante had demonstrated only moments before.

"The trick to this is to listen to your opponent, but remain detached from their emotions. It will allow you to anticipate their movements without getting distracted or overwhelmed," Jared said before he lunged.

Chloe easily dodged his attack. "Come on; don't take it easy on me," she said with a smile knowing he hadn't been. It was quickly becoming apparent that she had inherited her father's renowned strength and speed.

After several attempts, Jared was unable to get anywhere near his niece who, it seemed, was finding it very difficult to mask her amusement as she continually evaded her uncle.

"Like this?" Alexa asked on the other side of the room, attempting to replicate the movements Cami showed her as Dante approached, going through the motions slowly, at least for vampires, until she got the hang of fighting. Though Cami was supposed to be helping Dante with Alexa, she found herself mesmerized by the magnificent anomaly that was Chloe.

"Yeah; that was good," she said unable to pull her eyes from the youngest vampire. "Dante, you've got this under control, but I think Jared could use some help."

Dante chuckled from deep in his chest. "Yes; I fear our young friend is severely outmatched," he replied watching Jared fly several yards across the makeshift training area they'd set up in an unused storage room located in a rarely-used section of the compound.

Cami extended her arm to help Jared up from the ground. He took her hand, a look of defeat on his face which suddenly morphed to one of mischief before he yanked her down on top of him and captured her mouth in a fierce kiss.

Breaking away, she swiftly stood; putting a little distance between them while keeping her back to Chloe. "Jared, this is serious. You all need to be prepared," she chided. "Besides, we'll have plenty of time for that later," she added with a playful wink.

In a blur of motion and without any sort of warning, Cami went for Chloe. While Cami expected to catch her niece off-guard with the surprise attack, she instead found herself confused and spinning around, attempting to locate Chloe who had disappeared into thin air.

She looked toward Jared, who was doubled over with laughter; his eyes fixed on the ceiling above her head.

Reflexively, her eyes moved up and her mouth fell open.

"How are you doing that?" Cami asked with wonder as Chloe smiled down at her from her horizontal position against the high ceiling.

"Oops; guess we forgot to mention she can levitate," Jared replied appearing at a still-shocked Cami's side.

"What else have you failed to mention?" Alexa asked sharply, joining her brother, with Dante in tow. Having witnessed Chloe's rather rare feat, the pair had abandoned their own training for the time being.

Chloe glanced at her mother sheepishly.

Sorry, she sent, but it was apparent from Alexa's proud smile that she was far from upset.

My dear, sweet daughter; you are truly amazing.

"I'd like to try something," Dante said approaching Chloe and interrupting the telepathic exchange. "May I?" he asked gesturing for her hand. She looked at her uncle and mother with uncertainty.

He can sense abilities. If I touch him he'll know so much about what I can do, she sent.

Your aunt trusts him, so I trust him. But it is your decision, Jared responded telepathically. Alexa agreed with a nod of her head.

Chloe returned her gaze to Dante, looking into his kind eyes as she dove into his mind. She was surprised to find that, despite his pleasant and focused demeanor, his mind was a turmoil of worry and regret all centered on a beautiful face she recognized. The power of his emotions sent a pang into her heart and left no doubt in her mind about the kind of man he was. Pulling back from his thoughts, Chloe extended her arm with a smile.

Taking her hand, Dante closed his eyes and clasped both his hands around it. Almost instantly, the surge of her power flowed up his arm and over his body. His eyelids snapped open and he gazed upon her with awe.

"My God," he whispered. "I think it is fair to say that there isn't much more we can teach you, Chloe. Your abilities far exceed anything I have ever seen or felt. Indeed, there is none among our kind who could match you," he stated surely and released her.

"You're a mirror?" Cami asked, her eyes wide as she took a step back.

"I hate that term," Dante replied; his tone laced with irritation. "I'm sure you can understand why it's something I don't share."

Cami moved her head up and down almost imperceptibly. Up until that moment, she had never known a mirror, but she had been told stories about them as a child. Mirrors were said to possess the ability to detect the powers of others with a single touch and, if they so desired, take on or reflect those powers, thus the term 'mirror'. Mirrors could absorb energy and reflect it for a short time with little consequence; however, it was also rumored that one could draw so heavily on the strength of another, that they would steal their power entirely; and in some cases, their life.

CHAPTER 24 - *A Bond Challenged*

"Te amo, Alexa," Ethan whispered against her ear as he slid his arms around her waist and locked his hands together over her stomach. Alexa smiled lazily as his warm breath skated across her skin and she leaned back into his embrace.

"I've missed you so much, Ethan," she replied as he pulled her closer, pressing his growing erection against her backside and pulling a desire-filled moan from her lips.

The erotic sound froze his response in the back of his throat, flooding his blood with raw need and desire. He spun her around to face him, covering her mouth and dipping his tongue into her mouth demandingly as he rushed them across the room to the bed.

Alexa shot up off the bed, her eyes flying open as the climax ripped through her body. She called out Ethan's name into the darkness of the empty room. As the last tremors of orgasm passed over her thighs, Alexa let go of the sheets she had been fisting tightly and swiped at the tears which were sliding down her face as the feelings of pleasure were washed away by sadness.

As real as it felt, it had only been a dream. She was alone in her bed and Ethan was still gone; still suffering with no way to know she that was alive and waiting for him to come back to her. Alexa stood, intending to go to the bathroom, but fell back on the bed as a jolt of desire sprung up in the pit of her stomach.

The sensation was familiar, yet somehow different from anything she'd ever experienced. She closed her eyes and began to slide her hand down, hoping to ease the growing burn between her thighs, until a discomforting image flashed into her mind followed by an almost unbearable sense of guilt and remorse.

She recognized the sharp pain of guilt and immediately knew it was coming from Ethan; she was feeling him through their bond and, without thinking, she dropped her shields completely opening up the connection.

Alexa flew off of the bed and into the bathroom as the reality of what was happening exploded like a bomb in her heart and the contents of her stomach burst free from her mouth into the cold water of the toilet.

Ethan followed Lucias down the long corridor as commanded, all the while staring daggers at the back of the other vampire's head. With each day that passed, he became more and more himself and his hatred for Lucias grew; yet he was powerless to act on or express the powerful emotion. Despite the growing strength of his mind, the virus and its blood bond kept him completely obedient and under Lucias's control.

As was the case for all of Lucias's soldiers, he was expressly forbidden from speaking or acting against Lucias in any way. The handy little command prevented all manners of insubordination amongst the ranks of the army since, in Lucias's absence, the highest in command was to be afforded the same respect as Lucias himself.

"Ah yes, here we are; it appears everything is ready," Lucias said with a wicked smile, stopping just outside the door to his playroom and looking inside. Ethan stepped to the side; preparing to wait outside while Lucias indulged in whatever depravity he had planned with Molly for the evening, but Lucias remained in the doorway looking at Ethan expectantly.

Seeing the confusion on Ethan's face, Lucias gestured for him to enter. "Tonight's entertainment is for you, Ethan. As I assured you before, I know what you need to rid yourself of the pointless connection you feel to your dead mate."

Lucias stepped aside as Ethan approached, revealing Layla sitting naked on one of the large beds. Her glowing red eyes darted around the room, falling hungrily on someone who Ethan couldn't see, though judging by the sound of the human heartbeat and unmistakable scent, he knew Molly was waiting inside. Layla's body was coiled tightly like a snake as she inched towards the edge of the bed, the hungry look in her eyes shifting to something darker and more raw when her gaze landed on Ethan.

"You see what a generous master I am?" Lucias said in an amused tone as he walked into the room and joined Molly.

He took a seat in one of the chairs set up facing the bed that were obviously placed for optimum viewing of what was to come. Molly climbed onto Lucias's lap, feeling as giddy as a school girl and doing nothing to mask her enthusiasm as she waited for the promised entertainment to begin.

Ethan remained completely still in the doorway, a mixture of feelings washing over him as he realized what was expected. As much as he hated it, there was little he could do to stop the wash of desire that covered him as he looked upon Layla's naked beauty.

Feeling his body begin to respond, he closed his eyes, trying to focus on the phantom pull of his bond to Alexa which, until that moment, felt as if it remained only to punish him for what he had done. It was then he realized that the taunting pull was the last piece of Alexa he had left and he was overcome with grief, knowing that Lucias intended to use this woman to take it from him.

"Go to her," Lucias commanded before he licked up the side of Molly's neck. She moaned dramatically in response, as she squirmed on his lap.

As much as Ethan screamed at himself inside his own mind to stay where he was, his body moved obediently across the room where Layla waited.

"You'll have to go get closer; I have commanded her to remain on the bed until released. A regrettable, but necessary, precaution as long as Molly is in the room. Our new friend is freshly out of transition and unable to completely control her hunger for human blood," Lucias said as his fangs pushed through his gums.

"But later she'll be able to play with us, right?" Molly asked, tilting her head to the side, giving Lucias better access to her neck.

"Yes, of course. I am quite pleased to find you so eager to share me with another of my kind," Lucias remarked before he sank his teeth into her vein. He felt his cock jump as he thought of the other he wished to share both women with someday; his true mate whom he hadn't seen in nearly a century.

When the scent of Molly's blood hit the air, Layla's head snapped in her direction, breaking her focus from Ethan for the first time since she laid eyes on him.

Ethan stood mere inches in front of Layla, whose attention was still locked on the couple across the room.

Lucias released his hold on Molly's neck, sealing the puncture wounds with a swift swipe of his tongue before he spoke.

"Ethan, remove your clothes," he commanded as he slid his hand between Molly's quivering thighs.

The sensation of the bite already had her teetering on the edge of orgasm while she kept her eyes locked on Ethan. She had wanted the handsome vampire since the moment she'd greeted him boarding the plane in Eleuthera, but she knew better than to mention that fact to Lucias. While her master didn't seem to mind her taking pleasure with the humans she lured home, he'd made it abundantly clear she was to stay away from other male vampires.

In a matter of seconds, Ethan stood obediently naked beside the bed. With the wounds on Molly's neck fully healed, Layla's attention returned to him. The scent of her arousal flooded the air around them as her eyes fell upon his manhood. Even in an unaroused state, he was an impressive sight to behold.

"Don't be shy, my dear," Lucias encouraged as he continued to stroke Molly. "For now, Mr. Kellar is yours to do with as you please."

With Lucias releasing her to act, Layla's hand shot out and gripped Ethan's tender flesh without hesitation. The taking of blood was often a rather sexual act, so insatiable desire was an expected side-effect of the bloodlust evoked by infection.

Despite his mind's protests, Ethan was potently male and, though he hated himself for it, his body responded to Layla's demanding touch.

Lucias smirked, watching Ethan's hips thrust forward into Layla's hand. The smirk developed into a lustful smile when he felt Molly's body clench around his fingers as she cried out his name.

As the air in the room became saturated with tension and arousal, Ethan felt the grip of his control slipping further and further away. His mind was awash with the conflicting emotions of his beast and his soul; the beast pushing him forward, eager to ravage the woman before him, to take her with complete and primal abandon. His soul cried out with grief and regret, knowing the cause was already lost. With one last effort, Ethan closed his eyes and again focused on

Alexa, on the bond he still felt, opening up to it, praying it could somehow give him the strength to fight. But instead, the sensations he felt pulsing through the bond only strengthened the lust growing in his veins.

Suddenly, it was Alexa's touch sliding over his body, her scent filling his lungs, her face looking up at him with desire. And in that moment, even though he knew it wasn't real, Ethan let go, let himself feel Alexa as he covered Layla's writhing body and thrust himself inside her.

He wasn't gentle when he pushed into her over and again, but his pace and roughness were exactly what Layla's infected body craved as she clung to his back, drawing blood from the flesh covering his hard muscles. The smell of the red liquid reignited Layla's bloodlust, pulling a primal cry from her throat as she sank the sharp points of her fangs into Ethan's shoulder. He growled out with pleasure; so lost in the sensations washing over him, picturing Alexa and feeling her almost as surely as if she was the one there with him, Ethan reciprocated, piercing the vein at the base of Layla's neck. Releasing his shoulder, she cried out again, his bite sending a jolt through her body which set off a powerful climax.

The instant her blood hit his tongue, the pretense disintegrated. While he may have been able to squeeze his eyes shut and imagine it was Alexa lying beneath him, blood didn't lie.

Lucias sighed, watching the exchange while Molly moved up and down on his lap, as satisfied with watching the two taking each other's blood as he was with feeling Molly's tight flesh wrapped around him. Though it was not enough to create a genuine blood bond, Ethan and Layla's exchange was sufficient to create a temporary tie, which he was confident would erase whatever lingering connection he felt to Alexa.

In a blur of motion, Ethan flipped Layla onto her stomach before he pushed inside her again. While the guilt was nearly unbearable and he was screaming inside his mind to stop, to move away from this strange woman, his beast would not relent, pushing harder and deeper with each thrust. Ethan felt as if he had left his own body and was floating above, watching the events in horror and disgust as an orgasm pulsed through his body, finally quieting his beast.

He pulled away from Layla, looking to his master who was too consumed with his own pleasure at the moment to care what Ethan was doing. Lucias hadn't commanded Ethan beyond sending him to Layla and giving her lease to do with him as she pleased. So overcome with guilt that he felt physically ill, Ethan whispered, "Are you finished with me?"

"Mmmm," was her only response as she rolled over on the bed. Being so newly infected and in the absence of direct commands from Lucias, Layla's body and mind were functioning purely on the instinct to satisfy her baser needs. Pleasured sexually and full with enough blood to sustain her for several hours, she had no use for anything but sleep.

Taking her reply as affirmation, Ethan collected his clothes and sped from the room with every ounce of his speed, arriving in the bathroom of his quarters just in time to release the contents of his stomach.

CHAPTER 25 - *An Old Friend*

I know you can hear me. I'm sorry to do this, but I need your help.
Please.

Chloe opened the door and hurriedly ushered Dante inside, certain that many of her family members would be furious if they discovered him there, especially those who had learned of his power.

"I know why you've come," she said quietly.

"Yes, of course you do. I only touched you for a moment yesterday, but some of your power still lingers. I have never been able to sustain borrowed power for this long without great effort," he said holding his hand out towards a small bottle on the nearby table. Chloe watched as it lifted several inches off the surface before returning to its place in correlation with Dante's movement.

"I can only move small objects now, and the telepathy faded within a few minutes; but it seems that something about your abilities enhances mine."

"I saw about your kind in my aunt's mind. Could you really take all of my power?" Chloe asked, already knowing the answer; a part of her wanting him to do exact that. If she was ordinary, at least as ordinary as a vampire could be, Lucias wouldn't want her anymore. But she knew that even though he could, Dante wouldn't risk her life. With a sigh, she addressed the concerns bouncing through Dante's mind.

"My visions have been limited to two events, one which has already occurred. I don't believe the other is far off and there was something in it which will please you; Layla will come back to the compound with my father."

Dante dropped to his knees before her, a wave of relief washing over him as he battled the tears that threatened to spill from his eyes. "She's alive. Layla's alive, and she's coming home," he whispered and closed his eyes.

"Yes; she will come back to you," Chloe said as she reached out and stroked his hair gently. When her fingertip grazed the top of his scalp, a vision slammed down on her so hard and fast that she stumbled backwards beneath its force.

"What is it? Are you all right?" Dante asked in a panic, instantly on his feet with his arms around Chloe, steadying her as the vision formed.

With the contact, Chloe's power again began to seep into Dante and the images in her mind began to flash through his.

He watched with fascination as Layla's beautiful face came into view, so clear and vivid it was as if she was standing before him. Dante could only see the side of her face as she appeared to be transfixed on something off to the left.

"Layla," he called out, though he knew she couldn't hear him. Yet somehow, at that precise moment, she turned; facing him as the view moved outwards.

Dante yanked his hands back, releasing Chloe as if her skin burned him. "No, please; God, no," he whimpered as he closed his eyes and sunk back to his knees.

Though the contact was broken, the vision he shared with Chloe persisted and he was forced to watch helplessly as the glow of Layla's red eyes stared back at him, her naked body practically writhing on the bed as another man approached her. Before long, the man's large body completely blocked the view of Layla and the images began to fade entirely as the power he'd absorbed from Chloe dissipated. The man turned ever so slightly, giving Dante the tiniest glimpse of his face; before the view was blocked by the shirt he pulled over his head and the vision disappeared from his mind.

Dante began to shake uncontrollably as a whirl of emotions rushed through his mind, and as much as he knew it would hurt to see what would inevitably pass next between the woman he loved and the stranger in the vision, he opened his eyes and reached for Chloe's arm.

Reading his intention, Chloe moved away just in time, the only contact with Dante from the soft material of her skirt which grazed his outstretched hand.

"No good will come from you seeing anymore," she said, choking back her own sadness as the vision ended. "You saw her eyes; you know she is not acting on her own free will. She loves you, despite everything you may have done to stop her."

"Did you see who the man was?" Dante asked through his teeth.

"She will come back to you; the rest doesn't matter," Chloe said matter-of-factly, still struggling to deal with what she had just seen.

Dante opened his mouth to ask something else, but Chloe beat him to it.

"I don't know how yet, but she will be cured. Please just trust me," Chloe pleaded as she approached the door.

"My mother is waiting for you; the training helps her and she could use a friend right now. Both of you could. Just be careful to guard your thoughts around her," Chloe added before she closed her eyes and focused her senses. "It's safe now; move quickly before someone sees you," she whispered and opened the door.

Dante's only response was the breeze left in his wake which kissed her face as he passed by.

Chloe leaned back against the door and lifted her hand, watching as it trembled before her. Now she understood more clearly than ever what her grandmother had meant when she told her what a curse clairvoyance could be.

No matter how old, no child ever wanted to see one of their parents in a position like what she had just witnessed. Beyond that, her mother already knew and, as much as Chloe wanted to go to her and offer what comfort she could, there was something else she needed to do before it was too late.

Sliding her finger down the digital control panel, Chloe dimmed the lights and took a seat on the edge of her bed. Reaching around behind her neck, she unclasped the silver necklace which had hung over her chest since the witch, Tara, had returned it what seemed like a lifetime ago.

She dangled the delicate silver charm in front of her face, smiling as she closed her eyes and thought of the one who gave it to her when she was still very small.

"I was wondering when you would call on me, child," Barb said quietly appearing seated on the bed beside her. "I've been trying to contact you, but those shields of yours are something, even for someone with the power to reach beyond the grave."

"Oh, Barb; I don't know what to do," Chloe said, her chin trembling as she drew the silver charm to her chest for comfort.

"Hush now, my sweet girl. There'll be none of that, you hear? You just listen to what's in that good heart of yours and you'll be just fine. When the time comes, you'll know what to do, and just in case, always remember what you mean to us all, even him. Your power isn't just what you can do; it's what others will do for you."

Chloe swiped at her tears, feeling confusion at Barb's somewhat cryptic words which was unfamiliar. Normally, if she wondered what someone meant, she simply listened in on their thoughts. Apparently, even with telepathy as powerful as Chloe's, the thoughts of the dead were theirs to keep.

"Now, about your daddy," Barb continued, "You know he'll be coming soon and when he does, you need to show your mama how to cure him. They'll need to renew their blood bond to break the tie to Lucias, and to erase everything else that happened," she added, her ethereal form suddenly standing before the mirror across the room. "Her blood is the key, but you must wait until the last possible moment to show her. I think you already understand that, seeing how you knew to hide the rest of your vision from her. She loves you too much to let go on her own, so you're going to have to help her."

"I'm so scared," Chloe whispered, lowering her head in shame.

"Sweet girl, you'd be a fool not to be; but you're stronger than you know. Now, I'm afraid it's time for me to be going, but I think you should come over here and take a look at just how beautiful you are today."

Again confused, Chloe flashed across the distance to the mirror. "I'm not sure how—," she said into the empty room, stopping when she felt the loss of Barb's warm presence. Even though she knew she was gone, Chloe turned in a circle, scanning the room while holding on to the tiniest sliver of hope that she might be mistaken. Finding that she had been right, Chloe thought of Barb's last words and returned her eyes to her reflection.

She felt the blood drain from her face as surely as she saw it grow pale in the soft glow of the overhead light. Chloe wondered how she had failed to realize it when she'd chosen the ensemble, but there was no escaping what the pale pink blouse and gray skirt meant. The day of her vision was upon them.

"I was starting to wonder if you had forgotten," Alexa said, forcing a cheerful tone as Dante closed the door to their makeshift training room. Though she had only had one training session, she already felt stronger; more empowered somehow. At least she had before she'd gone to sleep. Since waking up, she'd spent the bulk of the morning lying on the cold tile of the bathroom floor, sobbing uncontrollably as she was forced to witness her husband, her soul mate, lying with another woman. Once she'd had the first glimpse, her emotions were so out of control it was impossible for her to raise a barrier to block the bond and the horrifying images it carried.

While a part of her wanted to remain there, wallowing in her despair, she fought with every ounce of her willpower to get up and make her way to the room in which she was standing. As much as it hurt, she knew she was too strong to give in to self-pity. Her family needed her; Ethan needed her, and no matter what happened, she would always be there for him.

"Sorry, just had something else I needed to attend to," Dante said trying to keep his tone light as he reinforced his mental shields. As soon as he entered the room, he sensed Alexa's unease; but in trying to deal with his own emotional train wreck, he quickly decided against prying into the source.

"Are you ready to begin? We won't have a lot of time; a group of soldiers is expected to arrive soon and I'm to lead a mission to the human's farm where we found the car used to abduct Layla," he explained, turning away as he unzipped his jacket, trying to push back the images of Layla from Chloe's vision, which flooded his mind at the mention of her name.

"Yes; I'm ready," Alexa replied before taking a deep breath and preparing her stance.

Dante dropped his jacket to the ground and, in a rush of movement, he was upon her. Alexa moved efficiently, countering each move and blocking his attacks. With each move, her straight lips began to turn up into a cocky smile. When Dante spun around, sweeping her feet, she easily jumped over his leg and countered with a punch that landed in the center of his chest and send him stumbling back.

"I'm sorry," she said, her hand shooting up to her mouth covering her smile.

"It seems I have been going too easy on you," Dante replied, a slight grin cracking his expression which had remained stern since his arrival. When he left Chloe's room, he wouldn't have believed that anything could dull the pain he was feeling; but somehow, as each minute passed with Alexa, it lessened more and more.

When he attacked again, it was at his full speed, which turned out to be slightly more than Alexa could handle as she found herself caught with one of his arms hooked under her neck and the other laying across her stomach, pinning her body to his.

"Now," Dante said with a chuckle, "this is probably a good time to work on release moves. If you're caught from behind, you should—" Dante started, stopping cold as Alexa's thought about how handsome he was entered his mind. Having been so focused on the training and blocking his mind from her, he'd neglected to rein in his own ability and had unintentionally absorbed her telepathy.

"I should what?" she asked, oblivious to the impact of her innocent thought. It was impossible to ignore how attractive Dante was; besides Ethan, she'd never seen a better looking man and those kinds of looks had an impact. In her case, combined with the focus needed for training, they were providing enough of a distraction to keep her from falling to the ground sobbing every two minutes.

Immediately releasing her, Dante took a small step back. Alexa spun to face him, her face confused until the slightest hint of his arousal tickled her nostrils. She opened her mouth to speak, but no words came. Her eyes fell to the ground while she struggled to find her bearings. She watched as Dante's feet inched forward in what felt like slow motion until there was almost no space left between them.

She wasn't sure why, but she looked up into his dark eyes knowing exactly what would happen when she did. Dante didn't disappoint, instantly closing what was left of the distance between their mouths as he slid his arms around her waist. Alexa moaned, parting her lips ever so slightly in an invitation he willingly accepted, sliding his tongue skillfully over them before slipping it inside to meet with hers.

Though it only lasted a few moments, that one kiss gave them both something they needed to move forward. They both loved other people and they would continue to love them when it was over, but for that little slice of time, they were free of the pain, of the hurt and regret which had consumed them before. The kiss gave them hope.

They moved back at the same time, breaking the kiss but remaining close as Dante stroked her cheek. No words were needed, their thoughts flowing freely through Alexa's telepathy, which he would share until they no longer touched.

With a deep sigh, Dante dropped his hand and stepped away. "Thank you, Alexa," he whispered.

She responded with a smile as she knelt down and picked up his jacket, passing it to him without a word before she disappeared out the door.

CHAPTER 26 - *Chloe's Sacrifice*

"Sir, that makes fifteen in less than six hours," Jester said in a panic, as he slid his chair to another monitor to pull up the location of the latest attack.

"Fuck," Commander Claesson replied, sliding his hand over his face, "How many soldiers are still on the compound?"

"Twenty-five; excluding us, the guards, and Cami, but Dante and his team should be returning any minute. The building at the back of Sean Taylor's property was deserted but, based on the weapons and gear they found, it is, or at least was, being used as a training facility for Lucias's humans," Jester replied.

"Like those who attacked Elijah in Indianapolis?" William asked stepping closer.

"Precisely; Cami was here when Dante called in so she took the photos he sent to her father in the lab. He confirmed that the gear was identical to what the human soldiers who destroyed his clinic wore."

"So Elijah and his wife are still holed up in the lab?" Claesson asked;

regarding William carefully.

"Yes; they've been working non-stop with some of your researchers, analyzing the sample of infected blood Jasmine found on her clothes. As I'm sure you can understand, they're desperate to find a cure as soon as possible," William replied.

"Of course; I just hope he's more successful in the endeavor than we were in the past," Commander Claesson stated; giving William a knowing look.

There had been an entire team of scientists working to synthesize an antivirus when the first round of infected vampires appeared nearly seven hundred years ago, to no avail. Technology had come a long way since then, so they were hopeful that a cure would be found. The real concern was if it would be found in time; both leaders knowing that, as an infected vampire, Ethan Kellar was an enemy their forces simply couldn't defeat.

"This area is only a few blocks from Blood Runners," Jester chimed in; pointing to a spot on the satellite feed which had just loaded on the monitor. "We could give Winston a call; maybe have his people handle clean-up since all we seem to be finding are bodies, and it's unlikely that this one will be any different."

"Make the call," Claesson responded, before turning to the High Commander. "It seems we're about out of time. The next wave of reinforcements won't be here until morning. If there are any more bodies tonight, I'm afraid we're going to have to enlist the help of a lot more civilians. Even with the witches' protection on the gates, we can't send out any more of our soldiers. Doing that will leave the compound virtually unguarded and, with one of our own missing, we can't take the risk."

"And what of the Boston coven; will the witches come to our aid?"

"They know what is at stake; I have Esther's word they will honor our alliance. But until we know more about Lucias's intentions, they will not leave the protection of their homes."

William nodded his understanding. "What do you think he's trying to accomplish with these blatant attacks?" he asked; slumping down into a chair.

Having spent the last several hours trying to appease the civilian leaders, and after many consecutive sleepless nights worrying about his daughter, William was beyond exhausted. The threat of widespread panic was imminent, as word of the violent deaths, which had been occurring in Boston since the sun went down, spread throughout the civilian vampire population. The body count was somewhere around thirty, consisting of a pretty even mix of humans and civilian vampires; all either dumped out in the open, or attacked within public view. It was a media nightmare, as evidenced by the three separate human news channels running the stories seen on the monitors that were mounted on the walls.

Thanks to some of The Elite's human allies, the murders were being attributed to a new drug, commonly referred to as bath salts; which had quickly become famous for the psychotic, and often cannibalistic, episodes it caused in its users.

"My guess is he's testing us. If he was looking for battle, his men would be waiting for us; and if his intent was to expose us to the humans, well, you know how easy that would be," Claesson replied; taking the seat beside him.

William cringed when the word zombie scrolled across the bottom of one of the screens. "If he keeps this up, it won't be long before the humans make the jump from zombie to vampire, especially if they get to one of the bodies before we do."

"The story was just picked up nationally," Jester said; pulling up the latest update.

"Shit; Thompson and our other contacts with Boston PD have been able to give us first pass on scenes, but if other outside agencies get involved, things will be far more complicated," Claesson observed, as he stood and began to pace the room.

William sighed heavily. "I suppose there's no point in putting it off any longer. I'll notify the civilian leaders in and around Boston and have them assemble teams from those amongst them who have been properly trained. I'll order them to keep the information local and need-to-know only, but you know as well as I do it won't keep for long. Their families and friends around the world will be warned within a matter of hours; not that I can blame them."

"My lord, if I may; I am of the opinion that the entire population should be informed of the threat. We are well beyond the point of maintaining secrecy amongst our own kind. It makes us more vulnerable; besides, we may not be far from the need to activate the human integration protocols," Claesson stated; his voice low.

"I hope it doesn't come to that," William replied solemnly though, with all that had happened, he realized his hope might well be in vain.

Lucias intended to rule completely; over humans and vampires alike. If they didn't find a way to stop him, the exposure of their kind was inevitable. Understanding that possibility, the vampire race's leaders and their human allies had developed a plan to minimize the backlash of their discovery.

"Sirs, I'm sorry if this is out of line, but maybe you should consider implementing those protocols preemptively," Jester interjected.

"Why in God's name would we want to do that?" William asked; sharply turning to the young vampire.

"Well, my lord; I've spent a lot of time following culture and trends with the humans online and in other media and millions of them are utterly fascinated by our kind, or at least the myths of our kind which have become so popular in recent decades. Even believing some of the worst stories about our people, many of them would be, well, thrilled to find out we are real," Jester responded; his tone growing more excited with each word.

"So you're suggesting that we reveal a secret which has been kept for millennia because you think some of the humans will be pleased that the monsters from their movies actually exist? And what happens when the excitement wears off and their fear sets in? How do you suggest we handle the remaining humans who are anything but thrilled to learn the truth? They outnumber us at least a thousand to one and, if history has taught me anything, it's that while a single human can be very kind, understanding, and compassionate, their species as a whole is intolerant and fearful of the unknown," William stated, feeling a chill run over his skin as he considered the catastrophic possibilities which lay before them.

"Yes; but how long before they find out about us because of these attacks, or whatever else Lucias has planned? Do we really want him to control our inevitable introduction to the humans? If their path to knowledge is lined with death and blood, who can blame them for their intolerance? But if we give them the truth now, show them we are not the threat, they could be our allies in the fight against Lucias and his army of infected," Jester added.

"Jester, take care how you speak to our lord and commander," Claesson warned.

"It's all right, Alek," William said, raising his hand. "Perhaps the boy is right. If we were to—"

William's words were cut off by the loud blaring of an alarm which sliced through the previously quiet air of the compound.

"What's happening?" he asked; watching as Claesson sped across the room and picked up the phone.

"Jester, lock it down now!" Claesson ordered; ignoring the High Commander as he hit a button and put the phone to his ear.

Jester's fingers skated over the keyboard efficiently, as he systematically engaged the emergency security protocols to secure the interior of the compound.

"Damn; no answer at the gate!" Claesson yelled over the screech of the alarm. "The compound has been breached!" he continued; turning to William.

He opened his mouth to yell something else right as Jester cut the alarm.

"All of the cameras in front are out," Jester stated; inclining his head toward the wall of security monitors behind the other men. The three of them had been so engaged in their discussions about the attacks, and the resulting television news stories, that they hadn't noticed when the security feeds had been cut.

"My lord, we must get to your family. The attacks must have been a distraction to weaken our protection here on the compound. Jester, you know what to do," Commander Claesson said and sped off after William, who was already gone.

Chloe took her hands down from over her ears, breathing a sigh of relief as the ear-piercing screech of the alarm fell silent.

She felt surprisingly calm, despite her knowledge of what was coming. Watching her mother pacing anxiously across the floor, she knew the source of her serenity. Her parents would finally be reunited, even if she couldn't be there to see it.

Alexa looked toward Chloe and threw her hands up. "How can you act so calm?" she said; her voice cracking as she spoke.

Before she could respond, the sound of the door sliding open got their attention.

"We need to move," William said, stepping inside.

"What happened?" Alexa asked, unable to pierce the strong shields of her father's mind.

"Someone has breached the outer defenses of the compound. We have to move to the training room. According to Commander Claesson, it doubles as a sort of panic room in case of an attack," he said; quickly signaling for both women to follow him.

The trio sped down the corridor, followed closely by William's personal guards; including Captain Erikson, who had remained posted outside of Chloe and Alexa's rooms since the start of the attacks in the city.

"What about everyone else?" Captain Erikson inquired when they arrived at the door to the training wing. With the compound on emergency lockdown, special security clearance was needed to move between the various wings.

"He went to the lab to collect Elijah and the others. They should be joining us shortly," he replied; quickly entering the code and standing aside for Chloe and Alexa to pass.

When the group arrived outside the training room, they found Commander Claesson, along with the rest of Chloe and Alexa's family, already waiting.

"My lord; once you are all inside, enter the code I gave you. It will engage the silver-plated security doors and panels. No one, not even I, will be able to gain access from the outside, and only the code will release the doors from the inside."

"Alek; you are not staying with us?" William asked; his voice full with concern.

"I cannot abandon my men. The intruders have not yet breached the building; only the outer grounds. We will hold them until reinforcements arrive if we can; but even if they break through, this room is impenetrable. There are enough supplies for weeks and a satellite phone to contact the outside. Jester's room is also secure; he will be able to run the entire compound from there and, when it's clear, one of us will come for you. For now, you and your family will be safe here," he said; placing a hand on William's shoulder.

"Captain, take the rest of the men and go with the commander. You will help secure the building," he ordered.

"But, my lord—," Captain Erikson began; only to be cut off.

"You heard the commander; this room is impenetrable. Your skills will be better utilized helping the soldiers hold the perimeter until help arrives."

The captain briefly glanced at Commander Claesson with disdain before nodding his understanding.

"Sir, let me come with you," Cami chimed in as the commander turned to leave.

Jared's jaw clenched as she dropped his hand and moved towards the door; but he remained silent, knowing with certainty that Claesson would deny her request and understanding why she had to make it.

"Your place is here with your family," Claesson replied; offering his hand with eyes full of sadness.

Cami looked at it for a brief moment, and then hurled herself at the large vampire; wrapping her arms around him in a tight hug, saying goodbye for what they both understood would be the last time. Though he didn't know it, she'd overheard the call he'd made to his wife and daughter from his office only minutes before, when he'd sent her and Jared to retrieve her parents from the lab. She'd told Jared to go ahead and had stayed long enough to know exactly how her fearless leader expected the night to end.

Reluctantly releasing him, Cami stepped back into the training room as the door slid closed between them. She stood there, watching Commander Claesson and the members of the High Commander's guard until the security panels dropped down, blocking the small window with the only view to the outside.

Cami closed her eyes as Jared pulled her against his chest, wrapping her in his strong arms as they stood in silent anticipation.

It seemed like hours had passed as Chloe sat on the floor leaning her head against her mother's shoulder; though, in reality, it had only been a few minutes.

Barely a word had been spoken among the group, as they all tried to cope with the uncertainty of what was occurring beyond the safety of the walls surrounding them.

Chloe looked around the room at her family, her mouth turning up into a sad smile as she grabbed her mother's hand and pulled it up to her face. Pressing Alexa's knuckles to her lips, Chloe inhaled deeply and closed her eyes.

He will be here soon. You must renew your blood bond; it is the only way to save him. I love you, Chloe sent telepathically.

"Chloe, what's—" Alexa began; but before she could finish, Chloe pushed the rest of her vision, the parts which she'd carefully shielded, into her mother's mind. Alexa's tensed, realizing her daughter's intentions, but before she could fully process what she'd seen, everything went black.

Chloe flashed to the door and entered the code she'd pulled from William's mind. She paused for the briefest of seconds to look back at her family, each of them lying unconscious on the floor around the training room as a result of the mind blast she'd sent out to incapacitate them. While she wished there was another way, she knew none of the people with her in that room would have ever allowed her to leave, no matter what visions she shared with them. They would all die to keep her safe; and if she stayed, that was exactly what would happen.

Uncertain as to how long she had before her family revived, Chloe reentered the code and sped across the threshold before the security panel fell back into place; moving with every ounce of her speed towards the front of the compound before it was too late.

Entering the elevator, Chloe reached out for Commander Claesson's mind and breathed a sigh of relief at finding that he and the other soldiers were still inside the mansion above; but the feeling was short lived. Through his eyes, she watched the wave of infected soldiers flying over the fence before he looked to the detonator in his hand.

Commander, please don't, she sent, trying to buy some time; knowing that if those land mines exploded, everything she cared about would be lost.

"What the—" he whispered in confusion, turning just as the elevator doors opened. "Chloe, you can't be here; go back to—"

The pulse of energy rattled the walls as it flew out from Chloe's body, knocking the commander and every soldier in the room to the ground. Before her fear could set in, she moved to the front door and pulled it open, stepping out into the flood of the security lights which lit the porch of the mansion.

No sooner than she came into view, three infected soldiers swooped in only to be sent flying back by the force of her mind. Realizing she was running out of time, Chloe sifted through the dozens of minds; searching for the one she needed.

I am the one you seek, she sent, standing up a little straighter as the rest of the infected vampires cautiously surrounded her.

Kaleb, like the rest of the vampires moving across the lawn of The Elite's compound, was surprised that, instead of a swarm of Elite soldiers, they were met by an unarmed, and breathtakingly beautiful, woman. Even more surprising was his father's command to halt their attack.

His eyes darted all around, to the roof, the windows; yet he saw no evidence of The Elite. While his father's plan had been to draw as many of them out of the compound as possible with the public attacks around the city, they never expected to find the facility so poorly guarded.

Using Layla to pass through the witches' protective spells, a small team of their men had easily taken out the guards and opened the gates for the rest of them to pass through.

"I will give you what you desire. I will go with you now, but only if you agree to my terms," Chloe said aloud, trying desperately to mask the tremble in her voice.

Kaleb felt his heart begin to pound when the delicate sound of her voice cut through the cool night air, and was suddenly overcome with a need unlike anything he'd ever felt before. When Lucias flashed across the distance and appeared only inches away from her, Kaleb struggled; using every ounce of his willpower to remain where he was, his fists clenched tightly at his sides as he watched Lucias caress a stray lock of her long hair.

"How very bold you are, though it would appear you have good cause to be so," Lucias said; glancing to the three unconscious men laying on the steps before he let his eyes drift hungrily up Chloe's body. "Tell me; how did you speak to me as you did before?" he asked; slowly circling her. "I am no telepath, yet I heard you in my mind as surely as if you spoke aloud."

"I can share my thoughts with others as I see fit. As I told you, I am the one you came here for," she replied; choking down the bile she felt rising in her throat as Lucias's perverse thoughts entered her mind. She battled the instinct to push up her mental shields; knowing that she needed the advantage reading his mind gave her.

"How remarkable; I expected a child and instead I find you, very much a woman. I must admit I am pleasantly surprised," he said in his best attempt to be charming, as he stopped in front of her and inclined his head. "I am Lucias,"

"I know who you are," she replied quickly. "I have only two requests; grant them and I will go with you without protest."

"Do tell," he responded; raising his eyebrows with curiosity.

"My father and the soldier, Layla; allow them to remain here and we, you and I, and all of your men can leave immediately," she said; cautiously taking his hand as she glanced at Ethan, whose eyes had

333

remained locked on her since the moment she'd stepped through the door.

The instant he saw her he'd felt as if the earth was shifting beneath his feet and, for the briefest of moments, believed she was a ghost there to torment him for all his failures. With Chloe looking so much like Alexa, it wasn't until she spoke that he realized she wasn't what he'd thought.

Shocked by the voluntary contact, Lucias stared down at their joined hands as Chloe tentatively stroked his knuckles with her thumb. "You give yourself to me freely then? What of The Elite; why have they not come to fight for you?" he asked; placing his fingertips beneath her chin, feeling a sense of power the likes of which he had never known.

Knowing that her family and The Elite could wake at any moment and that the demonstration of her power would please Lucias, she showed him a brief glimpse of her memory from the minutes before she'd emerged from the mansion.

"You surprise me, Chloe. It is not a feeling I am accustomed to," he said; looking to Ethan and Layla as he considered her proposal. As she'd expected, he was reluctant to relinquish the soldier who'd served as his key to the compound along with a vampire as powerful as her father; but like she'd hoped, he believed turning them over to The Elite could be used to his advantage. A slight smile turned up the corners of his mouth as he considered the possibilities of placing two of his infected within the walls of his enemy's home, like his own personal Trojan horse.

"There isn't much time. Do you agree to leave them, in exchange for my cooperation?" she asked; glancing again at her father. Though her eyes were filled with sadness at knowing that it could be the last time she would ever see him, she smiled and pushed into his mind.

Ethan's body tensed imperceptibly as the images of her memory flashed before his eyes. Suddenly he was back in his father's clinic, looking down into the greenish-gray eyes of his beautiful daughter for the first time, as she placed her tiny hand on his cheek and said one little word which would change him forever. *Dadda.*

Still under Lucias's command, Ethan remained obediently silent and still; but in that moment, all of the blood bonds and orders in the world wouldn't have been able to stop the lone tear that slid down his cheek.

"Very well," Lucias finally responded; pulling Chloe's attention back to him. "I will release your father and the woman. Consider it an early wedding present," he said; watching her closely as he pulled her hand to his lips.

"Thank you, my lord" she said; bowing her head to him respectfully. Sensing the minds of her family beginning to revive, she knew she had only seconds to get Lucias and his men off of the compound. "We must go now; there will be hundreds of Elite arriving at any moment," she said; embellishing the numbers to sufficiently motivate him to move quickly.

While he was curious to finally see his infected matched against The Elite in open battle, after spending centuries searching for her, he wouldn't risk it with Chloe present.

No; there will be plenty of time for that, he thought triumphantly, his body practically vibrating with the excitement and satisfaction of fulfilling a lifelong pursuit.

"Ethan, Layla; consider this your new home," he said; pulling Chloe across the short distance to stand directly in front of them. "Until you see me again, you may act freely. However, you will lay down your arms and wait for your new hosts to retrieve you and you will not speak a single word of me, my army, or my plans to anyone; nor will you ever raise a hand against my men," he commanded the pair, wanting to ensure that The Elite wouldn't be tempted to kill them on sight or try to use them in their fight against him. He turned to Chloe who, battling her true feelings, smiled, pushed up on her toes, and pressed a kiss to his cheek.

Satisfied, Lucias gave the command for the rest of his men to leave the grounds.

Standing just inside the protective mist of the outer gate, Chloe and Lucias were the last pair to pass through. Just before stepping across, they each looked back silently, one with eyes full of joy and triumph, the other with sadness and defeat.

The Fate Series

Choices of Fate - Book 1

Redemption of Fate - Book 2

Absolution of Fate - Book 3

For more information on titles by S. Simone Chavous
please visit

www.ssimonechavous.com

Acknowledgements

First, I want to thank all of my readers, every single one of you who took a chance on an unknown author and read Choices of Fate, giving me the encouragement to push forward in this crazy, and often brutal, world of writing.

To my family and friends, none of this would be possible without you. I love you all.

To the amazing bloggers and reviewers who work tirelessly for authors with only the satisfaction of doing something they enjoy as their reward, we couldn't make it without you.

And finally, to my fellow writers who have offered advice and encouragement along the way, especially all of you who I got to know in WFD, thank you from the bottom of my heart!

About the Author

S. Simone Chavous spent seven years as a tax accountant before deciding to pursue her true passion as an author. She lives in northern Indiana with her boyfriend, two beautiful daughters, and their rambunctious vizsla, Lily.

To learn more about S. Simone, please visit:
www.ssimonechavous.com

or connect with her on Facebook at
www.facebook.com/ssimonechavous

www.ingramcontent.com/pod-product-compliance
Lightning Source LLC
Chambersburg PA
CBHW070642180626
46817CB00006B/2215